Books by Maxim Jakubowski

Life in the World of Women
It's You That I Want to Kiss
Because She Thought She Loved Me
The State of Montana
On Tenderness Express
Kiss Me Sadly
Confessions of a Romantic Pornographer
American Casanova
Fools for Lust

I WAS WAITING FOR YOU

MAXIM JAKUBOWSKI

Published by Accent Press Ltd – 2010

Paperback ISBN 9781907016592
eBook ISBN 9781907726347

The story contained within this book is a work of fiction. Names and characters are the product of the author's imagination and any resemblance to actual persons, living or dead, is entirely coincidental.

To Silas and Taylor,
one day …

"Think of everything that has ever been said and everything that has ever been written, every book, every poem, every conversation, every scrap of paper, every encyclopaedia, in English, in Chinese, in French and Spanish and Italian and Russian and Korean and Arabic, in Swahili, in Farsi, and then think of your life. What are you next to all that? You're like one half of a letter in one word; that's your life, that is you front to back, up and down, over and out. But that doesn't make what we say and do less important. It makes it *more* important."

Scott Spencer
"Willing"

"I was born when she kissed me. I died when she left me. I lived a few weeks while she loved me."

Humphrey Bogart
"In a Lonely Place"

"We were perfect when we started
I've been wondering where we've gone"

Counting Crows
"A Murder of One"

This is the story of a man who often managed to fall in love with women he had never met.
You might call him a fool for lust.
A tale of longing, bodies, flesh like gold, and pain. It is also the tale of a minor league writer who was mistaken for a private detective.
It was the same man.
That man was Jack.

PART ONE

L'AVVENTURA

COITUS INTERRUPTUS, A BALLAD

THE CUBAN GUY TAKING her from behind was puffing and panting, nearing the finishing line in his race to orgasm.

Cornelia felt nothing. Neither in her body or her soul, let alone her heart.

What was the point, she wondered?

It was always like this.

Meaningless words. Hydraulics. Sweat.

No emotions.

Then her cell phone rang. It was lodged at the bottom of her handbag, but they both could clearly hear its insistent nudge.

She had no fancy tone. No classic song or silly sounds. Just a strong vibration followed by an insistent buzz.

The man inside her slowed. His tides of lust receding fast.

Possibly her body tensed, but Cornelia said nothing.

The phone kept ringing, then the sound died and there was a discreet mechanical click as the message function took over. In silence.

"It's OK," she said. "I'll check it later."

The man grunted and focused again on fucking her.

But whatever magic they had ridden the waves of had by now dissipated and his ardour was no longer the same.

He soon pulled out of her.

"I'm sorry," he mumbled.

The traffic noises outside his mid-range Broadway hotel room window somehow increased in volume.

"No problem," Cornelia responded.

He rose awkwardly from the bed.

Cornelia rolled over on to her back and pulled the white, crumpled sheet back across her naked body. She felt empty, again.

She remained silent.

The phone call she had not taken now separated them and the man was visibly in a hurry to cut their encounter short and be on his way.

Which was fine with her.

Cornelia had picked him up at the Oyster Bar beneath Grand Central Station. She'd been bored and the man had initially seemed clean and not too bad-looking. So she'd thought, why not?

He glanced back at her, and his detumescing cock stirred a little. Cornelia just looked him in the eyes and kept on saying nothing.

Finally, he looked away and moved toward the bathroom, grabbing his shirt and trousers on the way.

Five minutes later he was stepping out of the room, after reminding her that she could stay another few hours if she wanted as the room had been booked until three in the afternoon.

She nodded. Blew him a desultory kiss, but his back was already to her, in his haste to abandon the landscape of this latest sexual fiasco.

Cornelia sighed, stretched her long, pale limbs under the thin white sheet.

She closed her eyes.

* * *

The message was short and sweet.

"Call me. Today, if you can."

Ivan.

She took a cab back to her Washington Square Place apartment and rang him back from there, once she had showered and changed into a grey T-shirt and a pair of jeans.

"It's me."

"Good."

"A job?"

"Yes."

"I thought you wanted me off the scene for a few more months following last time's small mess."

"I did. But this is overseas, not on home patch. Have you got an up to date passport?"

"Of course."

"Fine. It's in Paris. You'll find the dossier in the usual place."

"Perfect."

"When can you leave?"

"Will tomorrow do?"

"Absolutely."

"Hardware?"

"Locally. A safe deposit box. It'll all be in the dossier."

"Fee?"

"Fifteen thousand."

"That works for me."

"And, naturally, we'll supply the return ticket. Business class."

"The least you can do at such short notice …"

"You're the best, C. You deserve a touch of luxury."

"Cheap and cheerful, that's me."

She could almost hear him smile on the other end of

the line. He had been her contact for two years now. They had never met. She had no idea what he looked like, although she guessed he must be in his mid forties. The voice was accent-less and impersonal. Businesslike.

Well, Cornelia reckoned, killing was just a business like any other, wasn't it?

And one she was good at.

At any rate, more interesting than sex.

A WALTZ OF LOVE AND LUST

JACK WAS ON THE rebound from yet another disastrous affair. Feeling distinctively sorrow for himself, drowning in a sea of regrets. Romantically inclined as he was, he would readily have stumbled into the abandon of alcoholism, but he didn't even enjoy the taste of booze. And it's an uphill task to get yourself dead drunk on fruit juices or Pepsi Cola. But he knew this small bar in a Paris side street, a stone's throw from the river, parked between a kebab place and a cheap souvenir shop. So there he was, now sipping his first coffee of the evening, attempting to stay awake, killing time, hoping some form of inspiration or another would strike and he would find out what his next book should be about. It had been over three years since his last one had been published, and the untamed ideas inside his head just kept on circling round and round, never quite connecting with any form of sensible plot, let alone believable characters. Or maybe, for the first time in ages, he was becoming scared of the loneliness of long distance typing?

A few decades earlier, he'd been a student here. Maybe taking yesterday's early morning business commuter Eurostar to Paris on a whim had been a further desultory attempt to reconnect with his past. The bar on the Rue St André des Arts hadn't changed much, although another alongside it had since become a Turkish takeaway and the smell of slowly revolving skewered meat and dripping fat just a few steps away kept on drifting across Jack's nose, unpleasantly reminding him that time had moved on. Anyway, genuine students seldom came to this part of Paris any longer since most university locales had been moved out of the Latin Quarter following the riots in 1968.

Once upon a time, he could spend endless evenings here with his friends during which they would unilaterally put the world to rights, arguing fiercely about politics and art, managing with practised talent to make their drinks last until closing time. Whatever would he have then thought about his present self: this grey-haired guy and his still unruly hair, this stranger who looked a lot like him but now had a wallet stuffed with cash, twenty-pound notes, euros and US dollars which he had no one to spend on.

Jack had switched to *citron pressé* and nursed it slowly, drowning the drink in sugar. He leafed through the current issue of a film magazine he'd picked up earlier at a kiosk. Most of the features were about new French actors and actresses he knew little about.

Many years ago, this place had been the very centre of his private universe, as he regularly missed lectures and sought comfort in the familiarity of these old-fashioned surroundings, the shiny metal counter, the sizzle and hiss of the coffee machine, his gaze invariably captured by the full-size glass window on the other side of which passers-by trooped by, many of them women, young, old and in between but all unapproachable and distant to him. With a quiet smile, he recalled the day Mary Ann Armshaw had walked in. Blonde and skinny, all-American and, then, his distinctive ideal of the perfect Yankee corn-fed beauty. She had not been alone, but her companion, also American, was on the curvy side and had dark hair to her shoulders. He had listened to their conversation as they sipped their coffees, unaware as they were that he was also English-speaking. They had arrived in Paris four days earlier, on a student exchange programme and both young women were still in awe of and scared of this new city which proved so different from their small Midwest town. None of his mates had been around that day so, on a whim, he had quickly decided to follow the girls when they left the café. For two hours, they navigated the small streets and corners of the Left Bank, with him never more than fifty metres or so away. They appeared quite aimless and fancy free, peering at shop windows, at buildings, walking along the busy streets as if they had all the time in the world. More than once he almost gave up the chase and returned to his flat. Had it begun raining that evening, he would certainly have done so, but the weather just about held. The day grew darker and one of the two young American girls finally noticed his presence in their wake and they quickly glanced at him observing them from a distance, quietly conferred and then made a beeline for the nearest bar. This was still the days when almost every other door led to a café in the Latin Quarter.

"You've been following us, Monsieur" the blonde girl said to him as he walked in and stood by the counter next to them.

He'd smiled. "Yes, I saw you in the other bar earlier."

She looked him straight in the eye. He held her stare.

"I often sit there in the afternoons …" he continued.

The darker-haired girl squinted a little as she gave him a closer look and it dawned on her that he was actually speaking English. And with no French accent.

"You're not … French?"

He sighed with relief. They were seemingly not going to prove rude or aggressive. They were now curious. The ice had somehow been broken.

"No, I'm a foreigner here myself … like you," Jack added.

"Oh."

He no longer recalled today what her friend's name had been, and her participation in the ensuing conversation turned out patchy to say the least. Two weeks later, she returned to America, having proven unable to adapt to the distinct charms and perils of Paris. Mary Ann Armshaw had stayed behind, and remained the full nine months of the academic year.

In addition to Jack, two of his friends, that he knew of, actually slept with her during that period, although he was sorry to discover later he was not actually the first and sly Marcel had breached her uncertain defences long before he did. He'd always been the quiet one. When his time came, she allowed him to do almost anything to and with her except touch her breasts. He still remembered those small breasts now as they rapidly became the very focus of his desire and he would on every single encounter try to get her to change her mind. But he never did succeed. Whenever a finger, let alone a whole hand, ventured inches forward towards her tits, she would begin to squirm uncontrollably as if the contact could have proved capable of setting her nipples, her very skin, on fire. Had he actually touched her there, he knew for sure she would have screamed like a banshee and thrown him violently off her and stormed off at great velocity in any random direction.

Anything but her breasts. Today, sitting in that bar, that haunt of his younger days, he could remember no other body part of Mary Ann Armshaw. Don't ask Jack what her features were like or whether she was tall or small, or how long her blonde hair was. Just her pale, small breasts and her name came to mind. He wondered where she was now and if she had married her high school boyfriend after her return home? And was now a mother, or even a grandmother? Or even alive?

This place was so full of strange memories. It had been ages since he had even thought of Mary Ann. Why now recall yet another woman he had failed to truly connect with? He pushed the magazine aside and drowned his glass. Should he stay or should he go? The weather outside appeared unsettled and it was too early to go eat, and if he stepped back to his hotel room, a ten-minute walk away from the Rue St André des Arts, he knew he would no doubt doze off trying to kill time and wake up way past midnight with an unquenchable appetite. He called out for a further espresso.

He watched all the women walk by outside through the bar's windows. There were men too, of course, but they were almost invisible to him. They came in all shapes, sizes, ages and colours, a melting pot of movement and limbs and lust.

He smiled.

Was he turning in old age into some sort of pervert who found every single unreachable woman trooping past out there an object of desire?

He chuckled quietly.

And silently answered his own question: no, he was not. He had always been that way: a dangerous dreamer, a fantasist, an unrepentant lover of the female kind.

And some had loved Jack back too.

But all too often in the wrong place or at the wrong time.

Like now.

He peered at the empty cup of espresso. The sugar had congealed at its bottom, but the taste was no longer present in his mouth. All he could taste was a bitter tang of loneliness.

Jack sighed.

Which is when the man walked through the door.

Outside, a deeper night was falling, darkness surrounding the narrow Paris streets like a blanket floating solemnly to the ground. The evening regulars at the café were making place for the night owls, another species of drinkers altogether.

The middle-aged man who had entered the bar gave him a rapid glance and walked towards his table. For a brief moment he annoyingly obscured Jack's view of the street and a sumptuous passing redhead with unending legs and a cinched leather jacket who had momentarily caught his attention.

The stranger had a broken nose and short, greying hair and was dressed in a long green woollen coat which reached all the way down below his knees. Under the coat, he was wearing dark brown slacks and a white button-down shirt open at the neck. He didn't appear to have shaved for a few days and the stubble across his cheeks and lower jaw veered patchily between black and white.

With no hesitation whatsoever, the stranger faced him and sat himself down on a chair across from the table where Jack had spent the last few hours in deep thought and reflections.

"I know who you are," he said. He spoke to him in French, but he had an accent Jack couldn't immediately place.

"Do you?"

"Yes," the man confirmed.

He wasn't in the habit of being recognised in public, but it was nothing to worry about. He had done readings and participated in literary festivals in several countries. Maybe that was the explanation.

"Great," he said. "What can I do for you?" he asked the stranger. There were deep, swollen red pockets under the man's eyes as if he had recently been crying a lot.

"I want to hire you."

"Hire me?"

"Yes."

Absolutely the last thing he had expected the man to say …

"To do what?"

He looked deep into Jack's eyes.

"To find my daughter."

"Are you sure it's me you want?"

"Yes, I read about you in the newspaper back at home. I also once heard you on the radio," he added.

Jack could now place his accent: he was Italian. He let him continue speaking in French, as he had begun.

"Did you?"

The Italian man nodded and lowered his gaze, as if he were now ashamed of looking at him and begging for help. The silence lasted almost a whole minute. Jack broke it.

"Do you want a drink?" he asked the Italian.

"Yes …" the stranger hesitated, "a glass of red wine, I think."

Jack called over to the bar and ordered the man's wine and another coffee for himself, a double this time. He somehow guessed he was going to need it, even though another part of him also knew the caffeine overkill would keep him awake all night. But then, what's new? It had recently been a frequent state of affairs, unaided by coffee.

The stranger grimaced as he drank his first small mouthful of wine.

Jack stirred too much sugar into his coffee cup. The embarrassed silence persisted.

"Tell me," he suggested.

The Italian man looked up at him once again, nervously tugged on his collar and launched into his explanation.

"I am a doctor. I specialise in gastro-enterology. I am from Rome where I work in a big hospital. Maybe you know it, it's San Filippo Neri, on the banks of the Tiber. I run the Digestive Endoscopy Department."

Jack naturally knew nothing about gastro-enterology. But there was a flash of recognition down in the pit of his stomach. A doctor from Italy? Surely not. His face deliberately impassive, he nodded sympathetically as best he could. It was visibly not his turn to ask questions right now. The other man continued.

"I have two children. A girl and a boy. My daughter is called Giulia. She is now 23. I know I shouldn't be saying this but she was always my favourite. She was a wonderful baby, always happy and cheerful. Dark curly hair from an early age and bright, oh so bright. We have tried to bring our children up right. I am very liberal, but she was always the apple of my eye and of course she soon knew it all too well and quickly became an expert in manipulating me to obtain almost everything she wanted. I didn't mind, of course." He wiped a thin tear away from the corner of his left eye. "When she became older, a teenager, both my wife and I were scared she might become too wild and unmanageable. There were a few difficult years, but we scrambled our way through them.

In her late teens, she would almost never spend any time at home, apart from sleeping, you know. She was like a gypsy, flitting from friend to friend, playing tennis, studying, seeing films, theatre plays and opera. So that she should not run risks like so many of her classmates riding on a Vespa, we even bought her a small car, even though we knew that some years later we would have to do the same for her younger brother when the time came; a major expense. She became so independent. Yes, we argued a lot. She was spoiled and selfish at times, but I know we were closer than most fathers and daughters usually are, even in Italy, you know."

The doctor caught his breath, picked up his glass to take another sip, even though it was now empty. He called for another one.

"No, maybe white this time," he said. "It wasn't very nice, I must confess … Algerian, I think." He smiled weakly.

"*Blanc, cette fois, s'il vous plait*," Jack corrected the order.

"Thank you," the Italian man said.

"Do you know why she left?" he ventured.

"If only," he answered. "She wasn't that much into boys, I know. She found most friends her age too superficial. Remember, she was … is terribly bright. Completed her degree at 21, spoke 5 languages, even began writing film reviews for a small magazine where my wife knew the editor."

"The reason girls usually leave home is because of love or infatuation," Jack suggested.

"I know," the man facing him said. "She seemed to be happier going out with girlfriends or as part of larger groups. Really. But then I suppose all fathers prefer not to think of real life and forget the fact that young girls cannot help but be attracted to sex. It's our modern society, isn't it? My wife and I met at college when we were only eighteen and sixteen respectively and married ten years later when we both had jobs and some form of security. She and I have never known others. Newer generations are different, I realise … Anyway, from time to time after she was seventeen or was it eighteen, Giulia would sometimes spend nights away from home, but she would always inform us in advance and we knew where she was staying most times, at a friend's or some other safe place. If she had a boyfriend, she would never tell us and we just hoped that, once it happened, it would be someone nice that she would bring home in her own time to meet us. But she never did bring a young man home. She was a creature of secrets. I tell you, she had all the opportunities, but she followed her own counsel. Once a year, we go on a camper van holiday somewhere in Europe, all together – Giulia would even help out with the driving – and then spend the rest of the summer in the country house we have an hour away from Rome. She never minded; never suggested she should vacation on her own, or even with friends."

He took a deep breath, anticipating the next question.

"She never wanted for money. I would always give her enough for her needs, and then she earned a bursary for her studies and worked a few hours a week at the university library. Somehow money never meant a lot to her. She seldom asked for more, unless she had a serious reason for doing so. Later she did suggest she could find a flat for herself and we argued a little about it, but she soon realised that with Rome property prices these days, it was something neither of us could really afford. It's then I think that she met this man. An older man. I knew nothing about it, of course. She would never tell me. But she did confide in her mother. Although, even to my wife she would not provide any details. Age, name, nationality, profession, all those sort of basic things. I have now learned it lasted over a year. I suspect he was the first proper man in her life, also. Before him, just cheap infatuations and clumsy fumblings but no close … relationship." He blushed. "But then something went wrong. Neither of us knows exactly what."

He fell silent, rehashing the events and memories in his mind.

"And?" Jack asked.

"It was visible something disturbing had happened to her. She was no longer the soul and life of the party. She began spending hours alone in her room. Became introverted and anxious, defensive whenever we would try to speak to her. Evidently, there was something wrong."

"What did you do?"

"What could I do?" he said. "She was doing a postgraduate course in journalism and publishing and had mentioned the possibility of an Erasmus exchange with a matching institution in Paris. I wasn't too pleased with the option of her being on her own in a foreign city, but she had done so a few years earlier when she had spent six months on a language course in Barcelona where I had made sure she stayed in a Catholic hall of residence, supervised by nuns; at any rate, this time I was the one who encouraged her to go to Paris on this course. Maybe I reasoned a change of place would do her good and the Giulia I had always known and cherished would return to us. I was wrong. Within a few weeks of arriving in Paris, she moved out of the apartment of the friend's family where we had agreed she should stay. Since then, we've been trying to reach her on her mobile phone number but she never answers. I still try four or five times a day. Maybe she's lost it. Or refuses to answer, I don't know what to think."

A veil of shadow lowered across his eyes.

"And you want me to find her?" Jack confirmed.

"Yes,' the Italian doctor said.

"You do know I'm not a private detective, Doctor, don't you?" Jack said.

The other man briefly looked away, as if this was a subject he would rather not discuss. He took a deep breath, then turned to Jack again, a note of pleading in his voice.

"Please," he asked. "If I went to the police, they would just tell me she is old enough to make her own decisions, and I have no evidence of anything criminal having happened. Just another young girl wanting to live her life. But, somewhere inside, I just know that's not the case. Not Giulia."

A curtain of silence swept across the two men, both sitting there in a bubble in the far corner of the Parisian bar.

"Why me?" Jack enquired.

Fearing the answer.

"She was always reading your books," the Italian replied. "I was always asking her why. I've never understood her interest, or for that matter anyone's interest in mystery stories. I used to read Agatha Christie and Giorgio Scerbanenco when I was still at the faculty, but never since. Normal people grow out of it, I thought."

"I see."

"And I read that short interview she did with you for her friend's magazine. She admired you."

"Did she?"

"Yes, it was always Jack Clive this and Jack Clive

that."

"So?"

"So, I thought you might have some idea where to look for her. I just couldn't face employing a real private investigator. It's stupid, I know. But, at the back of my heart, I thought that was what Giulia might have wanted me to do …"

Jack stayed silent. He had expected another explanation. A more personal one.

Before departing the bar, the Doctor left Jack a folder with photographs and a mass of other details concerning his missing daughter and made him promise to keep in touch. Inside the file, there was also a thick wad of euros. They hadn't, of course, even discussed a fee.

He was missing a daughter and Jack was missing all the women from his past.

It was a sorry state of affairs.

Or, looking at it from a different perspective, could it be the way to begin a new book? He'd always liked the simplicity of Raymond Chandler's books, when a client found Marlowe and launched him on his investigative ways. And didn't Marlowe invariably come across a woman or two along the way? Some might even have called this a challenge. Only time would tell.

L'AMÉRICAINE

CORNELIA TOOK THE RER from Roissy-Charles De Gaulle. A taxi would have been easier and more relaxed after the seven-hour plane journey, but she knew she had to remain as anonymous as possible. Cab drivers have a bad habit of remembering tall, lanky blondes, particularly so those who did not wish to engage in needless conversation and reveal whether it was their first time in Paris or was she coming here on holiday?

Because she knew there were countless CCTV cameras sprinkled across the airport and the train terminal, she had quickly changed outfits in a somewhat insalubrious toilet shortly after picking her suitcase up from the luggage carrousel, and by the time she walked on to the RER train, she now had a grey scarf obscuring her blonde curls and wore a different outfit altogether from the flight. It was far from foolproof, but at least would serve its purpose in muddying the waters in the eventuality of a later, thorough investigation.

The commuters on the train to Paris looked grey and tired, wage slaves on their mindless journey to work or elsewhere. A couple of teenage Arab kids listening to rap or was it hip hop on their iPods glanced at her repeatedly, but her indifference soon got the better of them and she wasn't bothered until they reached the Luxembourg Gardens stop where she got off.

She had booked herself on the Internet into a small hotel there the previous day. She checked in under the false name on her spare passport, a Canadian one she'd seldom used before. She took a shower and relaxed before taking the lift to the lobby around lunch hour, noticing someone new had taken over at the registration desk from the young woman who'd earlier checked her in. Cornelia then calmly walked back to her room and stuffed some clothes into a tote bag she had packed into her small suitcase and went down to the lobby again and left the hotel. Fifteen minutes later, she registered at another hotel, near the Place de L'Odéon, this time under her real name. This booking she'd openly made by phone from New York the day before. She was now the proud tenant of two separate hotel rooms under two separate names and nationalities. Both rooms were noisy and looked out on to busy streets, but that was Paris, and anyway she wasn't here for a spot of tourism. This was work. She settled in the new room, took a nap, and just before the evening walked out and took a cab to the Place de L'Opéra. There was a thin jiffy bag waiting for her at the American Express Poste Restante. Here, she retrieved the key she had found back in Brooklyn at the Russian grocery Ivan occasionally used as a dropout. She then caught another taxi to the Gare du Nord, where she located the left luggage locker which the key opened. The package was anonymous and not too bulky. She picked up a copy of *Libération* and casually wrapped it around the bundle she had just retrieved from the locker and walked down the train station stairs to the Métro and took the Porte d'Orléans line back to Odéon. In the room, she unwrapped the package and weighed the Sig Sauer in her hand. Her favourite gun. Perfect.

* * *

The Italian girl had always preferred older men. Some of her friends and other fellow students at La Sapienza, Rome's University, had always kidded her she had something of a father fixation, and indeed her relationship with her gastro-enterologist Dad was prickly to say the least, seesawing between devotion and simmering anger. At any rate, he also spoiled her badly.

But boys her age seemed so clumsy and uninteresting, coarse, superficial, so sadly predictable, and she found herself recoiling instinctively from their tentative touches all too often. Not that she knew exactly what she wanted herself.

Whenever asked about her plans for the future, she would answer in jest (or maybe not) that she planned to marry an ambassador and have lots of babies. When Peppino – the jokey name she would use in public circumstances for her much older, foreign lover so as to make him impossible to identify for her parents – queried her about this, she would add that the ambassador would also be a black man, a big man in both size and personality. He would smile silently in response, betraying his own personal fears and prejudices, only to point out that she'd be wasting so many opportunities by becoming merely a wife. After all, this was a young woman who by the age of 22 had a degree in comparative literature, spoke a handful of languages, and would surely make a hell of a journalist or foreign correspondent one day.

Her affair with the man she and her few friends aware of his secret existence had affectionately called Peppino had lasted just over a year and he had been the first man she had fucked. To her amazement, he had become not just a lover but her professor of sex; unimaginably tender, crudely transgressive, and the first time she had come across a guy who understood her so well their contact when apart became almost telepathic. However, he was also more than twice her age, lived in another country and happened to be married, which sharpened her longing and her jealousy to breaking point. The affair had proven both beautiful and traumatic, but eventually the enforced separation from Peppino could not be assuaged by telephone calls, frantic e-mails and mere words any longer. For her sanity, she was obliged to break up with him. Even though she also loved him. She had a life to live, adventures to experience; he had already lived his life, hadn't he? Now was her time. The decision was a painful one and he naturally took it badly. Not that her state of mind was much better, wracked by doubts, heartache and regrets by the thousands as both she and Peppino could not help recalling the days and nights together, the shocking intimacy they had experienced, the pleasure and complicity, the joy and the darkness. Sleepless nights and silent unhappiness followed in her wake and she had agreed to stay with a girlfriend from her exchange months in Barcelona who lived in Paris – ironically, a city he had always wanted to take her to.

It was a wet spring and the thin rain peppered the Latin Quarter pavements with a coating of grey melancholy. Flora had departed for the countryside and her grandparents' villa where a family reunion was taking place and left Giulia on her own in the apartment for a few days. Initially, she had looked forward to the prospect but now felt herself particularly lonely. When she was not busy and frantically exploring the city with other casual acquaintances, memories just kept on flooding back.

She was sitting reading a book at the terrace of Les

Deux Magots, sipping a cappuccino, half-watching the world pass by, women who walked elegantly, young men who looked cute but would surely prove dull in real life, she thought, when she heard the seductive voice of the bad man across her shoulders.

“That’s a quite wonderful book, Mademoiselle,” he said. “I envy you the experience of reading it for the first time. Truly.”

Giulia looked up at him.

He looked older. How could he not be?

Cornelia much preferred ignorance. A job was a job and it was better not to have to know any of the often murky reasons she was given an assignment.

Had the target stolen from another party, swindled, lied, killed, betrayed? It was not important.

Cornelia was aware she had a cold heart. It made her work easier, not that she sought excuses. She would kill both innocent and guilty parties with the same set of mind. It was not hers to reason why.

She had been given a thin dossier on her Paris mark, a half dozen pages of random information about his haunts and habits and a couple of photographs. A manila folder she had slipped between her folded black cashmere sweaters in the travelling suitcase, to which she had added a few torn out pages from the financial pages of *The New York Times* and a section on international investment from *The Wall Street Journal* to muddy the waters in the event of an unlikely snap examination of her belongings by customs at either JFK or Roissy. He was a man in his late forties, good-looking in a rugged sort of way which appealed to some women, she knew. Tallish, hair greying at the temples in subdued and elegant manner. She studied one of the photographs, and noted the ice-green eyes, and a steely inner determination behind the crooked smile. A dangerous man. A bad man.

But they all have weaknesses, and it appeared his was women. Younger women. It usually was. Cornelia sighed. Kept on perusing the information sheet she had been furnished with, made notes. Finally, she booted up her laptop and went online to hunt down the '*clubs échangistes*' her prey was known to frequent on a regular basis. They appeared to be located all over the city, but the main ones appeared to be in the Marais and close to the Louvre. She wrote down the particulars of Au Pluriel, Le Chateau des Lys, Les Chandelles and Chris et Manu, and studied the respective websites. She'd been to a couple of similar 'swing' clubs back in the States, both privately and for work reasons. She'd found them somewhat sordid. Maybe the Parisian ones would prove classier, but she doubted it. Cornelia had no qualms about public sex, let alone exhibitionism – after all she had stripped for a living for years now and greatly enjoyed the sensation, but still found that sex was an essentially private communion however effectless it could be. But then she'd always had an uneasy relationship with and perception of sex, and at a push would readily confess to decidedly mixed feelings about it.

Would sex in Paris, sex and Paris prove any different she wondered?

She rose from the bed where she had spread out the pages and photographs, switched off the metal grey laptop and walked pensively to the hotel room's small, pokey bathroom. She pulled off her T-shirt and slipped off her white cotton panties and looked at herself in the full-length mirror.

And shed a tear.

Sometimes, it just happened. For no reason.

*   *   *

The bad man had no problem seducing the young Italian woman. He had experience and a deceptive elegance. Anyway, she was on the rebound from her Peppino and a vulnerable prey. Had her first lover not warned her that no man would ever love her, touch her with as much tenderness as he? And had she not known in her heart that he was right? But falling into the arms of the Frenchman was easy, a way of moving on, she reckoned. She knew all he really wanted to do her was fuck her, use her and that was good enough for now for Giulia. She was lost and the excesses of sex were as good a way of burying the past and the hurt as any other course of action. This new man would not love her; he was just another adventure on the road. So why not? This was Paris, wasn't it? And spring would soon turn into summer and she just couldn't bear the thought of returning to Rome and resuming her Ph.D. studies and being subsidised by her father.

She rang home and informed her parents she would be staying on in Paris for a few more months. There were protests and fiery arguments, but she was used to manipulating them. She was old enough by now, she told them, to do what she wanted with her life.

"Respect me, and my needs," she said. Not for the first time.

"Do you need money?" her father asked.

"No, I've found a job, helping out in a bookshop," she lied. "But Flora's parents say I can keep on living with them."

The Frenchman – he said he was a businessman, something in export/import – ordered her to move in with him and Giulia accepted. She couldn't stay on at Flora's without revealing her new relationship.

At first, it was nice to sleep at night in bed with another person, a man. Feeling the warmth of the other's body, waking up to another naked body next to her own. And to feel herself filled to the brim when he made love to her. To again experience a man's cock growing inside her as it ploughed her, stretched her. To take a penis, savour its hardening inside her mouth, to hear a man moan above her as he came, shuddered, shouted out obscenities or religious adjectives and feel the heat waves coursing from cunt to heart to brain. Of course, it reminded her of Peppino. But then again, it was different. No fish face at the moment of climax with this new man, just a detached air of satisfaction, almost cruelty, as he often took her to the brink and retreated, playing with her senses, enjoying her like an object.

Day times, he would often leave her early in the morning and go about his work and Giulia would explore Paris, fancy free, absorbing the essence of the city in her long, lanky stride. For the first time in ages, she felt like a gypsy again, like the young teenager who would live on the streets of Rome and even enjoy sleepless nights wandering from alleys to coffee shops with a cohort of friends or even alone, drinking in life with no care in the world. In Belleville, she discovered a patisserie with sweet delicacies, near Censier-Daubenton she made the casual acquaintance of a young dope dealer who furnished her with cheap weed, which she would take care never to smoke at the man's apartment off the Quai de Grenelle. As with Peppino, she knew older guys secretly disapproved of her getting high, as if pretending they had never been young themselves. Neither did they appreciate The Clash, she'd found out … He would leave her money when he left her behind but she was frugal and never used it all or asked for more.

And at night, after her aimless, carefree wanderings, he would treat her to fancy restaurants – she'd cooked for him a few times at the flat but he was not too keen on pasta or tomato sauce or seemingly of Italian food altogether – and then bring her back to the bedroom where he would fuck her. Harder and harder. As she offered no resistance and her passiveness increased, the bad man went further. One night, he tied her hands. Giulia allowed him.

Soon, he was encouraged to test her limits.

She knew it was all heading in the wrong direction and she should resist his growing attempts at domination. But the thought of leaving this strange new life in Paris and returning to Rome would feel like an admission of defeat, an acknowledgement that she should not have broken up with Peppino, and broken his heart into a thousand pieces, as she clearly knew she had. Maybe this was a form of penance, a way of punishing herself? She just didn't know any more. Had she ever known?

One dark evening, after he'd tied her hands to the bedpost and, somehow, her ankles, he'd taken her by surprise and despite her mild protests, had resolutely shaven away her thick thatch of wild, curling jet-black pubic hair and left her quite bald, like a child, which not only brought back bittersweet memories of her younger years but also a deep sense of shame. She'd always insisted Peppino should not even trim her.

The next day, the Frenchman used his belt on her arse cheeks and marked her badly.

Sitting watching a film that afternoon in a small art house by the Odéon was painful, as Giulia kept on fidgeting in her seat to find a position that did not remind her of the previous evening's punishment. Her period pains had also begun, as bad as ever; she'd once been told they'd only start improving after she'd had her first child.

That night, the bad man wanted to fuck her, as usual and she pointed out that she was having her period. He became angry. He would have been quite furious had she actually revealed that she had once allowed Peppino to make love to her on such a day and the blood communion they had shared was still one of her most exquisitely shocking and treasured memories. He brutally stripped her, tied her hands behind her back and pushed her down on the floor, onto her stomach and sharply penetrated her arse hole, spitting onto his cock and her opening for necessary lubrication. She screamed in pain and he gagged her with her own panties and continued relentlessly to invest her. Giulia recalled how she had once assured Peppino as they spooned in bed one night how she would never agree to anal sex with him or anyone. Another promise betrayed, she knew. She grew familiar with the pain. She had never thought it would be so easy to break with her past.

Later, as she lie there motionless, the bad man said:

"Next week, I shall continue your education. I'm taking you to a club and I want to watch you being fucked by a stranger, or more, my sweet Italian girl. Time we tamed you."

He asked her for her mobile phone and took it away with him. Giulia just felt numb. Before he left the apartment, he retrieved her spare set of keys from her handbag and locked her in. They were on the fifth floor and she had no other way out. Giulia sighed.

It was a night full of stars and the Seine quivered with a thousand lights.

The taxi had dropped Cornelia around the corner of

Les Chandelles. She looked out for a decent-looking café and sat herself at a table overlooking the street, where she would be highly visible to all passers-by. She wore an opaque white silk shirt and was, as ever, bra-less. Her short black skirt highlighted her endless pale legs and this was one of the rare occasions when she had lipstick on, a scarlet stain across her thin lips. She'd ruffled her hair, blonde medusa curls like a forest, and slowly sipped a glass of Sancerre, a US paperback edition of John Irving's *A Widow for One Year* sitting broken-spined on the ceramic top next to the wine carafe.

The bait was set: a lonesome American woman on a Friday night in Paris, just some steps away from a notorious '*club échangiste*': L' Américaine. She'd found out earlier, through judicious tipping and a hint of further largesse, from the club's hatcheck girl who drank her pre-shift coffee here, that her target was planning to attend the club later this evening. The entrance fee for single women was advantageous but she felt she would attract less attraction if she were part of a couple. She'd gathered on the grapevine that lone men would often congregate here before moving on to the club, in search of a partner.

She'd been told right and within an hour, she'd been twice offered an escort into the premises. She hadn't even needed to uncross her legs and reveal her lack of underwear. The first guy was too skanky for her liking, and altogether too condescending in the way he spoke to her in the slowly-enunciating manner some automatically do with foreigners. She quietly gave him the brush-off. He did not protest unduly. The second candidate was more suitable, a middle-aged businessman with a well-cut suit and half-decent after shave. Even sent her over a glass of champagne before actually accosting her. Much too old, of course, but then there was something about Paris and older men with younger women. The water, the air, whatever!

They agreed that once inside she would have no obligation to either stay with him or fuck him, at any rate initially. Maybe later, if neither came across someone more suitable. He readily acquiesced. Cornelia knew she was good arm candy, tall and distinctive, a beautiful woman with a style all her own, and an unnerving visible mix of brains and provocation. She'd worked hard on that aspect of her appearance.

Despite its upmarket reputation, Les Chandelles was much as she expected. Tasteful in a vulgar but chic way; too many muted lights, drapes and parquet flooring, dark corners or '*coins calins*' as they were coyly described on the club's website, semi-opulent staircases leading to private rooms and a strange overall smell of sex, cheap perfume and a touch of discreet disinfectant not unlike the cabins of erstwhile American sex shop cabins or the tawdry rooms set aside for private lap dances in the joints she had once merrily navigated through.

She spent some time at the bar with her escort and enjoyed further champagne, and allowed him to show her some of the nooks and crannies of the swing club, where he appeared to be a regular. Now she knew the lay of the land. She offered to dance with him.

"Not my scene," he churlishly protested.

"It warms me up," she pointed out. He nodded in appreciation.

"Just go ahead," he said. "Maybe we can meet up later, if you want?"

"Yes," Cornelia said.

From the dance floor, she would have a perfect vantage

point to observe new arrivals as they trooped past on their way to more intimate areas of the club. She shuffled along to a Leonard Cohen tune and marked her area between a few embracing couples, embracing the melody with her languorous movements. She'd always enjoyed dancing, it had made the stripping bearable. Cornelia closed her eyes and navigated along to the soft music. Occasionally, one hand or another would gently tap her on the shoulder, an invitation to move on and join a man, a woman or more often a couple to a more private location, but each time she amiably turned the offer down with a smile. No one insisted, obeying the club's basic protocols.

Amongst the French songs she had not previously known, Cornelia had already delicately shimmied to recognisable melodies by Luna, Strays Don't Sleep and Nick Cave when she noticed the new couple settling down at the bar.

The girl couldn't have been older than 25 with a jungle of thick dark curls falling to her shoulders and a gawky, slightly unfeminine walk. Her back was bare, pale skin on full display emerging from a thin knitted top, and she wore a white skirt that fell all the way to her ankles, through which one could spy on her long legs and a round arse just that little bit bigger than she would no doubt have wished to have, an imperfection that actually made her quite stunning, what with deep brown eyes and a gypsy-like, wild demeanour that reminded Cornelia of a child still to fully mature. She wore dark black shoes with heels, which she visibly didn't need, as she was almost as tall as Cornelia. But there was also a sad sensuality that poured out from every inch of her as she followed her companion's instructions and settled on a high stall at the bar. The man ordered, without asking the young girl what she actually wanted. Her eyes darted across the room, looking at the other patrons of the club, judging them, weighing them. It was evidently her first time here.

Cornelia adjusted her gaze.

The man squiring the exotic young woman was him, her target. The bad man. Her information had proven correct. As she watched the couple, Cornelia blanked out the music.

Less than an hour later, she had innocently made acquaintance with them and suggested to her new friends they could move on to a more private space. Throughout their conversation, the Italian girl had been mostly silent, leaving her older companion to ask all the questions and flirt quite openly and suggestively with the splendid American blonde seemingly in search of local thrills. At first, the man appeared hesitant, as if the visit to Les Chandelles had been planned differently.

"I've never been with a woman before," the Italian girl complained to the man.

"Would you rather I looked for a negro to fuck you here and now with an audience watching?" he said to her.

"No," she whispered.

"So, we all agree," he concluded and pushed his stall back, and gallantly took Cornelia's hand. "Anyway, you can do most of the watching as I intend to enjoy the company of our new American friend to its fullest extent. You can watch and learn; I do find you somewhat passive and unimaginative, my dear young Italian gypsy. See how a real woman fucks."

Giulia lowered her eyes and stood up to follow them.

Once they had located an empty room on the next floor, Cornelia briefly excused herself and insisted she first had to walk back to the cloakroom to retrieve something from the handbag she had left there as well as picking up some clean towels, which their forthcoming activities would no doubt require.

"Ah, Americans, always keen on hygiene," the bad man said and broadly smiled. "We'll be waiting for you," he added, indicating to his young companion to start undressing.

"I'll leave my clothes too," Cornelia said, turning round. "Don't want to get them crumpled, do we?"

"Perfect," the man said, turning his attention to Giulia's slight, pale, uncovered breasts and sharply twisting her nipples while she was still in the process of slipping out of her billowing long white skirt. There were red marks on her butt cheeks.

When Cornelia returned a few minutes later, the bad man was stripped from the waist down and the Italian girl was sucking him off while his fingers held her hair tight and her head forcibly pressed against his groin, even though his thrusts were making her choke. He turned his own head towards Cornelia, a blonde apparition, now fully naked and holding a bunch of towels under her left arm.

"Most beautiful," he remarked, and released his pressure on Giulia's head. "Truly regal," he observed, his eyes running up and down Cornelia's body. "I like very much," he added. His attention now centred on her groin. "A tattoo? There? Pretty? What is it?"

Cornelia approached the couple. The man withdrew his cock from the Italian girl's mouth, allowing her to breathe better, and he put a proprietary hand on Cornelia's left breast and then squinted, taking a closer look at her depilated pubic area and the small tattoo she sported there.

"A gun? Interesting" he said.

"Sig Sauer," Cornelia said.

There was a brief look of concern on his face, but then he relaxed briefly and nodded towards the American woman, indicating she should replace Giulia and service his still-jutting cock. Cornelia quietly asked Giulia to move away from the man so that she might take over her kneeling position. The Italian girl, in a daze, stumbled backwards towards the bed. Cornelia lowered herself. As her mouth approached the man's groin, she pulled out the gun she had kept hidden under the white towels, placed it upwards against his chin and pressed the trigger.

The silencer muffled most of the sound and Giulia's sharp cry of surprise proved louder than the actual shot which blew the lid of his head off, the lethal bullet moving through his mouth and into his brain in a portion of a second. He fell to the ground, Cornelia cushioning his collapse with her outstretched arm.

"Jesus!" Giulia exclaimed.

She looked questioningly at Cornelia who now stood with her legs firmly apart, the weapon still in her hand, a naked angel of death.

"He was a bad man," Cornelia said.

"I know," the Italian girl said. "But …"

"It was just a job, nothing personal," Cornelia said.

"So …"

"Shhhh …." Cornelia said. "Get your clothes."

The young Italian girl just stood there, as if nailed to the floor, every inch of her body revealed. Cornelia couldn't avoid examining her.

"You're very pretty," she said.

"You too," the other replied.

Cornelia folded the gun back inside the towels. "Normally, I would have killed you too," she said. "As a rule, I must leave no witnesses. But I'm not big on killing women. Just dress, go and forget him. And me. You've never seen me. I don't know how well you knew him and suspect it wasn't long. Find yourself a younger man. Live. Be happy. And …"

"What?"

"Forget me, forget what I look like. You don't know me, you've never known me."

Giulia, still shaking from the shock of the summary execution, nodded her agreement as she pulled the knitted top she had worn earlier over her head, disturbing her thousand thick dark curls. The other woman was in no rush to dress, comfortable in her white nudity. Her body was also pale, but a different sort of pallor, Giulia couldn't quite work out the nature of the difference.

Cornelia watched her hurriedly dress.

"Go back to Italy. This never happened. It's just Paris, Giulia. Another place. A bad dream. OK?"

Back in the street, Giulia initially felt disorientated. It had all happened so quickly. She was surprised to see that she wasn't as traumatised now as she should have been. It was just something that had happened. An adventure. Her first adventure since Peppino. Under her breath, she whispered his real name to herself. "Jack". It all felt unreal. The Paris night did not answer.

She checked her handbag; she had enough money for a small hotel room for the night. Tomorrow, she would take the train back to Rome.

The Louvre was lit up and she walked towards the Seine, and towards the darkness. At her fourth attempt, she found a cheap hotel on the Rue Monsieur le Prince. The room was on the fourth floor and she could barely fit into the lift. Later, she went out and had a crêpe with sugar and Grand Marnier from an all-night kiosk near the junction between the Rue de l'Odéon and the Boulevard

Saint Germain. People were queuing outside the nearby cinemas, people mostly her own age, no older men here. She walked towards Notre-Dame and wasted time in a late-opening bookshop, idly leafing through the new books on display. She would have dearly liked to have a coffee, but none of the Latin Quarter bookshops also served coffee, unlike her favourite haunt, Feltrinelli's in Rome, where she had almost spent a majority of her teenage years. But she knew that if she walked into a café and took a table alone, someone would eventually try a pick up line and disturb her, and tonight she felt no need for further conversation.

Giulia then remembered that she had left her laptop computer and, more importantly, her passport at the bad man's place. And her clothes, although she was less concerned about losing them. She had never been that much a creature of fashion. More jeans and T-shirts and trainers, despite the nice things her new Paris lover had bought for her and ordered her to dress in. Back in Italy, she had always been swapping clothes with friends and acquaintances, finding a warm sense of comfort in second-hand clothes, which her aunt would often then adjust for her size. As they were leaving tonight, he had returned the keys to his apartment to her and she had dropped them in her handbag. She remembered the crime and mystery books she used to read. Surely, the police would not be investigating the man's death yet? She took a calculated risk and hailed a cab. She could be there in under ten minutes.

There were no cars with flashing lights outside the building. She slipped in, ran breathlessly up the stairs, put her ears to the door. There were no sounds coming from inside. In all likelihood he had not been properly identified yet. Just a naked man with a bullet through his skull. She unlocked the door and quickly ran through the flat. Picking up her few belongings, the computer, her toiletries. She couldn't see where he had put her mobile phone. Maybe he'd thrown it away. Damn! Looked at the bathroom mirror. Realised her prints were everywhere over the flat. But then reassured herself that the crime had not occurred here, so it was unlikely they would lift the prints. Anyway, she knew there had been other women here before he had taken her in, seduced her into staying as his pet.

She was about to run out the apartment, after barely four minutes flat – she had timed herself – when she noticed that the drawer under his desk in the study was still open. Just as they'd left for the club, he had considered ordering her to wear a heavy gold chain around her neck. All part of his sexual rituals, she knew. But the clasp had been too loose and he'd decided against it. They were already running late, and he'd neglected to push the drawer closed and lock it.

She peered inside. The necklace shone darkly. And beneath it a half dozen or so manila folders and a tidy bunch of bank notes tied together with a red elastic band. The money would prove useful, she reckoned. She hurriedly grabbed the drawer's contents and scooped it all into her deep and floppy handbag. Then pulled the necklace out and put it back in the drawer. It would evoke too many bad memories, she knew. And rushed out of the man's flat. Locked up behind her. Walked quietly down the stairs to the street. No one had seen her inside the building and the pavements outside were empty. She walked to the Place de la Bastille, where she caught a taxi to her hotel.

Back in the small room, Giulia slept soundly. A night without nightmares or memories.

* * *

The man in the Police du Territoire uniform handed her passport back to Cornelia.

"I hope you enjoyed your stay, Mademoiselle?"

L'Américaine candidly smiled back at him as she made her way into the departure lounge at the airport.

"Absolutely," she said.

FOLLOW ME AN ANGEL

THAT NIGHT, JACK DREAMED of Giulia. Of the warmth of her body in the bed at night, the scent of her hair. But every time Giulia woke up inside the dream and his hand tenderly advanced towards her in the darkness, she would draw back with a look of horror over her face and say, "Don't ever touch my breasts, ever …" just like Mary Ann Armshaw. And he would wake up drenched in cold sweat.

Realising that maybe he and Giulia were now actually in the same city. In Paris.

Not that he could appreciate the irony in this. That he had impulsively taken the first train to Paris to bury her memories. A place he had always promised to take her to, but then somehow circumstance and life had conspired against them and time had finally run out. Was this why she had come here, according to her father? Coincidence? Fate?

But then how had her father known where to find him?

Or was it all a bad joke being played at his expense?

He emptied the folder. Photos of Giulia. As a child, more recent ones he had never seen. Smiling at the camera, pensive, cooking pasta in the family kitchen wearing a white T-shirt that adhered to her skin and highlighted her jutting nipples, standing in front of

Warsaw's Old Square, driving the camper on some unrecognisable road.

Printed-out pages, with the addresses and telephone numbers, where known, of her friends. Some of whom he was aware of, from past conversations. Others unknown to him. Many of them Spanish. He idly wondered which were the two Barcelona University students she had gone to Mallorca with. One of them had made a pass at her, and she had been tempted, he knew. Had even allowed the young man to see her naked on the beach, sprawled across the golden, wet sand.

Jack swallowed the bile rising up through his throat.

He looked at every printed sheet of paper and every photograph again and again. Seeking clues, answers, a direction to follow until it all became a blur in front of his teary eyes.

Damn, he was no detective; he didn't even know where to begin this foolish investigation. He remembered that book he'd once written where the private eye was asked by a distraught husband to discover what had happened to his missing wife. Jack had tried to conceal from the reader that the detective in question had actually known the woman in question, and had in fact killed her, thus being recruited to investigate himself. He'd never been that good at plotting; had always been much better at characterisation.

He walked out to a nearby patisserie on the Rue Saint Sulpice, bought himself a couple of *petits pains au chocolat* and, on the short way back to his hotel room, a bottle of mineral water from an all-hours *épicerie* and settled at the desk in the narrow, fourth-floor room. He spread out the contents of the doctor's envelope and, across a few sheets of paper, attempted to list most of the things he still clearly remembered about Giulia: the friends she had mentioned, things she had said, places she had talked about, anything that could help him now find where she had taken off for. Was she even still in Paris?

Two hours later, his mind was still scrambled and despairing and he had a bad headache.

He needed to go online. Maybe he should find another hotel, one with a broadband connection.

Jack glanced at his watch. London was one hour behind but by now people would be out of bed there, he reckoned. He called up the contacts page on his mobile phone, and selected a number. The phone at the other end took ages before it was finally picked up.

A morose South London voice, emerging from the fogs of sleep, answered.

"Hallo …"

Timbers was a small-time hustler he had once been introduced to when he needed some inside information for a book he was working on. He wanted to know how one could get hold of an illegal gun south of the river. And Jack knew all too well that he was not the sort of guy who could venture into a pub in Brixton or Herne Hill enquiring about such matters, without running the risk of being beaten up at the back or wherever his curiosity would have led him to. He had the wrong look and the wrong accent, to begin with. Someone at the Groucho Club had once mentioned Timbers, another writer maybe and once he had made contact with the petty crook, they had improbably bonded and he'd become a mine of information. They hadn't seen each other for well over two years now, but had kept in touch with the occasional conversation over the phone every few months. Timbers loved reading mystery novels, and particularly enjoyed picking holes in plots and details, invariably pointing out that he could certainly do better should he ever find the time to actually write.

"It's Jack Clive."

"Wow, man, you've woken me up."

"I feared I would, sorry Timbs. But I'm abroad, in Europe, and wasn't sure what the time was back home," Jack lied.

"It's OK," Timbers said, stirring his mind, dragging it laboriously towards the shores of morning consciousness.

"I need some help. And couldn't think of anyone else to call, you see."

Jack could almost see the sly smile spreading across the other man's lips.

"Guns again?"

"No," Jack said. On the occasion of that initial encounter, he'd been treated to an hour-long treatise on models, calibres and a parallel history of South London establishments of ill-repute and villains. All that for something that warranted only a line or so in the novel. But Timbers visibly was thrilled to become the professor and showing off his knowledge of the darker side of life.

"Tell me, Jack, I'm all ears."

"I'm in Paris and need some information …"

"Mate, I haven't been there for ages, twenty years I think, know nothing about the place. You know me, it's a week of Sundays if I ever even cross the river here …"

"I realise that, Timbers, knew that already. What I need is some contact here who could maybe give me some assistance. Someone like you, see, but with local knowledge of things. Does that make sense?"

On the other end of the line, the gawky South Londoner chuckled.

"Ah, a French Timbster …"

"Exactly," Jack said. "Or should I say *exactement*?"

"For a moment there, I thought you wanted me to come over, had me worried, just not my scene … hmmm … tell me … legal or illegal sort of stuff?"

"Just information, really," Jack answered. "Lay of the land, suggestions and all that."

There was a brief silence.

"Can probably do, man."

"That would be just great …"

"I'll need a few hours. A couple of calls, check the guy is still around, see if he's willing to see you. Vouch for you."

"I understand," Jack nodded.

"I'll ring you back. This number?" Timbers asked.

"Yes."

"It's a deal mate. The moment I know, I'll be on the blower."

"Great, really great."

"I suppose a guy like you speaks French? Not sure how much my guy can communicate in English."

"I do," Jack confirmed. "Enough to make myself understood."

"So," Timbers queried, "your next story is going to be set in Paris?"

"No," Jack said. "Nothing to do with a book."

"Personal?" Timbers said.

"You could call it that, I suppose."

The call from London didn't come until the following day. Jack was given just a name and a number. Timbers had spoken to the man and vouched for Jack. "You owe me one," he'd said. "I know." "Good luck then; hope it works out for you."

It took him another couple of days to contact the guy in question. His number just kept ringing and took no messages. In the meantime, Jack kept on wrestling with his memories of Giulia in search of possible clues, evoking too many bittersweet memories of their past encounters and embraces. How they had met, the first night, the first touch, the kiss, the scent of her skin. He rang her father twice, in need of further information to clarify matters. He was back in Rome. Every time he spoke to the surgeon, he felt like a total fraud, but the snippets he garnered didn't help him make any progress. He knew why Giulia had come to Paris in the first place, but little of what she had done here for the past three months or so of her stay, outside of perfunctory university lectures and prudent evenings out with the friend with whom she had been staying until she had out of the blue moved out on some flimsy pretext. The friend, Flora, whom he'd questioned on the telephone, as she was initially reluctant to meet, had no explanations to offer; she was as puzzled as they all were.

Timbers' French connection asked to meet up with him in a bar off the Place Pigalle. In another life, he would have been fascinated to find out everything there was to know about the man, a stocky guy from Marseille with a lived-in face and piercing grey eyes, in his mid-fifties, who listened impassively to Jack's questions like a minor character in a Jean-Pierre Melville film, indifferent but attentive and secreting menace by the bucket load. But a small, sad voice inside him told Jack all of this was unlikely to ever make it into a book.

"That's not much to go on," he finally commented, taking a slow slip from his glass of pastis, and giving the photographs of Giulia Jack had brought along a somewhat perfunctory glance.

"I know," Jack said apologetically.

"Women go missing all the time in Paris," the man

from Marseille said.

"She's bright," Jack added. "I don't think she would have gotten involved in anything dangerous. Really. Let's not be over-dramatic here," he concluded. This was not a book and a damsel in distress to be rescued from the heartless clutch of traffickers in white flesh. Surely those days were over.

His interlocutor made no further comment.

"The family are happy to pay a reward, I would add," Jack said.

"Money's not the problem," the Marseillais said. "At any rate at this stage. I'm happy to do this as favour to our mutual friend in London. We go back a long time."

"That's generous of you."

"I'll ask around," he concluded.

They exchanged telephone numbers. Jack desperately wanted to ask the man how long his enquiries would take, but refrained from doing so. He had done a deal with the owner of his small hotel to stay for another week, at a slightly reduced rate. He had to be patient.

Later that day, he arranged to meet up with Flora, who had in all likelihood been the last known person to have seen Giulia before her disappearing act.

The young woman wore her hair cropped and short and preferred to just sit on the Boulevard bench than join him for a coffee. She was visibly nervous. She'd already told Giulia's father everything she knew, she said. She gave Jack a weary glance. As if she could see right through him. Had Giulia told her about him, their now defunct relationship, or was she just guessing?

"She just told me she had to … get away," Flora said.

"Was she running away from something, from somebody?" Jack asked, terrible visions of other men, tall, dark, swarthy pursuing Giulia.

"No," the young French woman replied. "That was in the past. She told me after she arrived that she'd come to Paris to forget the past, begin a new life, adventures maybe. She felt life owed her that …"

"Was she happy?"

"I think so. Those first weeks, we laughed a lot, went out dancing, she met a lot of my friends, she was cheerful."

"Do you think she might have met someone?" Jack enquired.

"Maybe, Flora said. "But if she did, she never mentioned it to me. Giulia enjoyed going out during the day, while I was at classes. Just walking about, you know. She always said she was something of an urban gypsy. She was also very secretive, kept to herself," she added.

"Oh, I know …" he said. Didn't he know it!

"She just told me she wanted to move out, that it was nothing personal, but she wished to be on her own, wanted to think and all that. But she was lying, I'm sure of that …"

"And she just packed all her stuff?"

"Yes. The last I saw of her was through the window – I was watching – as she began her walk towards the Métro station down the street, pulling her case behind her and that big rucksack of hers strapped across her shoulders."

"And she never phoned you again or got in touch?"

"No. I assumed she'd gone back to Italy soon after, so it was a surprise when her father came here to question me and my parents."

A thought occurred to Jack.

"Did she bring her computer with her when she came to stay in Paris with you?"

"Yes, she had a small Apple white PowerBook. But she couldn't use it much at our apartment. We haven't got a broadband connection, just a dial-up connected to the telephone. My parents are a touch old-fashioned. Giulia would sometimes go out to cafés or places where they had a free connection when she wanted to check or send mails."

Flora stole another furtive glance at him as he sat there deep in thought, adding every word, every snippet to his mental search engine. There was nothing to take notes about, he knew. He'd have no problem remembering all this. What little there was. Jack looked up, and his eyes intersected with hers. Her fingers were playing with a stray strand of wool defying the tidy alignment of her knitted scarf's thread. She avoided his gaze. As if she had been about to ask him something. "Who are you really?" "Are you the older man Giulia knew?" But whatever thoughts she was formulating did not translate into words.

"I'm sorry about all these questions," Jack said. "But her father does want me to find her, you see,"

Flora nodded.

They looked at each other in silence, too many unsaid thoughts swirling inside their heads. The conversation had come to an end. They formally exchanged telephone numbers – just in case – and shook hands and parted.

For a couple of days, Jack installed himself in the nearest Starbucks and sipped too many coffees while his laptop roamed the net for clues. There was no response from Giulia's old Skype moniker. Her profile there still listed her as living in Barcelona, which she had left almost eighteen months ago, and still listed only the fifteen contacts she'd had originally. No one had been added.

Evidently the account was dormant. Although Jack could not believe she would come to Paris without her computer. She'd never go anywhere without it, he was convinced. And it could be his only way of finding her.

She had no MySpace account, whether under her name or under the half dozen or so handles he knew she was likely to use. There were two other women there with the same name, but one was in San Francisco and the other in Reggio Emilia, and the photos on their main pages were quite unlike her and he did not believe she'd load a bogus photograph. In addition, the contacts for the two women showed no evidence of having any connection with the Giulia he knew, in addition to the fact their musical tastes would have literally made her scream.

There was a Facebook page though. And the black and white photo of a tall young woman dancing with her arms outstretched and her face in shadows was most definitely her. A new photograph he had never seen. He recalled her mentioning that a friend of hers had offered to shoot some pictures of her, and the shiver he had felt in his heart at the time. Not nude ones, surely. Jealousy already. She was wearing a short skirt, seemingly denim and a tight dark top which emphasised the flatness of her breasts. Her hair cascaded like a stream across her pale shoulders. Jack felt his stomach tighten.

The friends listed made sense. He recognised a few names, other girls she had sometimes mentioned in passing, from her film club and university, her brother, strangers he was unaware of, another writer she had also once interviewed at the film festival where they had first met. He made a request to become her friend, but she did not respond. Jack then blanketed her friends list. Only one reacted, a old school friend who hadn't seen her for two years and had no clue where she might now be. None of the others reacted, but the word must have gone out to Giulia that he was trying to track her down, and on the second morning he settled at the Starbucks table with a pastry and a coffee and connected to the web on an open wi-fi link, her Facebook account had disappeared. Although repeated Google searches still revealed, like ghosts, thin electronic traces of Giulia, synapses that ran across the screen that weren't quite there, like evidence left behind in the wake of her retreat. That photo, her name listed as part of a litany of names amongst her friends' accounts. Already the trail had grown cold. She was there somewhere but evidently did not wish to have any further contact with him again. As it was before her disappearance, he realised. Why would the circumstances have changed? How could she know that Jack was now helping out her family, rather than following his own agenda. Well, there was that too, he couldn't deny it, could he? Damn, he missed her so much.

He checked whether she was listed on Linked-In, but she wasn't. Another Internet social networking group, but one mostly business people used. Bebo was no help either. Or Twitter. This appeared to be a dead alley.

He closed the laptop and sat there silently. There was an old Simon and Garfunkel song playing in the bar. On the Boulevard outside, passers-by promenaded by in blissful oblivion, hurrying businessmen in suits and winter coats, beautiful women, all angles and curves under their finery, booted, lithe, each one another world of secrets he could never know. Sure, it could never have worked with Giulia. Jack knew that. It had been a war between his heart and the cold logic of the situation. Eventually, she would have grown bored with him, or he would have become incapable of pleasing her sexually or socially, the words would have run out, the silences would have taken hold and dug the grave of that ever so fragile love that still held them together in New York and all those other clandestine places he had taken her to. But never New Orleans, he sadly knew. Yet another promise he had never kept.

He felt like crying. A grown man at a corner table in a Paris Starbucks lost in his sorry thoughts. Not quite classy enough for Edward Hopper. A fool. A tear was brewing in the corner of one eye. He wiped it away with a single finger.

His phone rang.

"A man from Marseille tells me you are looking for information," the voice at the other end said in French.

"I am."

"Let's meet, then."

Antoine Franck had once worked for the French security services. He'd been recruited covertly whilst at university. He was bright and he was ambitious, but had no ambition to later move on to one of the Grandes Ecoles where the country's business elite were groomed. He underwent intensive training in intelligence matters and was later posted to the backwaters of Lagos in Nigeria where he managed to make the best out of an impossible place, and was later promoted to a small unit based in New York, which had been created to run discreet surveillance on United Nations delegations and identify possible sources of useful information. He was an apolitical man, but for him this was just a job, and patriotism was not a virtue that ever crossed his mind. In America, he flourished and discovered his forte was not as a man of action or a plotter in the darkness but as an analyst and gatherer of random facts with the uncanny ability to see through the murk of jungles of data and see the trees, the nuggets that would pay off. However, his insight into the clandestine financial dealings of others also provided him with a profound knowledge of the system and how it could so easily be subverted. He became greedy. Siphoned small, and then larger amounts of cash from offshore accounts held by friends and foes. Eventually, his transgressions were discovered and he returned to Paris in disgrace and jobless. He was philosophical about it, anything but angry and set himself up locally as a consultant in matters financial and discreet, offering his services to anyone who wished to manipulate the arcane loopholes of the financial underground: money laundering, setting up networks and connections which efficiently erased the trail of fraudulence. He quickly thrived. He had retained many of his contacts within the Intelligence community who were happy to use him for below the line activities, but also made him invaluable to those who lived on the other side of the divide between honesty and crime. A most useful man, with a foot in both camps.

He met Jack in the basement bar of the opulent Hotel du Palais Royal.

"So, you're the writer? Jack Clive? I looked up a few of your books. Interesting. But I don't read much."

"Yes," Jack replied, ordering a *citron pressé*. He just couldn't take more coffee, after his Starbucks residency of the past couple of days.

"I've never met a writer before," Franck said.

"Well, we look quite normal, don't we, no different from anyone else with a real job?"

Franck smiled. "Absolutely."

A waiter with a white regulation jacket served their drinks. Franck had ordered a glass of Sauvignon Blanc.

Jack diluted his lemon juice from the water jug and tore open all three of the sugar sachets he had been provided with and emptied them into his glass and stirred the whole lot in.

"Sweet tooth?"

"Indeed."

Franck quickly got down to business. "Why are you looking for the Italian girl?"

"A favour to her family," Jack said.

"I see." Franck weighed the information. There was visibly something on his mind.

"Did you find anything out, then?" Jack asked.

"Yes."

"So?"

"So I think there is a problem. A bad problem," the Frenchman said.

"Tell me."

"There is this man. You don't need to know his name, I think. A rather bad man, a dangerous man …" he briefly fell silent.

"And?" Jack's stomach was fast embarking on the agonising process of tying itself into knots.

"She was seen with him. Someone answering her description."

"Who is he? In Paris?"

"Yes, in Paris. He grooms young women …"

"Grooms?" A terrible spectre of obscene possibilities swished across his mind. The pain in Jack's midriff sharpened.

"A predator. A very accomplished one. He somehow manages to meet all these young women, has a talent for recognising those who offer the right potential. Initially, he seduces them. Then, gradually, he takes hold of them, mentally, not just physically and soon he convinces them it's right they be shared with others, trains them."

"Trafficking?" The images rushing across the back of his eyes were too much to bear.

"No. There is nothing non-consensual about it all. They become willing. That's the cleverness of it all. It never becomes illegal."

"I don't understand …"

"It's a whole other world," Franck added. "BDSM circles. Limited to a small elite but they always need new, fresh meat, so to speak. And he is one of the main suppliers. He's no pimp, doesn't sell them, just passes them on to others, to groups, once he has tired of them, sucked the will out of them, I am told. Ironically, there is nothing the authorities can do about the whole farrago. Various people are aware of his activities but he is beyond the law. Nothing can be done."

"And Giulia was seen with him?"

"Just recently. A young women corresponding to her description and the photograph I was provided with was seen entering a notorious *club échangiste*, a swingers club as you call them, on his arm."

"Jesus …"

"It gets worse …"

"How?" Jack felt breathless as the revelations continued.

"On the same night, this man was killed."

"How?"

"Shot. Looked like a professional hit. But she was with him when it happened. She was later seen leaving the club without him, though. There are no witnesses to what could have taken place inside the club. In those sort of establishments people cleverly always look the other way."

"It couldn't be her," Jack said.

"Of course not, from what you have told me she is not the type. But people change, you know; life intervenes."

"Certainly not," Jack vehemently added.

"But a lot of people might be seeking her out now. Not necessarily the police, who are possibly rather glad to be rid of him, but possibly his associates. And, I am told, others."

"When did this happen?" Jack asked.

"Two nights ago."

"So she might still be in Paris?"

"You know as much as I do," Franck concluded.

Jack was struck dumb.

"A nest of vipers, Mr Clive. I wouldn't like to be in your young woman's shoes right now."

"And you're positive she is the one who was seen with the man that night?"

"Yes, the doorman was positive. It's his job to remember faces. He's an invaluable source of information. I trust him."

Jack fell silent.

They promised to stay in touch.

That night Jack had nightmares of large, calloused hands roaming across Giulia's white skin, of her body stretched and tied to a cross, of whips and men in fierce boots and all the paraphernalia of BDSM he could summon from reading *Story of O* decades back. And every single cliché he could mentally summon hurt like hell. When it came to matters sexual, it took very little for his imagination to unleash.

Why did life sometimes turn into a novel, he wondered? Always the wrong sort of novel, of course.

DANCE ME

SHELTERING BEHIND DARK CLOUDS, a distant moon haltingly threw a light across the Washington Square arch. Cornelia paid the cab driver the fare from JFK and made her way up the steps to her building, swinging her tote bag behind her.

Inside her apartment, the message light on her phone was flashing. She ignored it. Slipped out of her coat. Glanced at her watch. Walked to her bedroom where she upended the contents of her bag onto the bed. She'd travelled light. She'd acquired essential toiletries in Paris at a corner *pharmacie* and left them behind at her first hotel. There was just a change of underwear and a couple of skirts, a spare T-shirt and the outfit she'd worn at the club. She had briefly thought of jettisoning the latter back in France, but since she'd actually not been seen wearing it that much, it would have been a bit of a waste, she reckoned.

For a brief moment, her mind wandered back to the moment of execution yesterday evening, the lightning flash of recognition on the man's face as he looked up from the small tattoo in her crotch to the weapon in her hand. The muffled sound of the shot and the eyes of the young Italian woman as she uncomprehendingly watched the scene unfold. Cornelia shuddered. She felt dirty. She hurriedly tore off the clothes she had worn for the flight.

It was the same after every kill. This delayed reaction. Not disgust at having killed another human being. Just emptiness. The adrenaline had now retreated from her system, and left her void, with a sense that her whole existence was meaningless. She didn't mind the killing. It was a job like any other, and in some cases she managed to pump herself up enough to actually dislike the targets she had been assigned. It was not even a question of morality. She sighed and made a beeline to the shower.

The water dripped, a Niagara of heat streaming across her wide shoulders. Her eyes were closed as she stood motionless, allowing the insistent warmth to surge through her body, cleansing her, waltzing her every thought away, when a phone in the other room rang. The cell phone she'd transferred from her bag to the bed cover. Barely a handful of people knew the number. Cornelia didn't move. The phone drifted into silence. A few minutes went by. Then it rang again. It could wait, she knew. It WOULD wait. The anonymous ring tone ceased again and the quiet returned, punctuated only by the water hiccupping down across her skin to the bathtub floor.

She dried herself briskly, dropped the white towel to the wooden floor, grabbed an old pair of jeans folded over the back of a chair and fumbled her way into them. Searched for a clean T-shirt and settled on a light V-necked beige Walkabouts on Tour one. Her leather jacket hung on its usual hook on the back of the apartment's door. It was old and battered, an imitation WW2 aviator's jacket, from which she had carefully detached all the irrelevant and pretentious sewn-on badges and insignias after she'd found it in a thrift store in San Diego a few years ago while on a job there.

It was approaching ten at night. As she locked the door behind her, the cell phone which she'd left behind, still on the bed, amongst her discarded clothes, rang again. She made her way towards the Bowery.

The club was half empty, even at this time of night. The recession was biting, and Wall Street types visibly had less cash to spend these days. Nor was it anywhere as opulent, or pretentious as the swing joint in Paris, Cornelia knew. Functional was the right word for it.

She'd checked on the way over whether she could work a shift, and Stangaler had agreed. Although he'd warned there weren't many big tippers around. Cornelia wasn't bothered. She just wanted something that could take her mind off the last job. Something she could do with her brain switched off. As she had walked down Lafayette, the thought that the Paris job was somehow far from over niggled her. Loose ends were always unwelcome and she suspected the Italian girl was one. Why in hell had she spared her? It had been a mistake, she realised. Hopefully, one that would have no lasting consequences. The girl had dark brown eyes and, following the surprise of witnessing Cornelia pull the gun from below the towel and her execution of the man who had dragged her there, there had been a shadow flying across those eyes that spoke of resignation, not of pleading as would normally be expected.

Maybe that acceptance of her fate, that sadness was what had momentarily touched Cornelia, interrupted her in murderous flight.

There were only three other dancers on tonight's bill. No wonder that her proposal to come and do an impromptu shift had been so cheerily welcomed.

It had been a couple of weeks since Cornelia had

worked last, but she kept a locker here with a couple of spare outfits and a bunch of discs pre-recorded with numbers she could dance to.

She changed into a black leather two-piece bustier and bikini bottom, each item garlanded with a plethora of zips, most of which only served a decorative purpose, then sat and pulled on a pair of matching thigh-high leather boots with pencil-thin five-inch heels. She'd always resisted wearing stockings for her act, unless specifically required to by the locale's management. There were already so many clichés in the stripping arsenal, and stockings had never pleased her. Fortunately, her dancing was sufficiently sexy (she preferred to call it erotic) for her to be forgiven her idiosyncrasies and there were at least half a dozen small clubs dotted across Manhattan who were happy to provide her with a stage on the occasions she made herself available. Cornelia never agreed to long-term residencies. She was strictly a freelance stripper. And, for convenience sake, she only worked in Manhattan, although word was reaching her that Brooklyn was fast becoming the in place. A better class of audience, it appeared. But, deep down, Cornelia only danced for herself, not for an audience. Take it or leave it.

From a hook on the far wall of the changing room, floating full of static across the make-up lamp, she grabbed hold of a thin wrap, all gauze and transparency.

She glanced at her discs and selected one. It had to be the right mood for today. On the other side of the curtain where the stage and its central pole stood, the sounds of a Beyoncé song were nearing their climax. Cornelia walked over to the sound and lighting technician's pokey cabin and handed him her music.

"Welcome back, gal," he said. "Been a long time."

"You know me, Pete," she said. "I have another life on the side." Little did he know.

"Good to see you again. This joint always needs a touch of extra class," he said. Pete studied sound engineering at Columbia and was in his final year. His job here paid the bills.

"It's good to be back," Cornelia said. "It's about time I exercised again. Been travelling. Too much food …" She'd almost mentioned she'd been to Paris before she caught herself. Too much information.

"Oh, by the way, you know that guy who's hung up on you. The Hedge Funder? He slipped me a few bills to let him know when you'd be in again. Should I?"

Cornelia smiled. One of her harmless regulars.

"Sure. Earn your money …"

"Any good books I should read?" Pete continued. He'd noticed early in her sessions here that she spent her spare time backstage reading, and was always happy to talk about the books. He'd thoroughly enjoyed her recommendations.

Cornelia was about to reel off a list of good reads she thought he would enjoy when the dancer who'd been occupying the stage stormed past them on her way to the dressing room. Her tape came to an end. Pete quickly pressed a button, and the muted sounds of a big band tune hit the speakers, the customary transitional music the club played between acts.

"Later," Cornelia said. "My turn."

She moved away from the cabin and crossed behind the curtain to the other side of the small stage where she would be making her entrance.

The music began.

A melancholy piano.

Darkness. Then a lone spotlight exploded, harshly

revealing her standing motionless on centre stage. Pale skin. Black leather. Blonde hair. Muted red lipstick.

Cornelia drew her breath, lazily extended her arms, reaching, stretching, her hands fluttered to the sound of the bass now underpinning the melody. The rest of her body remained frozen. The tinkling of glasses at the bar or at the scattered tables stopped; isolated conversations ceased.

A distant keyboard, organ or harmonium – the P.A. system was muddy and did the music no justice- quivered in the melody's background and Cornelia's head began to sway gently from one side to the other as the wall of sound began to grow in size and emotion. As if a statue was awakening from a thousand-year slumber. One hand grazed the translucent wrap that barely covered the top half of her body, and the thin material caught the light and shimmered. Her long, unending legs began undulating like a vertical tide from the stage upwards, ripples of movement moving towards her midriff.

Cornelia bends her knees, her body rotates on the high heels and her regal arse tightly constrained by the leather bottom is now facing the onlookers. She bends, offering the spectators a full view of her rump's curve. A steel guitar pierces the serenity of the dance and she straightens and pivots several times on her axis, her whole body now coming to life, tremors rippling between the white skin, the tautness of her stomach, the hard hills of her breasts laced within the black leather bustier.

She knows every eye in the room is on her. She closes her own eyes and accelerates her swaying, her dancing, her seduction.

One hand on the metal pole, she skips a figure of eight around it, head falling backwards, medusa hair swinging down between her shoulder bones, brushing against the small of her back, leg extended in front of her, a perfect horizontal line criss-crossing the metal pole. The rest of the music fades as she floats along on its melody and once again just the piano can be heard, dragging the tune onwards, lonely, sad, languorous, towards its inevitable lingering conclusion.

Her movements around the pole slow down until once again she stands motionless and someone in the audience rudely yelps. Within seconds, the music resumes, a new tune with heaving rhythms and relentless percussion unleashed. Cornelia nervously pulls the transparent, gauzy wrap away from her body, revealing the full domino visual effect of black and white, skin and leather, in all its glory, scattering the thin piece of material in her wake as she kicks a leg up and races across the stage and the abandoned wrap floats down towards the dusty dance floor.

Her body, all sinews now electrified and in the right gear, shakes and sways and glides like a whirlpool of movement, graceful, enticing, provocative. Cornelia opens her eyes again. Recalls her waltzing hand and without missing a step or a single planned tremor begins to pull the cord lacing the bustier across her front. The thin, black leather string effortlessly slithers back in her finger and soon the bustier gapes open, barely held up by her small, firm breasts. A skip, a jump and hey presto the bustier falls to the ground, but she is now with her back to the sparse audience, cupping her breasts in her hand as she bends again and offers them a final view of her arse in its black leather sheath, flesh far from invisible, perceived but still shielded from their hungry gaze, straining against the material.

One brief moment, the melody all but drowned in dissonance and reverb before the next bridge in the music intervenes and it flows, launches again in full flight, Cornelia's wandering mind alights on a fleeting memory: Paris. The swing club and its ornate chandeliers, the young Italian girl and the line of imperceptible hair fluff descending like an arrow between her belly button and her genitalia, the look in Giulia's eyes, but it's all a confused blur of movement and she returns to the present, and, now on automatic pilot, goes through the rest of her routine through a veil of indifference, exposing her pale breasts in full view now and, after a final change of tune, dives into her finale, with the right amount of flexing, bending, teasing and outright exposure, until all that is left of the leather two-piece is on the stage floor and she is fully visible, cunt unveiled, bare, as one final time she reverts to being a statue, motionless, legs apart, stance proud and upright, eyes piercing the darkness of the room, daring the punters to comment or even applaud, her jungle of blonde curls bathed in the sunlight of the lone spotlight like a basket of snakes, smoking, fierce, untamed. And then the light holding her captive at the very centre of the stage is switched off and it is dark night again. She keeps on standing there a while, a few shy claps in the audience, the sound of glasses clinking, being refilled, and that awful music they always put on in the intervals between the dancers.

Unseen, she moved off the stage and made her way towards the changing room, brushing against a Latina girl in a slutty outfit making her way towards the stage in their relay race of stripping and teasing.

She badly needed a shower again.

She'd been sweating more than usual. Maybe it was the jet lag? Couldn't really wait until she got back to

Washington Square. She couldn't stand the feel of it much longer, had to wash it off right now.

Dried off a quarter of an hour later, she was about to dress into her civilian clothes again, when the crimson lights above the changing room door lit up. She was the only dancer there right then, so it must be for her. A lap dance request. Not her favourite game.

She set her jeans back on the chair and grabbed her work outfit again.

It was her hedge funder. Her current greatest fan. They came, they went. Never meant too much to Cornelia. He'd certainly made good time getting here after being advised of her presence, she reckoned.

"Hi," he greeted her, with a large smile on his face.

"Hello," Cornelia walked into the small private cubicle. He was already sitting on the settee, his legs apart, jacket off. He was wearing totally uncreased black corduroy trousers which had probably never been worn before and his customary starched white shirt. His idea, no doubt, of leisure attire in the rush to reach the gentleman's club from his downtown condo.

A fifty-dollar bill had been placed on the worn green settee's corner. He knew the routine. He'd been visiting her over six months already; had probably spent most of a thousand bucks on lap dances with her in that space of time.

"How are you? Been on vacation? Anywhere nice?" he asked.

"Nowhere special," Cornelia replied, stepping towards him and positioning herself above his knees, ready to straddle him.

She unhooked her top. Leaned in towards the middle-aged guy, catching a whiff of his deodorant, or was it after shave, observing with detachment how his sandy hair was perfectly sculpted and trimmed.

"Music?"

"No need," he said. Strains of the music playing onstage a few curtains away were leaking through all the way to the cubicle anyway.

"A silent lap dance, eh?" Cornelia said.

"The best," he remarked. His eyes alighting on her pink nipples now almost grazing the crisp material of his shirt as she leaned forward, barely making actual contact with him. He took a deep breath. Cornelia was now sitting on his knees and to an unheard rhythm began grinding her arse against his thighs, shifting her weight from one thigh to the other with metronomic regularity, balancing, slipping and sliding. In an instant he was visibly hard. Her head fell towards him, and her jungle curls fell across his forehead, caressing him, whipping him gently. The hedge funder threw his head back and his chest heaved, the white shirt momentarily wiping against her jutting nipples.

Three minutes can sometimes feel like a wilderness of eternity.

Cornelia never offered any extras. Just a basic lap dance. No frottage. No unzipping the punter's trousers and helping him manually to climax. No lips or mouth on his cock, let alone his face or any other part of the man's anatomy. She had explained the rules the first time he'd called for her after her show. Naturally, on the initial occasions, he had suggested more, offered more cash, but she was not prepared to change her rules. For him or anyone else. She had made that clear.

The allotted time ran out. Cornelia began to rise.

"No. Stay," he asked, his hand extending to the jacket draped across the other side of the settee and pulling out a further bank note.

"It's your money," Cornelia remarked and began to grind into him again.

"No need for that," he said. "Just talk …"

Again. He always wanted to talk. But Cornelia was not into conversation. This was a job, that was all. She felt no need for bonding or extraneous manifestations of friendship. Just keep it professional.

"Fine," she agreed. Still sitting on his knees, his bones now pressing hard into her flesh. Tiredness rushed across her body. Maybe it had been a bad idea to come and work so quickly after the transatlantic flight.

"You never say much, do you?"

"That's not what I'm here for, is it?" Cornelia replied.

"I realise that, but … it would be nice to know something about you, wouldn't it? After all, you seem intelligent … and with all due respect, not like your average sort of lap dancer …"

"So, I'm articulate and I can spell and I don't have a Bronx accent … Does it make me any sexier?" Cornelia asked her customer.

"Absolutely," the hedge funder said, with a soft chuckle. "And you have a sense of humour, to boot …"

"Thank you, kind sir."

His tone changed. His eyes looking darkly into hers.

"Listen, you're fucking beautiful but I just don't understand why you do this … as much as I enjoy seeing you strip and these private sessions, you could do so much better for yourself … really … I don't know what brought you here but if I can help you …"

Cornelia sharply interrupted his hurried flow.

"YOU listen. This is what I do. This is want I want to do. I won't give you a sob story about my journey to get here. There was no journey. I didn't grow up disadvantaged, I wasn't abused or abandoned on some sidewalk bereft of everything following a wounding affair of the heart. I have no bad luck story to bore you with or gain your sympathy or your pity at that …"

Her head drew back and Cornelia straightened. On the P.A. across the room, on the stage where another girl was now performing, they could recognise the strains of Springsteen's *Born in the USA*.

The man opened his mouth wide, as if to protest against her tirade.

Cornelia continued.

"Look, I don't wish to be saved. I'm not drowning, just dancing. Because I like it, because it's what my body is good at and if the pleasure I provide is worth a few bucks all the better.

Why is it so many of you men always want to invent some complicated story full of sound and fury to explain why we shake our butts on a badly-lit stage exposing our bodies to all and sundry. I'm not on drugs, I'm not a single mother and I know what my personal vices are and can happily live with them, thank you. And the very last thing I'm seeking is some Wall Street prince to ride in and save me from the gutter. There is no story to tell and no cry for help in my darkness. I don't need the questions, or the pity. Just try and understand that and we'll get on fine and I'll keep on showing you my tits or spreading my legs for your delectation and private fantasies. It doesn't come free of course, but you know that already, and beyond that I'm not for sale."

Her punter was now fully silenced.

Cornelia glanced at the man-sized watch on her wrist.

"So, you still want to know the reason I'm a stripper?" she asked him provocatively.

Puzzled, he said "Yes."

"I do this because I collect books," Cornelia said. "And now your time is up. I have to leave now. See you."

She rose from the couch and still proudly topless swiftly stormed out of the narrow lap dancing area and made her way back to the artists' changing room. She was laughing inside from the dazed look on the man's face, his lips pursed like a fish's mouth. Because for once she had actually told him the truth. Well, maybe a half truth: the dancing and stripping paid for the basic bills, but her freelance contract killing did actually pay for the rare books she liked to collect. As vices went, she could think of much worse.

The weather was still mild for the time of year and Cornelia decided to walk home, rather than take a cab. She needed the fresh air to clear the fog of her jet lag. She meandered up Broadway, made a detour through Chinatown and then reached Houston. There was a midnight movie playing at the Angelika, but she decided against it. Somehow she was not in the mood right now for an indie with an emo soundtrack. There was a fifty/fifty chance she would fall asleep halfway through anyway. She noted the film would still be playing for the next few days. There was no rush.

A nagging feeling of unease had settled on her mind.

The Greenwich Village comedy clubs and bars disgorged their hordes on to the quietly lit streets as she made her way North. Bleecker Street. Thompson. Sullivan and finally the shores of the darkened park.

The cell phone she had abandoned still sat on the table. It vibrated, then buzzed. Cornelia first ignored its insistent sound and moved over to the kitchen, took a sip of apple juice from the half empty carton in the fridge and then finally picked the phone up. There were six messages waiting. She held it to her ear.

"Hello."

"Where the fuck have you been?"

"Here and there," she said.

It was Ivan. She didn't think she'd ever heard him swear at her before.

"Don't you pick up your messages?" he asked.

"I'd left the phone at home and gone for a walk."

"Damn, woman, you should have been in touch with me the moment you landed at Kennedy. Reported back."

"Sorry. I was tired. Didn't think. I would have called you in the morning."

"Very unlike you."

"So, sue me …"

"Cornelia, you've fucked up."

"Have I?"

He snorted on the other end of the line.

"How?" But Cornelia knew. She'd broken one of the basic rules. Leave no witnesses.

"You know very well what you've done, girl. I'm disappointed with you, really."

It had been barely 24 hours since the hit. How could they have known? Was there someone else at the Paris club, observing, checking matters out?

"Why did you spare the other woman?" Ivan continued. "You know it's not on. And don't go telling me you took pity on her. There's no place for sentiment in this business. You of all people know that."

"It just happened, Ivan."

"Well, the shit has hit the fan, my dear."

"Let me guess: the doorman reported back?"

"No matter how it happened, Cornelia. I'm having bad pressure applied. The customers are furious …"

"Even if the girl talks, to the French police or

whoever," Cornelia protested. "Worst possible case, all she can do is describe me. There is no open connection to you or your principals."

"That's not the way they see it, I'm afraid," Ivan said.

"I'm sorry, Ivan. I've let you down. I'll forego the payment and reimburse the expenses. And the cost of the Sig Sauer, which right now is at the bottom of the Seine. It was disposed of soon after the job, I threw it from a bridge. It won't be found."

"That's just not good enough."

"So?"

"Not only did you let the girl go, but she is thought to have then taken some documents from the hit's apartment. She has to be found."

"Me?"

"You're the only one who really knows what she looks like. She hadn't been introduced yet to the man's associates, so apart from the doorman at the club who only caught a quick glimpse of her, no one else can now recognise her."

"Oh, Ivan …" she began to plead.

"Go back. Eliminate her."

"A tall order …" Cornelia said.

"You've always been resourceful. Anyway, you have no choice. You messed it up and I've been instructed to the effect that if the young girl is not found and those documents retrieved within ten days at most, it's you who might have to pay the price. I'm sorry."

"Who are these principals of yours?"

"You know I can't tell you that, even more so in the present circumstances."

"It would help to know a little. Might explain who she is and where I should be looking out for her …"

"I don't even know that, Cornelia, you realise. And

there is no way I can ask. You know how it works: every link in the chain must remain just a voice on the phone …"

"And right now I'm the link that sticks out like a sore thumb …"

"Yes."

"Damn."

"I'd hate to lose you, Cornelia. I've always liked you and you're good at the job. Quirky but efficient. I'm still surprised you could have made such an elementary mistake, what with all the experience you have."

"No one's perfect."

"There's a flight out of Newark tomorrow at three in the afternoon. Be on it. Usual arrangements at the other end. You know the drill. Get it right this time, please."

"I will."

"Clean things up once and for all. That's all you have to do. They wanted you scratched, you know. Asked me to assign your case to another operative, but I pleaded for you. Got you this second chance. It would have been too much of a waste."

"I understand."

The phone in her hand went dead.

Cornelia felt ever so tired right now. She stripped and dropped onto the bed. Pulled the covers around herself and sleep finally caught up with her.

LIKE A LILY TO THE HEAT

GIULIA LOOKED AT THE cash she had retrieved from the bad man's drawer. There was more there than she had initially thought. Sitting up in the narrow bed of the small hotel room on the Rue Monsieur le Prince, she pulled the red elastic band from the bundle and began counting the euro notes.

She could survive on this for several months, she reckoned. Easily.

She realised she had no wish to return to Rome and bury herself in the deadly, familiar routine of studies and family. It would be an admission of defeat. There surely had to be something more to life. Paris had begun on the wrong foot. She had been too weak, goal-less. A mistake she was determined not to make again.

Having wrapped the elastic band around the cash again and transferred it to her rucksack, she looked at the half dozen manila envelopes she had picked up from the drawer in her haste to leave the dead man's apartment behind. Surely not more money? She pulled them towards her across the grey sheet that reached to her waist.

She opened one, and then the others. Just files. Dossiers with names and random information. Some of them had photos attached. Of young women. Images of their faces looking sadly into the camera. Others of their naked bodies shot against a dark photographic studio background, impersonal, stark, like a series of pieces of meat put up for sale. Giulia shivered. Leafed rapidly through the mass of files that had been divided between the envelopes. No, there was no file on her. She didn't recall the man having taken any pictures of her. Yet. Was he planning to set up a file about her, had the fatal incident at the *club échangiste* not happened? Another woman in a catalogue. She had no wish, right now, to read the text that accompanied each woman's photograph. In French, anyway, which would take her ages to decipher. There was something creepy about all the documents. She stuffed the envelopes into the rucksack, rose from her bed and quickly showered, She needed a walk. Some fresh air. Time to think.

She was wandering through the bird market just to the north of Notre-Dame when the helplessness of her situation struck her. She was alone in a foreign city, she had severed all her ties to the few friends she had here and had no wish to return and attend the courses she had been following. It had only been an excuse to leave Italy again, and allow her father to subsidise her. She already had her degree; what was the point of further qualifications when the job market in Rome was worse than it had ever been and over two-thirds of graduates could only get macjobs and still lived with their parents late into their twenties? And she had been the witness to a murder. Was it even safe to stay here?

Maybe she could go to Barcelona. She still held bittersweet memories of the city, its friendly campus, the Ramblas on Sant Jordi's day, the beaches. The man who had joined her there. Just two years ago now; how time had flown. Or should she take a flight to America, any flight, go as far as she could from Europe? San Francisco maybe? She realised she had enough funds to do so. But what then? A question she still couldn't find the right answer to.

The grey waters of the Seine lapped against the stone walls of the quays and Giulia shivered. Warmer weather, that's what she needed.

She stopped. Her nose was dripping. She hadn't brought warm clothes with her to Paris. And made her mind up right there and then. Rapidly retraced her steps back to the small hotel. Repacked her few possessions, settled her bill and walked down to the nearest Métro station on the Boulevard St Germain, the entrance opposite the banks of art cinemas and took the first train towards the Porte d'Orléans. Half an hour later she was standing in the vast and noisy departure hall of the Gare d'Austerlitz. The vast station momentarily felt like a film set, a ghost town littered with lingering extras waiting for the invisible director to call the shots and set them in motion.

Jack was stuck in a rut. Philip Marlowe by now would have called up his cronies in the police force, followed half a dozen red herrings, possibly come across murderous but beautiful twins or little sisters and been bashed over the head several times and woken up dazed and dishevelled by a lake or in some derelict industrial warehouse, but at least he would have made progress in his quest for the missing person or object he had in a fit of romantic generosity agreed to look for. Alongside consuming endless sips of whiskey. Jack didn't even have a clue where to venture to even get beaten up properly. Damn, it was easy on the page. Marlowe would never give up on a case.

It was evening. Autumn was slip-sliding into winter

and he was sitting at his usual table in the small café in the Rue St André des Arts, with a notepad open at an empty page on the table next to his glass. Clueless. His phone rang.

"Hello?"

A woman's voice, soft, shy.

"Mr Clive, can I call you Jack, it's Eleonora Acanfora. I knew Giulia. Her father, il Dottore, told me that you are looking for her. I also want to find her. I would like to help. I am in Paris. Arrived this afternoon by train. Maybe we can finally meet for first time?"

Jack had heard of Eleonora when he and Giulia were still seeing each other. She was a photographer in Salerno, south of Naples, who had accompanied her to take snaps on the occasions Giulia had been asked to interview movie directors or actors for the small semi-professional film magazine she sometimes freelanced for. Which was how Jack and Giulia had originally met.

He remembered Giulia mentioning how much she liked Eleonora. They had even, she had once confessed to him, swapped skirts.

"Hello, Eleonora," he replied. "It's been a long time. I was worried that you'd grown offended with my e-mails … Anything you can do to help would be gratefully appreciated."

"Good."

He gave her the address of the café. She joined him there an hour later.

Out of curiosity, the year before, Jack had once visited Eleonora's website. Initially, to see whether she had ever taken shots of Giulia he might not have seen before. It was in fact more of a blog illustrated with frequent photographs and with a hyperlink to a flickr account where the rest of her images were archived under an assortment of categories. Often reading other people's blogs was like peeking into the lives of strangers with total impunity, a compelling variation on voyeurism and one a writer found it difficult to avoid. More so as Jack always could find time to waste on the Internet; like all writers he held the art of procrastination in high regard and online research was always a perfect excuse not to write quite yet. He had begun to scroll through the previous six months of Eleonora's entries. More short sentences or zen-like thoughts possibly lifted from books she had read. She didn't post every single day, and the journey hadn't taken that long.

The initial sojourn inside Eleonora's life had touched him more than he thought it possibly could, in addition to the fact she represented a final link to Giulia after their break-up. She didn't use her blog as a diary, like so many other bloggers he had come across did, but in a strange way it was even more intimate. The respective entries were merely evocative, if puzzling titles "darkness', "red room", "blue room", " hold me", "street with no name", "raindrops on wire", "take my soul", "the surface of water" and so on, some accompanied by a photograph, others by a short poem or an excerpt from something she had recently read, a book or a haiku. Reading through the actual lines and sensing how apposite each photograph was to the words or the enigmatic title, he sensed the weight of a monumental sadness. This was visibly a woman in pain. And she moved him. There was also music embedded in the website which could be heard at the click of a link once he turned the sound back up on his computer. Some of the music he knew, some he did not recognise and was eager to identify as it also spoke of inner desolation, yearning and desire, all tropes that also anchored his own soul. And in strange ways her connection with Giulia made this surreal in a bittersweet way.

Had Jack not been in mourning for Giulia, he would have mailed Eleonora right there and then, with a myriad questions and an unhealthy curiosity for deciphering the story behind the story.

He recalled the conversations they had had about her friends. Was Eleonora the one who loved opera, or was that another, Simone maybe?

Slowly the memories coalesced. Eleonora was the friend from early schooldays who wanted to be an artist and had discovered she had a born talent for photography (and liked modern jazz, not opera …) but was not yet at a stage where she could make a living from it. She had not gone to university but the two young women had nevertheless kept in regular contact. Eleonora worked in her brother's computer store in Salerno, but spent most of her leisure time in Naples and was always miserable in love, embroiled in an on-off-on relationship with a local musician – a piano player Jack thought he remembered – who treated her badly but that she couldn't quite jettison. This was enough information for Jack's unbridled imagination to pen whole stories in the gaps between her blog entries and illustrations, and think he understood Eleonora a little better.

There had been a loop of hypnotic guitar music on her website one week which had caught his imagination. He had e-mailed her, asking her to reveal its provenance. It was from the soundtrack of a movie he had already seen, but at the time it had not struck him as so compelling that it was now, accompanying her words and her images. They had then begun an intermittent correspondence, in which Giulia's name or existence was deliberately never alluded to. A week or so later, she had posted a short sentence from one his books that had been translated into Italian – in fact some lines he could not even recall writing. Something to the effect that the bodies of women so quickly erased all evidence, traces of previous lustful excesses. Was it a signal to him or just something intimate that she recognised in herself?

A few days later, Eleonora began posting a whole series of new photographs, self-portraits, and Jack learned in an otherwise distant mail that she had broken up with her man. Again.

Every new photograph that appeared on the website – and by now, Jack was hunting them down almost obsessively at regular intervals, like a story developing, a page-turning plot, revealed another part of her, like a chameleon shedding layers of skin or pretending to be someone else. Her face, dark as night eyes, an aquiline, proud nose, wild dark, unkempt hair. And always, a sadness, a beauty made in darkness.

Some of the photographs revealed her in various states of undress, unveiling long legs, a pale shoulder, acres of white skin, her stomach, the swanlike line of her neck, the timid birth of breasts (none of the images were ever truly explicit), the shadow of her bones beneath the skin, the long-lasting pain in her eyes of coal, her strong waist (above black panties). He sometimes felt like printing up each and every image and trying impossibly to assemble them into a whole jigsaw portrait of her, but there would always be parts missing, as if yahoo or whichever server hosted her site did not allow sexual parts to be posted to a flickr account. So, Jack being Jack, he would wildly fantasise, imagining her on a bed, walking out of a shower in an anonymous hotel room. Jack had always had a perverse talent for dreaming.

Eleonora never offered him any encouragement and

the little correspondence they exchanged was cryptic and mostly one-way traffic as she seldom clearly answered any of Jack's questions. Which became highly frustrating as she usually took a week at least to answer Jack's invariably longer e-mails. But every new photograph she posted online felt to him like a veiled, personal message.

He thought of her a lot. Maybe because of the connection with Giulia. The fact they both happened to be Italian. And attractive.

But he didn't even know the sound of her voice.

Or the smell of her skin.

Let alone the taste of her lips. Or the texture of her hair slipping through his fingers.

From all those images on his computer screen, he knew intimately the shape of her back, the curve of her knee, the black shiny boots she once wore, a dress, a top, the ring that circled one of her fingers, the coat that buttoned at her neck, the deep sense of yearning in the deep pool of her eyes. He wondered unendingly what it might feel to sleep with her in the same bed, to feel the warmth of her body as they unconsciously switched positions at night in a bed too small for two, what her eyes would look like in the morning as she woke by his side. Harmless dreams.

One day, Eleonora had written to him, asking if he thought it would be easy for her to find a job if she ever came to London. She felt she had to get away from southern Italy and her present, confining surroundings. Just to get away from things. As Giulia so often did. Jack knew that she had seldom travelled outside Italy, except for two trips to Germany when her boyfriend's band had toured there. It felt to him like a cry for help.

He cautiously answered that in all honesty it might prove difficult as he was aware that her spoken English was halting (they both wrote to each other in their own, respective language) but he was happy to do all he could to help.

It took Eleonora another fortnight to answer. Just a few words. Not really an answer. Telling him she was trying to sort herself out. Then their patchy correspondence had just petered out.

Out of gallantry, he had sent her flowers for Valentine's Day months later. Roses, of course. As he used to do for Giulia when they were an item. She took a photograph of the flowers and placed it on her website as a blog heading. Enigmatically titled "Thanks, J."

One week later, a new stream of photographs began to appear on Eleonora's website. A plate of sushi on a restaurant table, the boyfriend (Henry Miller to her Anais Nin) sitting across from her in the same restaurant.

Then, as the days went by, a succession of photographs of Eleonora with her boyfriend, both topless, in unchaste embrace, sitting on a bed, against a wall, holding hands, fighting almost, touching, littering the horizon of her blog. One followed by another, relentlessly. Like an unfolding newsreel. Forever witnesses of afternoons and nights there were spending together – or, it once occurred to Jack, maybe they were earlier images of when the couple had been together and this was just a final visual requiem. To Jack, the other man almost looked like a Neanderthal. Rough, unfeeling, not the sort of guy he could ever understand Eleonora being attracted to. Every single time he logged on, Jack began to fear that the next image he would uncover might actually see them actually fucking.

For several days in a row, the images continued. Never had Eleonora appeared more beautiful and lost. There were now daily photographs of Eleonora and the other man, no text, no titles, no haikus. Then one day it just stopped and the blog stopped being active.

Maybe it was best this way, Jack had decided. What was he thinking of, falling for a woman he had never even met? And a friend of Giulia's. It would have been like treading on thin ice, surely?

He sent Giulia yet another e-mail; asking her where she now was, and why she still refused to communicate with him, assuring her that he still missed her abominably and shackled himself to his keyboard to finally write another book. Yet again, Giulia refused to answer his pleas.

Six months later, Jack deleted everything he'd written. It just didn't feel right. Once upon a time, the longing he felt inside was capable of generating stories, feelings. Now it was just a parade of words full of emptiness.

He'd packed lightly and taken the next morning early train to Paris.

He recognised her the moment she walked into the café. She was so much shorter than he had expected. All those photographs he had seen of her had not prepared him for this. Jack smiled.

"Sit down," he invited her.

They both looked at each other.

"Is nice to finally meet," Eleonora finally said.

"It is. Really," Jack answered. "It's so good to see you. Have you taken time off from your brother's store?"

Eleonora's smile broadened. She wore all black from head to booted toe.

"Oh no," she said. "I not work there any more. For four months now I just do official photography at Naples clubs and music places. Tomorrow, if you want, I will show you my new portfolio. Is all pictures of musicians. I manage to become official photographer for many Naples venues where they have music. Is six months contract. Not pay too much but is still good. Better than my brother's shop, for sure."

"That's wonderful."

"But then, il Dottore, Giulia's father, he come to see me and ask if I hear from her this year."

"Have you?"

"No. I not even know she had come to Paris. She stops communicating totally after she finish with you. I not know if sadness or not. But she was always such good friend when she was happy, I decide I must do something. But now I not sure what."

"Welcome to the club," Jack said.

"But then I think that maybe together we know enough about Giulia. We have ideas. We talk and know where to look, no?"

"Maybe."

"Il Dottore, he give me a bit of money and I have some of my own. I just I feel I owe it to Giulia. She help me when I was sad with Henry, you know."

Jack knew. She would call him Henry after Henry Miller, and she thought herself as Anais, an Italian incarnation of Anais Nin. He'd seen the photographs. The images of their bodies together in the stark black and white photographs.

Eleonora read his thoughts.

"Is over with Henry," she told Jack. "Finally. I make break. Is better. For good."

"Eleonora, it's none of my business. You don't have to tell me, you know," Jack pointed out.

"Is better to be honest, Jack."

She leaned towards him over the table and Jack caught a whiff of her perfume and smiled.

"Why you laugh?" Eleonora asked.

"Just smiling, Eleonora. Just smiling," he said. "Your perfume?"

"Yes?" she said quizzically.

"I recognise it. It's Anaïs Anaïs, isn't it? By Cacharel?"

They both laughed.

"So, you and me, together, we find Giulia? OK?"

"Yes, Eleonora, we find Giulia. That's a deal."

But at the back of Jack's mind, there was another nagging question worming its way through to the surface. What would happen when they found her? Or if they didn't?

Just four Latin Quarter blocks away, unknown to them, Giulia had earlier finished paying her latest hotel bill. For two weeks now, she had been flitting from place to place, eking her funds out, having graduated down to low-grade two star hotels in a bid to make the money last. Time to move on, she had decided.

Giulia had transferred all her meagre belongings into a large, newly-acquired rucksack she had slung over her shoulders for now, after having been defeated by the complexity of its straps and appendages. In her right hand she had her customary deep-bottomed canvas bag with her laptop and other essentials.

She'd taken the Métro to the train station.

The departure hall reverberated with a cacophony of noise. Light shone through on this grey day through the station's cantilevered glass roof. She spotted random clusters of policemen examining papers at the entrance to various platforms and she nervously moved back into the main concourse. Her heart skipped a beat.

Surely this was routine; didn't concern her.

She noticed a sign for the public toilets and zigzagged towards them between the ever-shifting crowds of travellers.

She washed her face with cold water and then, impulsively, disposed of the stack of envelopes and their shady dossiers into the nearest waste bin and quickly buried them under a mass of crumpled paper napkins. Why was she even carrying the stuff? It was the past and she was severing her ties once and for all. Yesterday, Rome, her studies, Jack, Barcelona, that week in New York, the bad man, the murder and now Paris.

Giulia walked back into the bustling railway station and looked up at the ever-shifting jumble of destinations, times and platform numbers on the large, high electronic indicator board.

All she really knew was that she wanted to go south. She grabbed a slice of lukewarm and tasteless pizza at the station's central cafeteria.

Anywhere south.

Giulia knew her heart sought sun and warmth.

The louder sound of cheerful, laughing voices reached her ears, catching her attention. A group of young men and girls burdened with heavy backpacks were making their way to the platform where the TGV to Madrid was parked. Giulia glanced at the indicator. The train was scheduled to leave in a quarter of an hour. She looked down and saw the group being waved through by the bored cops. Three young women in jeans and tees, and four tall boys with untidy long hair, some with basketball caps, most wearing sweat shirts bearing logos of various American universities. Which didn't mean they were necessarily Yanks, Giulia knew. It was just the sort of thing that was fashionable with European students, she had discovered.

It occurred to her that if she hadn't taken different roads in her past life when alternatives had presented themselves and she had made the wrong choice, she might well have been part of that group, carefree, laughing her head off at bad jokes, slightly tipsy even. She looked down at her legs, her scuffed trainers. After all, didn't she dress just like them? Wasn't she even in all likelihood more or less the same age?

Giulia made up her mind.

She swivelled round and rushed to the ticket counter and bought a one-way student rate ticket for the train to Madrid and ran to the platform. The cops had moved on to another part of the railway station by now and she wasn't delayed at the gate.

She stepped on to the train. She had no reserved seat. She was still catching her breath when the doors closed with a soft electric hush. There was a deafening moment of silence then the wheels shifted into gear, slowly at first, then exponentially faster as the whole train shuddered and followed and moved out smoothly, the now empty platform unrolling like a movie through the windows.

Giulia began her journey through the train, until she came across the earlier group of young men and women all sitting together in a compartment towards the front of the train. They were quieter now. One of the girls also had dark corkscrew curled hair, just like Giulia. And one the boys, who was growing a beard which was still a faint wisp on his chin, wore the same trainers, she noted, although his were still quite new and cleaner.

"Can I join you?" she asked.

Gentle, smiling eyes looked up at her.

Someone said "Yes" and two of the young men shifted apart to create a space between them where she could sit and offered to haul her bag onto the elevated luggage rail above them.

"My name is Giulia," she said. "I come from Italy."

"Hello, Giulia, " one of the girls said, greeting her.

"Where are you going?" Giulia enquired.

"Spain, and then maybe some of the islands. No firm plans, really. We're all quite open-ended."

Some were French, one of the girls was Spanish, a boy with darker skin had Middle-Eastern looks.

It sounded just the thing for today, Giulia thought.

"I'm travelling too. No particular destination. Can I join you?"

They all laughed and Giulia took her place alongside them.

YOU OWN ME

THIS TIME AROUND, CORNELIA found herself a mid price three-star hotel in a Montmartre back street, which principally catered to the tourist trade. Best hide herself in plain sight amongst the ever-shifting crowds of foreign faces, where she would not stand out more than necessary, between incoming and outgoing coaches and corralling tour guides. She had taken the customary precautions and changed outfits at Roissy following her arrival, and booked in under an assumed name and a stolen US passport she'd held on to for years, unlike her previous trip. It would help muddy the waters if anyone was seeking her out as a result of the hit, earlier that week. There would be no official record of her having been in Paris already.

She didn't plan to make a similar journey to the American Express Poste Restante offices in Rue Scribe. For one thing, she didn't think she would need a weapon. For now. In addition, even if she wore a wig, it was too much of a risk visiting the same place so soon after the initial call. She would have to find other ways of getting hold of a gun, when the time was right.

She had no clue where she could find the Italian girl who had witnessed the shooting. Or even where to begin looking. For all she knew, the young woman could already have left the city. Maybe returned to Italy. But

Cornelia had been informed that the girl had returned to the man's place and taken something Ivan's principals badly wanted. Did this mean that she knew more than she should have and was in fact no innocent bystander?

The key to the problem, Cornelia decided, was to find out more about the man she had been employed to kill. If she discovered what he used to do for a living, what he was and the possible reasons for the contract, it might shed a light on the Italian girl's role, and consequently her whereabouts. A call to Ivan would not generate any answers to that particular question, she was aware. The organisation or man who had generated the hit knew of her existence, she recalled. How?

"Yes," she said quietly, sipping from a cup of jasmine tea, and distractedly taking bite-size chunks from a melted cheese skewer in the Japanese restaurant she was eating in, towards the south side of the Luxembourg Gardens, her first hot meal in two days as she always turned down airplane food.

The doorman at the *club échangiste*.

Who had seen Giulia leave, without the man who had brought her along to the club. A tenuous connection but the only one she had right now. She hoped he would be on duty this evening, and not having a night off. She paid for her meal in cash and took the Métro back to Montmartre and her hotel and slept for six hours like a log, recharging her batteries for the likely task ahead.

Cornelia began her surveillance of the Chandelles in the same café around the corner where she had sat the earlier evening. The club only opened its doors at ten in the evening, but there was no doorman on attendance until around midnight, in view of the few customers who bothered to arrive this early. It was raining quite hard by now and Cornelia had to squint to get a better view of the man's face when he installed himself by the club's entrance, shielded from the weather by a thin stone ridge that protected the door and its immediate neighbourhood from the elements. He was holding a large black and white umbrella, and his collar was pulled up around his neck. But he looked familiar. It must be the right guy. Stocky, ruddy-faced, buzz-cut hair, muscular.

It was going to be a long night, Cornelia knew. She took a cab back to her hotel and changed into warmer clothing and returned to the area around two in the morning. She knew he would still be there. The café was closed by now, and there was nowhere else to keep a watch on the club's entrance but a bus shelter with the right vantage point. By now, the arriving customers were thinning out and very soon were overtaken in numbers by departing couples the doorman would walk solicitously to the kerb under his umbrella until a cab came along. Which they always did quite rapidly. He must have a phone to call them, she reasoned.

Cornelia munched on a couple of chocolate bars to keep her energy levels up, as she waited in the cold for another few hours. Finally, nearing four in the morning, the lights on the first floor of the club went off and a few straggling punters exited. The rain was now thinning. The attendant pushed the door open and walked back in. Cornelia hoped it was just to get his gear or another coat. She didn't care for waiting much longer. Within minutes, the rest of the staff filed out, waving at each other or engaged in deep conversation. The doorman was amongst them, now wearing a long black leather mac that gave him the appearance of a Gestapo cop in a war movie. He began walking at a brisk pace towards the Opéra. Keeping a hundred metres or so away, Cornelia followed. Half an hour later, she knew where the man lived. A 1930s building in the Rue Montholon, between the Gare de l'Est and the Gare du Nord, a quiet residential quarter that didn't appear to have changed much in character for half a century at least. Watching outside, Cornelia identified his flat when a solitary light lit up a window on the first floor just a minute after he'd walked through the main door. At this time of night, the rest of the building's facade was in the dark and it would have been too much of a coincidence for a light to go on in the wrong flat to coincide with the man's arrival. So far, so good. She even knew his name now: the list of tenants could be found by the row of letter boxes under the entrance arch. There were only two flats on the first floor and the other one happened to be a dentist's surgery. The man looked nothing like a dentist.

He would be sleeping for a few hours now, she guessed. During which time she had to formulate her plan of action. Cornelia sighed and walked away. The journey back to her Montmartre hotel would do her good, help her concentrate, she hoped. It was a bit like trampling through thick fog, never knowing what she would come upon next. She'd trained herself to kill, mentally erasing all forms of morality and personal doubt or guilt. Just a job. And Cornelia knew she was good at it. Sometimes, awake in bed back on Washington Square Place, she stayed awake counting all her past hits, like sheep in the night, even forgetting some of the jobs. She never quite reached the same number of bodies she was responsible for on every separate occasion. They already faded in the mists of memory. But this detective palaver was not something she was used to. Give her a name, a place, a face, a gun and she could aim the deadly weapon at the right person at the right time. It was clear cut. Easy.

By the time she reached her room, she had regained her resolve and abolished the seeds of doubt. All she had to do was pretend this was all a prelude that would lead to another hit. The club's doorman. Then she would move on, maybe to his associates. Then, rolling back the plot, this would lead her to Giulia and this time she wouldn't fail. Just a matter of being utterly professional again. Settled, then. However, she was intrigued by the fact that none of the local newspapers she had read through since she'd returned to Paris had carried any mention of the murder at the *club échangiste*, and there was no report of the body being found. She would normally have expected an incident in such a high-profile locale to make minor headlines at least. Were the police keeping it under wraps for one reason or another? Or had people at the club managed to hush matters up or disposed privately of the body? In the latter case, this meant there was more to the affair than she had been told, and there were some questions she could possibly get some answers to, she reckoned.

The blonde American woman bumped into him on the street as he was returning from the *boulangerie* late that morning. He'd picked up his morning baguette and was holding a plastic carrier bag with a litre of milk, a tin of Nescafe and a kilo of apples he'd bought just before at the *épicerie* across from the square. He was turning back into the Rue Montholon and she was walking in the opposite direction and must have stumbled over some crack in the pavement as she fell across him, grabbing the lapel of his jacket as she attempted to retain her equilibrium, before sprawling across the pavement. It all happened in a flash. Joseph Nicolski dropped the plastic carrier bag and, helpless, watched it fall to the ground and heard the milk bottle shatter.

The woman looked up at him.

"*Pardon, Monsieur. Vraiment pardon,*" she said, getting back on her feet, instinctively pulling down the short Burberry skirt that had hitched up midway across her thighs. There was a quick flash of white skin. Was the damn woman not wearing panties?

"*Pas de problème. Juste un accident,*" Nicolski said, almost apologising himself.

She had a foreign accent. American, he thought. He'd once been based for just over two years in Chicago when he'd still been boxing. Her shoulder length hair was straw blonde. A real blonde. No way it could be peroxide. She frantically reached for the spilt contents of his carrier bag, separating the coffee tin and the half dozen apples from the mess of glass and milk.

"Don't. There is no need, is just an accident," he said in English, as she scrambled in a forlorn attempt to rectify the damage caused by their accidental collision.

He extended his hand forward, inviting her to stand up from her somewhat undignified position with one knee on the dirty pavement.

She rose gracefully. Tall. Thin. For a brief moment, Joseph thought there was something familiar about her face, but he couldn't quite pinpoint where he might have seen her before. Student, tourist? he wondered silently.

"I'm sorry. So, so sorry," the American girl said, visibly embarrassed by the whole brief incident.

"It's nothing, really," he said.

"You must allow me to pay for the milk," she looked down at the bag's contents still scattered across the pavement. "And those spoiled apples. I insist."

"*C'est pas grave*. You don't have to," Nicolski said.

"No, no, I insist," she replied, pointing to the *épicerie*

where he had just completed his small shopping minutes before just a few metres behind him.

Joseph shrugged his shoulders.

She smiled and took him by the hand and dragged him gently back towards the shop where, still apologising effusively about the accident that had brought them together, she paid for another bottle of milk and another bag full of apples. As they were walking out of the store, she looked down at her legs and swore under her breath.

"What is it?" he asked.

"See," she pointed to her left knee, where she had been kneeling down. Badly smudged. "I hope the skin under the dirt is not broken," she added.

He peered at her long, svelte legs. "Appears OK to me. You should be all right."

Looked up. Her eyes were dark brown. Unusual in a blonde. Rather striking, he felt.

"Listen," he heard himself saying, "I live just over there. Not far at all. If you want, you can come up and clean your knee. No problem."

"Really?' she innocently asked.

"Don't we French have a reputation for being gallant?"

Her beaming smile was the greatest reward.

Piece of cake. Playing the role of the naive American abroad came easy to Cornelia. Maybe she should have become an actress.

Joseph wasn't a bad fuck. Not her first French guy – that had been the exchange student she'd met some years back in a Boston bar, who had introduced her to a few interesting variations on the standard sexual themes – but a decent lover who, at least, took his time and was relatively unselfish.

"So, tell me about this place where you work?"

Nicolski explained the concept of the French *club échangiste* to her.

"Wow, sounds classy even," Cornelia noted. He now knew her as Rita. She never gave anyone her real name when out on jobs, and seldom used the same one twice. Nor was it the name listed on the stolen passport she was now using. "We have them in some cities in the States. Not that I've ever been to one, you understand. But they're supposed to be somewhat sleazy, you know. Once, in New Orleans, some guy did suggest we go to one, but it just wasn't my style. Trust the French to do it properly, eh?"

Joseph Nicolski grinned. "Of course."

"Swinging at home is still in the dark ages. Car keys in fruit bowls, middle-aged suburban couples wanting to be naughty and daring and all that," she said, giggling under her breath at the mere thought.

"We have that too," Joseph told her. "I understand that in the French provinces, the clubs people go to are less sophisticated. It's inevitable. Just the local bourgeoisie getting their kicks, being naughty. In Paris, we do things better, we're more sophisticated. The Chandelles is one of the best. It doesn't make you feel cheap …"

Cornelia licked her lips, pouted. She was sitting up naked on his bed, the crumpled sheets tipping over the edge. The doorman was by her side, leaning on his elbows, his hairy mass sprawling in all directions, his limp cock still leaking down his thigh and her rump.

"I'm so curious," Cornelia said. "Do you think you could smuggle me in? Just for an hour or so, maybe? I'd love to see the place. Please?"

"Maybe," the man said.

"I'd behave. Be discreet. I can be …" she insisted.

"Maybe," he said again.

"I wouldn't go with other men," Cornelia pointed out. "I'm not a slut. I'm monogamous," she added, laughing softly. "Only one man in any city …"

She had earlier explained to Joseph that she was touring Europe, wanted to spend a whole year moving from city to city, had already done London and soon planned to move on to Berlin and Barcelona and maybe Rome. Her father was a rich banking executive and this was his gift to her for having graduated. Once the year was over, she would be returning to America and would no doubt settle down. There were many suitors. But she wanted to enjoy life to the full until then. A magnificent packet of lies.

Joseph relented. "OK. you can come with me tonight. But you must dress sexy. To fit in."

"Absolutely," Cornelia pecked him on the cheek and then lowered her mouth towards his dormant cock to revive him. Tasted herself there. Joseph was happy to cooperate.

"You'll be the death of me, young lady," Joseph said, as he felt the velvet caress of the young American woman's tongue across his mushroom-shaped head. He closed his eyes, abandoned himself to the feeling.

He came quickly. Undaunted, she eagerly swallowed his seed like a genuine little trooper. These foreign girls sure were craftful, he reflected, slumping back on the bed.

She rose. Damn, she was a sight for sore eyes, tall, straight-backed, pale-skinned, high-breasted and so proudly naked. He felt confident that given another hour he could manage another erection. He smiled to himself.

"I have to go clean up a little," she said, tiptoeing across his cold linoleum floor toward the neighbouring, small bathroom.

"That's fine," the club doorman said.

He heard her switching on the shower, hoped she didn't mind cold water; at this time of the day, the house's central heating was far from efficient. Soon, he had dozed off.

By the time he woke up mid-afternoon, she had expertly tied him up with some rope she had probably found in the compartment under his kitchen sink and immobilised his feet and hands with neckties. The moment he stretched his eyes open, Cornelia, waiting at his side, quickly forced a couple of handkerchiefs deep into his mouth, and he became unable to speak. She was fully dressed again, putting him at yet another disadvantage. How the hell had she managed to do this without waking him, he wondered idly before panic set in?

"What is this?" he wanted to say, but the material stuffed past his lips only allowed him to grunt or moan.

"I have some questions, Joseph, and I expect answers," the young American woman said. Her tone was cold and there was no longer anything innocent about her at all. Just a quiet, determined ruthlessness.

He nodded.

"Good."

His eyes were wide open, staring at her. He was still in a state of shock. How could this have happened? What the fuck did she want?

"Last week, there was an incident at the club, wasn't there? Someone was killed."

Joseph's head went up and down in agreement.

"See, it puzzles me: there hasn't been any report in the papers or the news. Has it been hushed up? And if so, why? And by whom?"

Cornelia paused as she watched the man began to realise what this was all about.

She continued, "And then there's the curious case of the young woman you spotted leaving the premises later without the man who had brought her along, the man who was killed, as we both know. You mentioned her to someone. I would like to know who."

She looked him in the eye. Her gaze had the hardness of blue steel.

As Joseph gathered his senses, there was now an air of defiance about him. She quickly punctured this when she raised her hand, and let him see the sharp Swiss Army knife she had come across earlier while going through his drawers.

He blinked.

"I'm not showing off, Joseph. Just want to show you I do mean business." She smiled at him, but this time around there was no sense of play or flirtation any longer.

He shivered.

"So," Cornelia continued. "I need some answers. And I want them now. No wasting time." She pointed the unfolded knife at him. "I'm going to take those handkerchiefs out of your mouth so you can speak, but don't even think of screaming, calling for help or anything stupid because I would not hesitate to use this one moment." She glanced down at his cock hanging limply between his thighs. Joseph lowered his eyes, indicating his understanding of the situation.

"Open wide."

She pulled the crumpled wet material from his mouth

Joseph gazed at the knife Cornelia was now holding and the cold stare of her eyes and determined expression. She was not joking. But surely she wouldn't cut him? Or would she?

Maybe he could reveal a little to her, pacify her and she would then relax the interrogation, and he would somehow gain an opportunity to get the upper hand again. He closed his eyes one brief moment, remembering how it had felt to make love to her, how pliant she had been, how soft, how her thighs had clenched his, the deep sigh when he had entered her the first time. All lies, pretence. No mere American tourist girl, this. He could sense the ice-like sense of danger that now radiated around her. How could he have been such a fool?

Cornelia waited, observing his silence.

"Know what, Joseph, I've always been a great fan of French novels. I was wondering whether you'd ever read Octave Mirbeau's '*Torture Garden*'?"

He hadn't. Indicated so.

"Thought so," she added. "Takes place in China early in the last century, how a man suffers the death of a thousand cuts, one little nick at a time, a cut here, a slash there, until his whole body bleeds and hurts through every pore of his skin. It takes an eternity for a man to bleed to death. Although I do seem to recall they also do quite a few other charming things to him, though. Did you know that a penis can, under the right circumstances and treatment, actually ejaculate blood? Very imaginative." She waved the Swiss Army knife in front of his eyes.

The doorman blinked.

"So?" she asked.

"The owners of the club didn't want to attract adverse publicity and police attention. The body was disposed of."

"Good," Cornelia relaxed. "Now tell me more."

"No one knows anything about the young girl who

came to the club that evening with the man who was killed. She was new meat, so to speak. Probably some kid he'd picked up somewhere and wanted to put through the motions …"

"The motions?"

"He was a regular patron. Often brought new young women there. Was known to share them with other members of his circle. I think he held shares in the business, so they turned a blind eye to his activities. It's all one big bordello, anyway. No difference really between suburban or Parisian swingers, or the predators who would use the club as their stamping ground. A fuck is a fuck, ain't it?"

"But you reported her leaving without the deceased to someone? Who? Why?"

"They are very important people. They were the ones who asked about the young girl."

"And you told them the same thing you are telling me? That you don't know who she is or where she might have gone?"

"That's correct."

"So no one's the wiser?"

"Indeed."

"How convenient," Cornelia remarked.

Her bound prisoner was now sweating heavily. She leaned towards him.

"His circle of friends. Tell me more about them, these people who come there with more than just swinging on their mind. Women trafficking?"

"Not at all," Joseph replied.

"Explain."

"They're into BDSM, you know, masters and submissives, slaves even. But for them it's more than play. It's a way of life. They have international connections. It's not just a network of bourgeois thrill-seekers; they are very serious about it."

"Too many fools who've read *Story of O* and have mighty delusions of grandeur," Cornelia ventured.

"Don't kid yourself," Joseph said. "These people are dangerous. And powerful. You'd be a fool to get involved with them."

"I am involved, whether I like it or not," Cornelia pointed out.

The Frenchman nodded.

Without a word of warning, Cornelia waved the knife and the blade slashed across the naked man's stomach, just below his navel.

Joseph roared. "Fuck. Why did you have to do that? Fucking hell!"

"Just to show you I am deadly serious," Cornelia said, wiping the fleck of blood on the knife's tip on a towel that was lying around. The cut was not deep.

"That was totally uncalled for," he said, catching his breath.

"Yes, it was. Just a taste of what I might be provoked to do if I find you lying to me."

"I haven't. I'd never seen the girl before, nor again after that night, I bloody well swear. No clue who she is or where she might have pissed off to."

"I need the names of some of the dead man's associates."

"They're dangerous. I can't," Joseph protested.

Cornelia's hand took a firm hold of his dangling testicles and squeezed. "Next time, it's the knife I'll use," she warned him.

"Bitch …"

"And being offensive will make no damn difference."

"You can't get away with this …"

"I have so far," Cornelia said.

The man sniggered and was about to spit at her, but he reined back his anger, thought better of it. She'd get what was coming to her if she messed with those people, Joseph knew.

He just hoped they would not blame him for her interference.

"Spill," she insisted. "Now."

Joseph provided her with the names of three men he knew had been involved with the murdered man and were active in the circle. He did not have their addresses or telephone numbers but advised Cornelia that the information in question must be stored somewhere at the club. Hinting that if she let him out, he might obtain it for her. Cornelia smiled.

He was no longer of any use to her.

"I've given you what you wanted," Joseph said. "Will you let me go now, come on" he enquired. "At least, let me dress, this is so undignified."

Cornelia did not answer. She stood up, looked down at his naked, immobilised figure, moved the knife to her other hand and expertly cut across his neck at an acute but premeditated angle.

Blood spurted. She stood aside to avoid being caught by the thin torrent geysering from his throat. The words forming around his lips ended up a gurgle, his eyes wide open in amazement and he slumped as the realisation he had barely a minute to live dawned on him.

By then, Cornelia had already turned her back on him and was calculatingly trashing the small apartment. Making it look like a burglary gone wrong would delay any official investigation into his death, she knew. She then untied the body's hands and legs and rolled him out across the floor, where she wetted a rag and cleaned his limp cock of any secretions that she might have spilled when he had fucked her. Not that she believed the authorities would waste too much forensic time on the dead club doorman.

It was only midday.

THE LIFE IMAGINED

BY THE TIME THE train reached Madrid, Giulia felt as if she had rolled back the years. This instinctive camaraderie with the other boys and girls in the travelling group reminded her of those final years at college and the initial time at La Sapienza University back in Rome. Laughs, sipping from bottles of beer, smoking joints, silly jokes, loud conversation. It just felt natural again. As if the past unending months of older men and anguish had not even happened. Instead of small cafés off Piazza Navona or Manzoni around the midnight hour, it was just a railway carriage hurtling through the landscape and heading towards the blessed South.

They all communicated on a simpler level, unburdened by thoughts of the future, fear of consequences, any form of calculation. It was like a massive weight being taken off her shoulders. Her mind was in a haze, but totally at rest, as she slumped back in her seat, leaning against Paolo, the Portuguese boy with the shaven head, relaxed, blissfully retreating from the real world.

In Madrid, someone knew of a friend of a friend who had a spare room, where they all slept that night, sprawled between sofas and spread across the wooden parquet floor cocooned in sheets and blankets and sleeping bags. The aimless conversation went on well into the small hours and morning easily bypassed them. The rest of the day was spent wandering across the city, pausing in gardens and tapas bars for smokes or food and by evening there were already two more group members, picked up almost by accident, a local young woman with a leonine mane of hair and her Swedish boyfriend, a tall blond Viking with dreadlocks and a skeletal frame.

They all agreed they wanted to continue the journey southwards, and most of them expressed the wish to reach the sea, where they could lounge for days on end until another better plan occurred to them. One member of the initial group was unable to come along as he had made arrangements to meet friends in Sevilla a few days later, but promised he would attempt to convince his mates that they should all assemble a week later at the beach they had agreed would be the group's next port of call and rejoin the fray. The news was greeted with another round of drinks. Someone was despatched to the main railway station to investigate the timetables.

Paolo's eyes pleaded poverty and Giulia agreed she would pay for his ticket. She could still afford it.

That same night, he shared his sleeping bag with her. There were too many others in the room for them to be able to fuck with any relative discretion, but once inside cuddled up to his musky warmth, she slipped out of her T-shirt and knickers and slept naked against his skin, which brought back memories of that one night almost centuries ago now when she had lain naked with her tennis instructor. It felt comfortable if weird to be sleeping with someone again like this, chastely, listening to the other breathe softly, heartbeat against heartbeat.

"This is nice," Giulia said, but the boy was already sleeping. Whispers and sighs flittered across the room, the sound moving between couples and singles and other random combinations of bodies huddled together. Not everyone had decided to be as discreet as she and Paolo, what with the familiar halting melody of hushed lovemaking hopscotching its merry way between the walls. Giulia guessed it must be Stieg and Marta. She smiled.

By the time they all reached Tangiers ten days later, the group had fragmented and half of the original Paris contingent had scattered to be replaced by other young kids on the summer trail. Giulia had kissed Paolo on the ferry from Gibraltar and slept with him properly the same night on the African side of the waters in a sultry cheap bed and breakfast room. He had proven clumsy if tender, and came too fast. Had Jack and her Paris seducer spoiled her, she wondered? She was sensual by nature, they had all told her, but surely not all young men were as inattentive to a woman's desire. Or was there something twisted inside her that men her age could not satisfy? The next morning at breakfast, out of frustration and anger, Giulia had a bad argument with Paolo and he took the next ferry back to the mainland. Which now made her the only unattached female in the small travelling group.

Marta had come across some good local dope in the market that same morning. They both sat on a balcony overlooking the blue sea passing the handmade roll-up between them. The stuff was very strong, and Giulia imagined she was floating in the air even as she could feel the cold stone of the terrace under her bum, barely shielded by the wafer thin material of her long white linen skirt. As if she were in two places at the same time. Observing herself. Serenely detached.

"What about you?" Marta asked. She was Hungarian, dead on beautiful with her medusa hair now haloed by the Mediterranean sun like a crown of fire.

Giulia blinked. "What about me?" She hadn't even properly heard the question. Or followed the gist of the other girl's conversation, her monologue, for some time now.

"What brings you here?"

"I don't know. Really," Giulia answered, taking another puff, inhaling deeply and feeling a haze of sloth shroud her whole soul.

Marta was peering at her.

"Well," she added, hesitating, "I witnessed a murder back in Paris and I didn't want to get involved with the police and all that. It was accidental. Nothing to do with me. A bad coincidence. But I just don't wish to talk about it."

"What did you do? Before?"

"Just studying. I have a degree in languages, but not actually sure what sort of job I want to do. Probably journalism or publishing. That's what my thesis was about. Citizen journalism."

"What is it, citizen journalism? Sounds communist," Marta chuckled.

Giulia sketched a half smile across her dry lips. She felt sleepy.

"No, it's all about how ordinary people can do personal sort of journalism on the Internet … You know, sort of going beyond blogs and all that."

"Oh …" Marta observed. "I never even learned how to use a computer."

"Really?"

"I was never interested."

Giulia remembered that it had now been ages since she'd even logged on. Her laptop's battery, long dead, probably badly needed recharging. Anyway, this small place where they were staying had no Internet access and she had no desire to go into the town hunting for a cyber café. In all likelihood all she would find in her mailbox would be more messages from her father or Jack claiming how much he missed her or Eleonora worried about her whereabouts. She didn't feel guilty that she had gone off the map. She had drawn a line, needed this time for herself. Even if it hurt others. This was her time to be selfish, she reasoned.

She took another puff from the joint. Felt blissfully light-headed.

"This stuff is strong," Giulia remarked, "so what about you?"

"Just a boring story," Marta replied. "I wanted to see the world, I suppose. Wanderlust. Did a few bad things to get the cash."

"What sort of things?"

"A couple of films for a Dutch company. Porn. Amateur stuff. Pretend casting videos done in a hotel room. Just a means to an end."

"What was it like?" Giulia enquired.

"Felt very dirty afterwards but, like you, it's something I don't want to talk about much. I've drawn a line. The moment I had the money, I left Budapest. They were hoping I would do more, but it was never my intention. I met Stieg on the road. He's okay. I like the way he smells. Different somehow from the guys back in Hungary. Strange, no?"

"Yes, life sure is strange," Giulia remarked. "Even if I still haven't a clue what it's all about, family, men, sex, adventures, somctimes it makes no sense." Her mind was sinking in a haze of dope. It was relaxing. It was good.

"Stieg knows this place two hours down the coast to the east," Marta said. "Some sort of artist's colony. Very remote. Almost private. Apparently the grass you can get hold of there is not only terribly pure but also quite cheap. We're talking of heading there in a few days. Maybe you should come with us?" she suggested.

The initial group Giulia had been travelling with since Paris had now fragmented to all corners of the south and she had no longer had any loyalty to it. She hazily recalled Marta's earlier words, "a means to an end".

"Sure," she nodded. The African sun above was sensually wrapping her into a warm cocoon of laziness. She knew she should get up and move out of it, or her pale skin would burn badly, but it felt difficult to summon the necessary energy.

Marta's voice punctured Giulia's reverie.

"Our room's shower is not working properly. Do you think we could use yours, Giulia? I do love this weather, but it makes me sweat like a pig." There was a thin sheen of perspiration on her forehead and cheeks.

"Of course," Giulia said.

They both rose unsteadily to their feet and walked into the shade. Stieg was at the bar downstairs nursing an absinthe and daydreaming. Flies buzzed. The three of them slowly walked past the tiled central patio of the building and down the corridor to Giulia's room.

Once in her room, Giulia collapsed onto her bed and watched Marta and Stieg undress. They looked beautiful. Shiny. An innocent form of nudity. Stieg winked at her as he slapped Marta playfully on her rump and then took her by the hand and led her to the narrow shower stall.

Giulia took a final puff from the dregs of the joint now beginning to burn her fingers and listened to the sounds of water, laughter, splashing and then lovemaking.

She lowered her right hand and slipped it under her white linen skirt and inside her panties and touched herself. The hair that had been shaved away in Paris was growing again.

The next morning they all packed their few belongings into a rucksack each and ventured down the coast towards the colony. The bed and breakfast owner agreed to store Giulia's laptop and her winter clothes while she was away. In her own mind, she knew there was little certainty she would even return.

Eleonora had moved into Jack's hotel. She had her own room but for a week they would spend most of their days together. Speculating. Comparing notes. Evoking memories. Growing ever more familiar with each other. They visited Flora again but failed to extract any further information that might prove useful.

Unlike Giulia, she was allowed to eat spicy food so Jack introduced her to some of his favourite eating places in the Latin Quarter. The Japanese kebab place a few doors away from the hotel, Chez Bebert the couscous restaurant on the Boulevard St Germain, the Korean BBQ near the Bastille, the Crêpes stand near the Luxembourg. All places he had once wanted to take Giulia to, naturally.

Sitting together at a large wooden table in the hotel's reception area, laptops facing each other, they had systematically explored their respective inboxes for Giulia's old e-mails, a process Jack found painful as it evoked too many memories and reminded him of the so many words of tenderness and affection she had once bestowed upon him. Searching for forgotten words, throwaway remarks that might give them a clue to her present whereabouts or intentions.

"I'm no longer even sure whether she even loved me once," Jack remarked.

"She did," Eleonora answered.

"Really?"

"Yes, she spoke to me so much about you. And she wrote to me about it too. Here, in some of her mails. Do you want to see?" she asked, ready to move her computer across the table.

"I'd rather not," he said. They had agreed at the outset that they would refrain from looking back at the past under a microscope darkly. Some things were better left private.

Eleonora fell into a deep silence. Jack's mouse danced a distracted fox trot on the rubber pad as he moved on-screen between past messages.

She looked up and gazed deeply into his eyes. "What did you see in Giulia?" she asked him.

Jack pondered at length. He didn't want his answer to be flippant.

"Life," he finally said.

Eleonora squinted.

"She was so lively, almost childish at times," he added. "Selfish, but in a healthy way. She made me look at things in a new way, in a positive way. Just one look at her and the whole day felt better, something I wouldn't have to struggle through. Essentially, she made me a better man. Not someone who had seen it all and become a cynic. She became life itself for me."

"That's true. She is a force of nature. Always so cheerful. And determined. Nothing could ever make her change her mind once she had decided on something. Like the time, she borrowed her father's camper and drove us to Venice for the film festival ..."

"Could she be there?" he suggested. 'Venice?" he wondered briefly.

"Something inside tells me it can't be Italy. She'd feel

a sense of defeat having to return to her own country, I believe."

"You're probably right. But then the Giulia you knew is not the one I did …"

"I know. After she met you, it's strange. On one hand, she was so happy but also, on the other hand, there was a sadness about her."

"My melancholy can be contagious," Jack stated. But he knew this was not the sole reason. He had not been fully available then, and this had been like a worm eating away at her mind and her insides. He had proven incapable of giving all of himself. And Giulia was young and when she wanted the world, she wanted it now.

"It's not just you," Eleonora pointed out. "When I was with Henry," she said, "I was both happy and sad. That's what love is, isn't it? One goes automatically with the other."

"But does it always have to be this way?'

Eleonora didn't answer. She scrolled down her screen. Looked up at Jack.

"I think it was in Barcelona she was happiest," she remarked.

"That's true," Jack said. "It was her first time away from home on her own, before San Francisco." Giulia had been arguing with her father for months to allow her to go on the student exchange programme. Her first genuine taste of liberty, of independence.

"I visited her there," Eleonora said.

"Me too," Jack said. Which they both knew.

Eleonora snapped her laptop screen down.

"She's left Paris. We both agree on that. People often return to places they have been happy in, don't they?"

"So they say," Jack confirmed.

In books, yes. In real life?

"We should go to Barcelona," Eleonora decided. "I know the names of some of the friends she met there. Boys. Girls too. The bars she enjoyed drinking in."

"Maybe."

"We have to do something," she said. "Have you any better ideas?"

It might work. It might also make things worse, Jack reflected, returning to the steps of Parc Güell or that café on Plaza Catalunya where they'd had their first serious row.

How would he feel setting foot in Barcelona again? At least, they could stay in a different hotel, not the Condal where the uniformed men manning the reception desk always gave him strong disapproving looks or smirked when he picked up his room key, hand in hand with a young woman visibly half his age. As Giulia had been. And Eleonora was too.

"Barcelona it is," he said. He would confront the ghosts of the past. He had little choice.

The beach went on for miles. Sand of gold and the sea a shimmering blue against a cloudless horizon. They had travelled across a set of undulating dunes for half an hour after abandoning the main coast road as it bent inwards. It was as if a desert extended straight into the warm waters of the Atlantic, melting into the rhythm of the lapping waves as they caressed the shore with white endless tongues.

Giulia caught her breath. It was like a vision of paradise.

In Italy, most beaches were heavily regimented, with deck chairs and parasols organised into geometric configurations, straight lines and right angles that allowed no fantasy or freedom. She had been told there were some unspoilt, wild beaches in Sicily and Sardinia, but she had never had the opportunity to go there.

As far as her eyes could see the sea merged with the sky.

"Worth the journey, no?" Stieg remarked.

The two young women agreed.

"There is a small village a further three kilometres down the coastline, I gather. With a few shops where one can get food and drink, and a handful of buildings and a scattering of huts, it's pretty basic but I'm told most people stay in tents on the beach at this time of the year."

"Feels like the end of the world," Marta remarked, gazing at the sun-scorched vista unfolding before them until the distant point where land and sea melted into each other.

Giulia followed the couple as they marched briskly down the sand. By the time they reached the colony the sweat was pouring down her back and her whole body felt as if she was wading through an open-air sauna. She should not have worn jeans.

It was just a hodge podge of fragile beach shacks and dozens of tents of all colours dotted in a zigzagging pattern across the sand beyond the reach of the tide line.

"We're here," Stieg shouted out.

"Is this it?" Marta queried, visibly disappointed by the Spartan aspect of the place. They could hear voices further down in the water where the stick insect silhouettes of a dozen or so people were playing around in the sea. A red and green flag floated above the nearest tent.

"Isn't it great?" Stieg remarked, throwing down his heavy rucksack to the sand, taking the weight off his shoulders. Giulia did likewise. All she could feel was the discomfort of the heat holding her body in a vice.

"I take it all back," Marta said. "It's not the end of the world, more like the beginnings. Before civilisation established itself."

Giulia could understand it. It was bare, sparse, primitive.

Next to her, Stieg was pulling his soiled T-shirt off above his head.

"Let's swim," he shouted out. "Wash all the grime of the journey away …"

Marta enthusiastically followed his example. Giulia copied her and slowly unbuckled the belt of her jeans. By now, Stieg in his haste had already stripped totally, and stood there naked, the sun already deepening the deep tan of skin. Giulia looked away. Turned to Martha as she unbuttoned her wet shirt. The Hungarian girl was down to her smalls. With no hesitation, Marta unclasped her black bra and swiftly pushed down her matching panties. Giulia hesitated. She had on occasion gone topless on beaches, but had never stripped down in public totally. She peered ahead. The others in the sea all appeared to be nude too.

"Come on," Stieg said. Marta giggled. "It's the way we were all created. Naked. You'd stand out, if you were the only one here to keep your bikini bottom on. Don't be such a prude, Giulia."

Her two friends began running towards the soft lapping waves, leaving her behind. Sounds of laughter breezed across the beach, or was it the shriek of distant birds? Giulia braced herself and stripped. She felt self-conscious about it. Her small breasts, the whiteness of her skin, the increasing bushiness of her pubes, the size of her bum. Only five men and members of her family had ever witnessed her naked.

She took a deep breath and trooped down to the edge

of the water, dipped her toes in. It was surprisingly warm. Stieg and Marta were already well beyond the crest of the waves, up to their waist in the sea, splashing water at each other and shrieking with delight. Giulia raised her arms and waded in.

Barcelona had proven a dead end. No one there had seen or heard of Giulia since she had completed her Erasmus exchange programme and duly returned to Rome, although many had fond memories of her and expressed dismay at the news she had disappeared. Eleonora had tracked down a girl who had been in the same Catalan Literature class at the University and had visited Giulia in Italy six months later, on which occasion the three young women had all met up for a late night drink in a joint off Via Veneto which had always been one of their teenage haunts. The Spanish girl, Mariana, had remembered how Giulia had once mentioned she had spent a wonderful time in Sitges, a beach resort thirty minutes south of the city.

Jack and Eleonora had conveyed this sparse piece of news to Giulia's father who had flown in to Barcelona for the day to enquire about the progress, or lack of, of their investigation. Giulia's uncle, his brother, was a pilot for Alitalia, so members of the family had easy access to cheap flights.

They met up in the café of a bookshop that Giulia had been known to frequent, a few blocks off the Ramblas.

"I still don't understand why she has left," the surgeon said. "She never missed for anything at home, you know. She was spoilt even."

"She just wants to live her life, Dottore," Eleonora pointed out. "I'm sure it's nothing personal against you or your family."

“But why run away?” he sighed.

Jack stayed silent.

“I’m sure she’s all right,” Eleonora said. “Once she has satisfied her curiosity, she will come back, I am sure.”

“I hope so,” her father said. “Her mother and I worry so much.”

“None of us believe any harm has come to her,” Jack intervened, not that he had any evidence of the fact. They all looked at each other with concern. The possibility of suicide was like an elephant in the room.

“She wouldn’t,” her father firmly said. “I just know. Not my daughter.”

He had to make his way back to the airport. They walked him to the coach stop on Plaza España.

“Any news, we will be in touch. Absolutely,” Jack assured him. Eleonora nodded approvingly and kissed the doctor on both cheeks. Jack and he shook hands.

It was the last week of the tourist season, fiesta time, much fireworks the following weekend they had been informed at reception, and they had been unable to get two separate rooms in the same hotel. He had offered to place a cushion between them in the large king-size bed they would have to share on this night, but Eleonora had just shrugged her shoulders in response. They both felt emotionally drained, sensing that their hapless quest was reaching yet another dead end.

Jack woke up several times during the night, as he usually did. A thin sliver of moonlight peered through the open window which looked over a panorama of flat roofs and terraces where a variety of neighbouring houses hung their washing out to dry overnight. Eleonora slept soundly, the warmth of her body reaching him in peaceful waves, the muted sound of her breathing like an even serenade. Her partly naked back faced him. She was wearing a long purple silk night-gown. He, just his underpants. He had turned his back to her when she had changed before bedtime. Once, he realised she was also awake and looking at him in the darkness, the cadence of her breath now different. Were they both thinking the same thing? Or of the same person? He kept his eyes closed, willing sleep to return.

At five in the morning, he woke again, noted the time on the LCD of the radio alarm on the bedside table. In her sleep, Eleonora had moved nearer, and was now barely an inch away from him. Somehow, the thin blanket had been pulled away to her side and Jack was now only half-covered. Not that it was cold by any means. Jack turned over. The movement was more instinctive than deliberate as he navigated in a blur between sleep and consciousness. He just wanted to smell her, decipher that distinctive sweetness in her fragrance. As if she was sensing this, it was Eleonora who shifted imperceptibly and slid over the sheet until their bodies met.

Spooned.

Through her skin, he could feel her heartbeat, its strong vibration swimming across her skin like electricity. Jack's arm was in an awkward position, unready as he had been for Eleonora to bridge the gap between their bodies and he knew that if it remained where it now was under his flank, he would soon cramp badly. He pulled his arm out and his hand grazed her rump. Her night-gown had hitched up during her sleep. Her softness overwhelmed him. He knew she was now awake. Neither said anything.

His hand slowly journeyed across the skin of her arse. It felt as if she was on fire. Silk and flames.

He felt himself hardening. His cock growing against the back of her thighs. There was no way she could not feel his arousal. Eleonora could have moved away to her side of the bed, but she didn't.

Now fully awake and encouraged, his heart beating the light fantastic, Jack moved his wandering hand away from her rear and moved it upwards under the thin material of her slip until he reached her right breast, cupping its firmness, almost weighing it. He extended his finger until it grazed her nipple, landing on its sharp promontory, rubbing against its uneven texture then circling it slowly but steadily. Now it was her time to harden.

Eleonora moaned.

"You OK?" Jack whispered.

"Hmmmm …" Her voice had deepened.

Another lengthy curtain of silence settled across them. They both had known for a few weeks that this moment might come. There had been an inevitability about it. They had always been attracted to each other, even when they had both been with others. Only a sense of betrayal had slowed the progress of the lust.

"Yes," Eleonora said. The sound came from the depths of her throat.

Jack's fingers sharply pinched her nipple while he adjusted his position so that his cock now faced her opening. Immense heat radiated outwards from her. He breached her tenderly. She was very wet. They docked. Below the distant and invisible ghost of Giulia. As if she were giving them her blessing.

The Atlantic night was littered with a million stars. They had spent the day swimming, playing in the waves and snoozing on the beach, Giulia carefully sheltered from the sun's rays naked under her old *Strangers in Paradise* T-shirt, now punctured with small holes, and the billowing white skirt. Her pale skin reddened much too fast. Tomorrow, she had decided, she would acquire a sun hat at the shack where you could also find sunglasses, shawls, second-hand tourist souvenirs and all sorts of African knick-knacks. They'd found a free tent and stocked up on mineral water, fruit and cans at the hut where food was on sale, dispensed by little black kids in djellabas sporting sparkling ivory teeth who spoke pidgin English and always appeared to be taking the piss out of the visiting foreigners and hippies who'd migrated down here.

Half a dozen fires burned at regular intervals along the beach, with small groups of young people huddled around them. Guitar playing here, off-key singing there, lazy conversations drowning the sound of the waves dying against the shore. Most of the kids in the group Stieg, Marta and Giulia had now joined around the campfire came from Eastern Europe, boys with hair down to their shoulders, unkempt, rangy, girls with plump lips and voluptuous curves. Everyone was still naked after the afternoon's exertions.

Joints were passed around and Giulia, light-headed, relaxed. Her mind floated in a soup of warm pleasure. Sitting cross-legged, now oblivious to the fact that everyone could see all the way inside her, beyond her burgeoning-anew forest of pubic curls no doubt, she took yet another deep puff from the thick hand-made cigarette making its leisurely way around the circle. A hand landed on her shoulder just as she we was beginning to lean back, on the point of blissfully dozing off.

"Hey, *piccola signorina,* try this one," a stocky guy with a severe buzz cut so unlike most of the other men at the colony, was handing her another joint. "This is the real stuff, the good stuff. I see you're a fan …"

Giulia extended her hand and took the new cigarette between two fingers and brought it to her lips. Inhaled.

Jesus. It was powerful . A wave of drunkenness surged across her brain and she could feel the vibrations extend like tendrils through every cell in her body.

"Wow," she mumbled, "this is good. Really good." All of a sudden she felt as if she were pinned to the ground.

She closed her eyes to surf this powerful new sensation.

Someone laughed. Close to her or was it maybe miles away?

Giulia could feel the blanket of the night surrounding her, protecting her, as every single past memory haunting her until today slowly began fading away into the gulf of yesterday. She felt in the darkness for her bottle of water and drank the rest of it down in one single gulp. Then inhaled again from the magical joint that killed all bad memories. Sighed. Then cried a little, a thin line of tears gliding down her warm sun-streaked cheeks. She was floating on air. A pair of hands lowered her head to the ground and settled her on an improvised cushion created by wrapping a partly-empty rucksack with some discarded piece of clothing.

The joint was delicately taken from her fingers.

Did she actually sleep or was she just daydreaming?

An instant later or maybe it was already hours beyond the stroke of midnight, Giulia opened her eyes. There was a chant swirling across the campfire, drunken or stoned voices singing an old barely recognisable sixties song in unison. Marta was dancing, her wild hair flying, obscuring the crescent of tonight's moon; another couple, right by Giulia's side, were embracing, limbs entwined, murmuring sweet nothings or could it be gentle obscenities into each other's ears. Giulia looked around, here was a tangle of legs to her left, all moving tentatively as if their dance had slowed down and was unfolding in deliberate slow motion. As she moved her head, a powerful wave of dizziness engulfed her. With difficulty, as if fighting against a river's current, Giulia peered up at all the legs, the unsynchronised ballet gesticulating in front of her eyes.

Overcome by sudden nausea, all she could register was the four or five cocks dangling just inches away from her face, as the men continued their unstable movements in a parody of dancing. Her eyes focused on the varied penises. Dark, pink, long, thick, cut and uncut, floating in the shadow of the thin slice of moon, illuminated by the sparks from the camp fire.

She tried to raise herself but she was still too disorientated and she stumbled. To regain equilibrium, she had to grab hold of one of the dancing men's legs. It was the guy with the buzz cut. She was so close to his crotch that she could even smell a trace of urine rising from his semi-hard cock. He was circumcised. Memories came flooding back like an uncontrollable torrent. Giulia's throat tightened.

A hand settled on her head, guiding her even closer to the rising cock of the man.

"Good girl," someone said.

The penis made contact with her parched lips.

The other men in the circle all moved closer.

She remembered the large sunflower sewn to her old tote bag in Barcelona. She smiled as if she compared herself to the flower, she was now its apex, its centre, and every cock surrounding her was a petal.

She half-opened her lips and allowed the man's penis to enter her mouth. Closed her eyes. The group began to clap as she started sucking the thick meaty trunk.

The first man came quickly, but as he retreated from her taking a few steps back nearer to the campfire, another cock was presented. She swallowed and opened her mouth wide open. This was unreal, she thought, her stomach tingling, knowing all eyes were on her, as if she was putting on a show for everyone there on that endless beach.

She serviced them all. One by one. By the end she felt hollow and the effect of the pot had begun to fade, and her mind was now in turmoil at what she had just done so willingly. No one had even attempted to force her. Although mentally disembodied, she had somehow called them to her, to her mouth, her warmth, like some crazy form of primeval earth mother. And they had answered her call and the circle of men had naturally converged towards her.

It occurred to her that every man had tasted sort of different.

But tiredness now got the better of her, and Giulia slumped to the ground pulling her scattered clothing around her and quickly fell asleep.

At dawn, she awoke. Stieg and Marta were no longer there, but many others, some strangers, others whose faces she recognised still from yesterday, were curled around the embers of the fire. It was like a topsy-turvy landscape of bodies after a battle.

Her head was now quite clear although she had the beginnings of a migraine. She rose, throwing the remnants of her improvised clothing aside, and headed towards the sea to cleanse herself. Naked in some twisted form of paradise, she reckoned.

PART TWO

LE FEU FOLLET

DANCING IN THE DARK

ONE OF THE MEN lived in Germany, so Cornelia concentrated on the two others for now. She was aware that the trail was unlikely to lead her to Giulia. The Italian girl had probably disappeared altogether, fled back to Italy, reintegrating a world of deceptive normality, and was unlikely to ever be a threat to anyone again. Good for her. But Cornelia had now been forced to intervene twice in this sorry affair and felt she had no choice but to retrace her way up through this network she'd uncovered. Maybe it was a sense of duty, being professional to the end, that now motivated her.

She hoped that, if she could ascertain why the kill had initially been sanctioned, she would be able to assess the danger and take the necessary action.

Getting to meet Enrico Santaclara proved relatively easy. A brief period of surveillance outside his suburban villa in the Neuilly area soon pinpointed his routines and he, like most men, was ready to be deceived by a woman's good looks and sexual candour, and within a week she had inveigled herself into his life and his bed.

He lived alone behind the high gates of the expensive, sprawling property with its wild, untended gardens, in a large, sparsely furnished house of polished, wooden floors and echoing rooms. Untouched art books littered the coffee tables and expensive prints and erotic lithographs adorned the white walls, turning the labyrinth of interconnected rooms into a private museum open only by personal invitation. The kitchen was all shiny copper pans and dark, imposing black ovens and a massive ebony-coloured fridge freezer which could feed a regiment for weeks in the event of a nuclear war, but in Cornelia's presence Santaclara would only use the microwave. Or maybe she hadn't yet graduated to the point where he would condescend to cook for her or allow her the liberty of the kitchen. It all somehow reminded her of a stage set, every single detail perfect but awaiting the spark of life to take on the necessary added dimension that would make it resonate. In fact, there was also something theatrical about Enrico Santaclara.

The man was silver-haired, tall and lean, his voice clipped but suave and his Italian accent melodic, whether he was speaking French or English, the latter he spoke with an easy fluency, serenading Cornelia with suggestive sweet talk from the moment he realised her ready availability and evident curiosity. With him, she had quickly realised that there was no point pretending to be a naive tourist and, instead, made no secret of her worldliness and possible experience. The best way, she felt, to seduce a seducer.

She had informed him that she was in Paris for several months attending an advanced business studies course, paid for by her hedge fund employers back in Boston, but had quickly established the fact it was pretty useless and unlikely to teach her anything she didn't already know, so was now just enjoying most of her time in the French capital to relax, philander and see whatever came up. Her name was Marti. A diminutive for Marlene, a name she didn't truly like to be used in her presence, she had told him. The explanation appeared to satisfy him.

He turned out to be a good lover, ardent and enduring, just a tad rough at times, which she had expected from his connections with the network she had uncovered in the course of her perfunctory investigation. Demanding too. Cornelia didn't mind the exercise in the slightest. A girl had to do what a girl had to do, and anyway body parts were just body parts and she preferred her relationships with no emotional strings attached, and enjoyed pretending that the men were in control.

"You like?"

"I like," Cornelia replied with a hushed tone in her voice, as the man's nose dug into her mons and his tongue brushed up and down her clit, arousing her, playing with her, pleasing her. She was tied to the bed, her hands cuff-linked to the metal bedposts, her ankles held wide apart with thin silk strips connected to a pair of leather belts nailed by metal studs to either side of the bed on the wooden floor.

She squirmed as Enrico's warm, halting breath streamed across her bare stomach and the pressure against her cunt increased and he slipped a couple of fingers inside her, stretching her open.

"You still like," he asked. His fingers digging deeper, while his tongue tirelessly kept on brushing up and down against her hardening nub.

"Hmmm, hmmm …" she nodded.

It was the first time he had bound her. She had offered no resistance.

"Good," he mumbled, his lips occupied, lapping up her now flowing juices. "Ah, you taste nice …"

"Am I a slut if I tell you it feels so sexy to be tied up, to feel helpless and at your mercy, at a man's mercy?" Cornelia whispered.

He raised his head from her genitals and looked at her

with a cruel smile spreading across his lips.

"Not at all, Marti. It's natural. Very natural. It means you are reconnecting with something that lies deep inside you, a kernel of your own sexual identity. You crave to submit. That's what it is. Goes back to when we were cavemen. Things have changed since in society, but there is that fire still buried in the depths of your mind and body, the essential law of domination and submission, of men and women. The true balance. It's good you accept it. Really good."

She didn't need any lectures.

But she quietly moaned again as another finger opened her wider. The pleasure was real. There are some things you can't disguise.

"Good girl," Enrico said. He looked her in the eyes. "Now I'd like to blindfold you. Is that OK? If there's anything you don't like, object to, all you have to do is say so, you know. I'll stop. We can even agree on a safe word. Look at it as an adventure, see how it goes, no?"

"OK," Cornelia said.

Shortly after her sight was taken from her, still spread-eagled across the bed and obscenely open to his touch and explorations, she felt a cold, large object being inserted into her. Then another at the rear after she had been lubed up and he had raised her rump by placing a hard cushion under her to facilitate the angle of penetration.

Next came the nipple clamps.

She held her breath. This she didn't like. But she offered no resistance or objection.

She blanked her mind totally, banishing the genuine pain he was now casually inflicting on her, moving into a mental zone of both appreciation and indifference. At the same time, the adrenaline flowed freely inside and her endocrine system booted into action and she could even perversely manage to enjoy the way she was being defiled. It made no sense, but then she was no an average woman and she had long been aware that there was some sort of broken short circuit within her senses and soul that allowed her to do these fundamentally bad things or accept certain things to be done to her and her body. Cornelia had dabbled in the arcane rituals of BDSM on previous occasions. It had left her unscarred, if puzzled. But if this was what it took to properly close an inopportune chapter in her life, she was willing to go through with it with her eyes wide open.

She felt trussed and stuffed like a turkey when Santaclara brutally took hold of both her ankles and forced her spread legs even further apart. It made her sinews scream, as he forced her open to a yet more revealing and humiliating angle. Cornelia just hoped he wasn't about to immortalise the session by taking photographs. That would be too tawdry. And she would then have to later locate them and destroy the evidence before the fool spread it over the Internet or wherever it served his kicks.

'You like the view," she joked, her voice rasping.

"Very much so. Somewhat pornographic, to say the least," Enrico said.

More ridiculous than arousing, Cornelia reckoned. But it took all tastes.

"Just don't put a carrot down there," she added, with a mocking tone in her voice. "I don't think the colour orange conjugates elegantly enough with my skin shade."

Santaclara chuckled.

"It's good you have a sense of humour. A virtue seldom seen in American women," he said. "But do take this seriously, Marti. I see you're no novice, though."

"I've dabbled," Cornelia said.

"And it excites you?" he asked.

"Sadly, yes."

"That's what I thought. I think you'll make a very good subject."

"For what?" she asked, as he tightened a new pair of thin leather buckles around her ankles and began adjusting a spread bar between them to maintain the impossible, strained angle between her legs.

"If you enjoy this sort of play, this scene, my dear Marti, I believe I can answer all your dreams and beyond. It doesn't have to stay here. We could make it a long journey further down this intriguing road."

"Surprise me," she said.

"I will," Enrico said, behind her back. "But enough of your repartee, young lady. I want you respectful, and silent." His fingers moved to her mouth, pulled her lips apart and placed a ball gag there which he fastened at the back of her head.

"There," he said, satisfied with the paraphernalia she was now encumbered with.

Cornelia didn't appreciate the fact she had been silenced. It turned her into more of a victim than she wanted to be. She no longer had access to the humour that could defuse the sordid side of the power exchange. The bastard visibly knew all about the psychology of domination. She drew her breath, speculating as to what would come next.

"Let's put this slut through her paces," Santaclara said.

Initially, he attempted to break her physical resistance with a clever and ever fiercer catalogue of implements, from paddle to whip, until the sore skin of her buttocks screamed to high heaven and blood almost burst through the deep, raised lines of purple criss-crossing her arse cheeks. Cornelia steadfastly refused to emit the slightest sound. This only encouraged Enrico Santaclara to test her will further. He moved her around on the bed and pulled Cornelia to her feet and attached a different set of metal clamps to her nipples to which he connected small weights and then did the same to her labia. Her whole body was now on fire, pain and anger coursing like a whirlpool through her veins.

He marched Cornelia out of the bedroom and down to a cellar with padded walls. Here she was fitted with a dog collar connected to a metal chain, a leash which he pulled her by and then ordered her down to her knees, where she was made to crawl like an animal on all fours while still having to prevent the thick objects stuffed deep into her vagina and anus from falling out, parading subservient in a circular motion with her chin downwards and the ball gag was briefly removed and she was allowed to drink some lukewarm water from a dog bowl on the cold stone floor to avoid getting dehydrated.

Satisfied by her performance so far, Santaclara pulled her up to her feet by the metal leash, almost choking her in the process, ordered her to raise her arms and attached her wrists to a pair of metal links fixed to the cellar's ceiling. With the spread bar still holding her long legs wide apart, Cornelia was now like a picture of crucifixion. Fortunately for her, the improvised dungeon did not appear to have a wooden cross or nails.

Now she was standing, the weights attached to her parts grew heavier and ever more excruciating and an involuntary tear of pain streamed down her cheek. Observing this, the man cruelly smiled, pleased with his performance and her reaction to it so far.

“Good girl,” he said.

And then punched her hard in the pit of her stomach. Cornelia exhaled violently and was unable to draw breath for a moment or even bend in reaction, totally immobilised as she was, which made the impact of his fist even worse. It would leave a bad bruise, she knew. Oh, how he would be made to pay her back for all this when the time came. But first she must play along, as distasteful as it was proving, and find more about the network he was involved in.

Santaclara walked away and out of the cellar, not saying a word, steps echoing on the stone, leaving her alone for a short while. This allowed her to regain her composure and concentrate on banishing the pain. She tried to disconnect but there was an undertow of want still playing with her cunt. There was no way she could suppress it.

When he returned, no doubt suitably refreshed, the smell of cigarette smoke on his breath, Cornelia felt like shouting at him under the ball gag to fuck her then, fuck me now. But he smirked, observing her needy expression and calmly denied her that pleasure. This was edge play.

The games continued. The man certainly had a fertile imagination and a clear-cut talent for keeping her on the thresholds of pain and pleasure combined holding back on any sort of reward or personal gratification until she was almost mentally begging for relief or further humiliation.

By the time he tired, Cornelia could hardly hold herself together, physically or mentally, and when he untied her and loosened her bonds, one limb at a time, she couldn’t help herself from collapsing into his expectant arms, which he held aloft anticipating her fall.

“There, there,” he remarked. “That wasn’t so bad, was

it?”

Cornelia tried to say something in some vain form of defiance, but her throat was too dry.

“Let’s take you upstairs, where you can relax a bit, have a sip of water, put something on, Marti. I like you: you have attitude, pride. You know you could have asked me to stop at any given time, but you didn’t. You seemed determined to test your limits.”

“You have no idea of my limits,” she spat out, straightening herself and forcing herself to raise one leg and then another to demonstrate she could walk up the stairs unaided. His hand playfully caressed her sore, marked buttocks as he walked behind her.

“But you enjoyed it, didn’t you?” he asked. “You were visibly in the zone. So wonderfully wet.”

She glanced down at her thighs. She had leaked badly, dried secretions of lust like snail trails marbling her pale white skin.

There was no way she could even deny that she had found pleasure in the pain, in the experience.

“It was … fascinating,” she said, fumbling for the right word.

“A most interesting way of putting it, I’d say.” They were now back on the ground floor of the house. He guided her to a large bedroom and pointed out the en-suite bathroom.

“You can clean yourself up there, my dear. Do join me afterwords in the study. I think we might have a lot to talk about. But take your time. I’m sure you have a lot to reflect on.”

She had found a white bathrobe and wrapped it around her weary body. Tiptoed on bare feet back to the living areas. Santaclara was sipping a cognac in the study.

There was classical music playing. She recognised the melody, but couldn't name it. She had always been a rock 'n roll sort of gal. He offered her a glass. Cornelia downed it in one gulp.

"Made you thirsty, hasn't it?" Enrico pointed out and poured her another glass full. This time, Cornelia slowed down, brought it to her nose and sniffed, inhaling the drink's harsh sweetness. She took a deep breath and then tipped the glass to her lips, allowing the burning liquid to swirl around her mouth before it continued its obligatory way down to her throat, soon warming her whole body.

"It's good cognac," she said.

"Vintage" he said. "Only the best."

Cornelia sat on the leather sofa, finally able to relax, as if landing after a long flight, nerves no longer tingling but in a pleasurable, serene state of *satori*.

"You came through that really well," the man facing her said.

"Was it a test?" Cornelia enquired.

"You could call it that."

"Tell me more," she asked.

"Women like you interest me."

"Not just for sex, you mean?"

"Precisely," he said.

"Is that why you didn't fuck me? It would have been fine with me, I wouldn't have minded in the slightest."

"Any slut can provide sex," Enrico continued. "Or any foolish girl who thinks being submissive is just an expression of love, worshipping her master and all that, read the usual books once too often and opens her leg out of sheer romantic instinct. One should never trust a book."

"It's true. I am not romantic, by a long way," Cornelia confirmed.

"You have inner strength, Marti. You are evidently in possession of a fierce intelligence. You understand it's not all about the meat of bodies, holes and penetration. Pleasure can turn out to be so much more. On a higher plane."

"I suppose so."

"So why did you engineer our meeting?" Santaclara suddenly asked her.

"Engineer?"

"Don't take me for a fool," he said. 'An attractive young woman like you doesn't throw herself at a man so readily. Let alone allow herself to be used as you have been. I'd rather you came clean. Now." There was a hint of threat in his tone of voice.

"I was at the Chandelles the other day when that man was killed."

"Really?" A worried look spread across his features as he absorbed the new information.

"Someone took me there, a guy I sometimes go out with back in the States. He'd read about the place in a guide book on Paris sex spots. Just as we were about to leave, there was this commotion. We were in a private room, across from where it happened. The man I was with was unaware of what had occurred, but I had gone to powder my nose between scenes and noticed all the staff running around in a mild state of panic. I saw you giving out orders. It's just that the next morning, and the following days, there was just nothing in the papers or on the news. I was just curious, you know."

"So you thought you'd arrange to meet me?"

"Well, yes. A right little Nancy Drew and all that, there must be a reason it was all hushed up, no?" She sketched a pleading smile.

"Are you sure you wish to know?"

"Well, you might say I've gone to great lengths to find out, no?"

"So you have. But you know what they say about curiosity, don't you?"

"Enlighten me."

She learnt that the man who was killed at the Chandelles club was a long established acquaintance of Santaclara and his associates. A group of them were actually the true owners of the establishment, although this was concealed through a series of dummy companies through which other more conventional businesses were also funnelled in order to muddy fiscal waters. It could be said that what they were engaged in was not actually illegal, even though in the eyes of many it could be seen as morally dubious. The men had all met through their frequentation of BDSM circles and tastes for domination.

Initially they lurked on the Internet in a variety of adult chat forums where they had advertised themselves as a group of dominant men offering women the opportunity to partake and be the objects of group sex, gang bangs even, on a purely anonymous, discreet and safe basis. It was surprising how many had proven interested and found the courage to go through with the events which normally took place in hotel rooms or the specially-appointed cellar of one of the men's houses or the basement of another's high-street fashion store. The open invitation had attracted women of all ages and social status, from nurses to doctors, teachers to bank executives and, more appetisingly, even school girls or students.

As Santaclara carefully pointed out, the women came willingly. There was no money involved at this stage, so it couldn't be said that prostitution was involved. Why they attended voluntarily and offered themselves knowingly to a group of unknown men for such prolonged episodes of sexual exploitation and degradation was between the women and their conscience. Nymphomania, overbearing curiosity, a longing for submission both psychological and physical, it wasn't for the men to reason why. Most of the women satisfied their urges, unnatural or not, and some would even return for more, become regulars of sorts, who would then graduate to open air parties in semi-public places, dogging excursions and, once the Chandelles was acquired by the main instigators of the group, to special events organised there to which outsiders were invited, after careful screening.

"Charming" Cornelia remarked.

"It's what they wanted. They were never forced to participate," Enrico pointed out again. "Things were always made very clear to them from the outset. It was their decision alone to become involved. On every occasion a new girl agreed to be fully used in the manner we had explicitly explained to her, she would meet every single member of the evening's group at the hotel bar for drinks before we would go up to the room. Until she had crossed the door into the bedroom, she always had the opportunity to pull out. A few did. We accepted that, and that would then be the end of the matter."

After the group's activities expanded into selected exclusive evenings at the swing club, their reputation quickly grew. They were not offering professionals, whores, but normal women who, in order to satisfy their sexual needs, proved eminently willing and available for even the wildest, or even perverse, occasions. The women were never paid, although from a certain stage onwards the new punters they collected did; after all, the club had to earn its keep, didn't it?

"And what happened to women once they had satisfied their lust and were no longer of interest to the group? Surely, it wasn't possible for them to go on doing this for ever. Everyone has limits, and anyway wasn't fresh meat always needed? It's like a vicious circle, a conveyor belt, no?" Cornelia enquired.

"Exactly," Santaclara said. "You've put your finger on it. That's where the problems began."

A member of the initial group had got it into his head that, after they had tired of certain women, maybe he could keep on exploiting them for profit, rather than discard them with relative elegance and kindness as had previously happened. Well, they had been well groomed and he felt it would be wasteful not to recycle them, so to speak.

"How?" Cornelia asked.

Santaclara frowned. The whole matter was evidently quite distasteful to him, although all the other activities he had been discussing did not present him with any problem, it appeared.

The bad man in question had somehow made a connection with a network through which women were traded from country to country, mostly to wealthy collectors. A lot of money was involved. He was beginning to funnel some of the women through that dubious pipeline.

"Sounds like slave trading to me," Cornelia remarked.

"Maybe. But he was clever. He was one of the best groomers in the group. Had always been the best of us at discovering new girls, not only on the Internet, sometimes he'd pick them up in the street, in bars. He had a way, a *je ne sais quoi*, which always succeeded in convincing the women in question they were acting of their own free will. He could spot them, as if there were something written on their forehead that said 'submissive' or just naive. After the women grew tired, after their initial thrill had exhausted itself, he was very good at talking them into risking the next step."

"Selling them?"

"Yes."

So, Cornelia noted, the sordid puzzle was all now coming together.

"Who ordered his death?"

"He was becoming something of an embarrassment. He had left us no alternatives."

No wonder they had hushed up the kill and disposed of the body with no unwarranted publicity. What a nest of vipers she had dipped her toes into.

"Who? Your group?"

"Not just us. His activities were becoming too public. He supplied girls to the network, but also double-crossed them when convenient and traded with Arabs. That was a step too far for everyone. We can't condone white slavery."

"How delicate of you."

"Some of us hold important positions in business and even government. We have connections. We made contact with the network he had been dealing with. Explained the problem we were facing to them. We all agreed something had to be done to curtail his activities once and for all. We sanctioned the action but they organised the particulars."

"I see."

"I don't know who they used or how. But it happened quickly. Very professional, I must say."

Cornelia repressed a small grin.

"So that's what I caught a glimpse of," she said. "What a story. And whoever did the job left no clues or witnesses."

"Actually there was a witness. Most unfortunate," Santaclara said. "A young Italian woman the man in question had brought along to the club that night for some form of further initiation. We knew nothing of her; he'd probably picked her up shortly before. She'd been living with him for some weeks but he hadn't yet introduced her to any of us."

"What happened to her?"

"In the confusion, she slipped out of the club. Went on the run. Probably scared out of her wits. We don't know her name. She stole some of the man's files but tried to dispose of them in a railway station, in all likelihood as she was leaving the country. A friend in the police retrieved the papers for us, so no harm was done."

"Are you or the network still looking for the Italian girl?"

"We aren't, but I understand people in the network are concerned she might have caught a sight of the killer they employed for the job. However, that's no concern to us."

Cornelia felt a tinge of disappointment. She'd reconstructed the whole story, but she was nowhere nearer finding Giulia or getting Ivan's clients off her backs. This was yet another dead end. There would be no point getting Santaclara to spill further beans. Her problem was now back in the States.

Santaclara poured her another glass.

"So what am I to do with you, young lady?" he asked.

LIFT ME UP

JACK AND ELEONORA CHECKED out of the Barcelona hotel just off Diagonal and hailed a cab which took them to the principal railway station where they boarded the local train going down the coast.

Forty minutes later they had arrived in Sitges. A popular beach resort which they both associated, albeit for somewhat different reasons, with Giulia. The tourist season was coming to an end, and already many of the restaurants facing the promenade were closed, shutters up for the winter, and the main stand which sold ice-creams, waffles, sweets in all colours and *churros* was boarded up. The locals and visitors from the city paraded up and down the long walk until midnight. The first thing they noticed was the sheer number of pregnant women around. By next summer, there would be a logjam of prams and buggies joining the late night ramblers here.

Jack's gaze was distant as they walked towards the gothic promontory formed by the old town fortifications from Napoleonic times, which separated the main shore from the San Sebastian area and, a stone's throw beyond, the new leisureport. Between the cemetery on the hill and the port stood a rocky area where new apartments were being built all over the hills all the way to the railway line which bisected the town. Further up a succession of small beaches lay, a trio of narrow coves harbouring one of the town's gay beaches as well as an unpoliced one where nudity was tolerated.

"You are very pensive," Eleonora remarked.

"I know," he answered, emerging from his private thoughts.

She looked up at him. Guessed.

"It's here you came with her, isn't it?" she asked even as she knew the answer. "That's why she kept on mentioning Sitges in her letters to me."

Jack nodded.

"She's like an invisible third person in our relationship, isn't she?" Eleonora pointed out. They were now descending the narrow stone steps separating the beach area from the recently developed pleasure harbour which was self-enclosed, and where the hotel they had booked into was situated.

"Same hotel?" she asked.

"Actually, no. We stayed in a small place in the town itself. All the places overlooking the sea were full. It was a very short notice trip for both of us."

"How you say, it's a small mercy," Eleonora remarked.

They silently took the lift to the second floor, both too tired to walk up the stairs after walking miles that day. The windows of the long corridor at the back of the hotel looked onto a wall of rocks, where the cliff had been carved into to create space for the construction of the hotel, loose stones held back by a curtain of barbed wire.

After boiling some water for coffee, they settled on the balcony overlooking the marina port where a geometrical jungle of small boats spread out, some already mothballed for the coming colder season. Further out on the jetty wall, wild cats roamed. Muzak crept through the air as the parade of restaurants below their balcony came to life.

"Where do you want to eat?" Jack asked. "In the port or should we walk back into town? Whatever suits you best."

It was as good a way as any other to break the rising blanket of silences that was beginning to separate them Eleonora didn't respond. Jack persisted.

"I know you were good friends, close friends, but tell me, if you will, was there ever more?"

She lowered her eyes as she answered.

"No …" then hesitated.

"You wouldn't have minded?"

"Exactly. But she never responded if I say something in that direction, or touch her when we talk or walk …" Jack thought he saw her blushing, but the light of day was failing, and he couldn't be certain.

He placed a hand on her knee.

Eleonora shuddered.

"I don't think she ever was into other women, you know," she whispered.

And began to cry.

Jack rose from his chair and took her into his arms.

They had become fools for lust, thrown together by their loneliness and the ever-present ghost of Giulia. They had come together by accident, bodies colliding quietly as their travels and this parody of an investigation they were conducting brought them closer to each other. But there were no deep emotions, just the mechanics of sex, the call of a warm body in the night, as if mere friendship was not enough.

He couldn't tell Eleonora that once he was inside her, thrusting, grasping, sweating, he could not help himself thinking of Giulia, and wishing it was her instead and sometimes closed his eyes and imagined her face, the soon to be forgotten texture of her skin, the different rhythm of her breath at the instant of orgasm. As if to conjure up her presence like a magician of the flesh using his darkest spells.

And, in all likelihood, Eleonora opened herself to him, to his cock, all the time picturing Giulia's plump lips wrapping themselves around it, welcoming Jack's penis into the hot cavern of her mouth. Yes, she and Eleonora had kissed once, mouths open, tongues clashing, but it had been out of affection and both had been drunk anyway after a birthday party in the moat by the Colosseum organised by Giulia's father for her nineteenth. A mad moment she had never been able to forget. Or the time they had instinctively held hands during an emotional moment at the opera together, although she now couldn't recall any longer whether it had been a Verdi or a Puccini aria. Yes, the cock stirring inside her had known Giulia's intimacy. It was what tenuously held them together. It was a terribly vulgar thought. It was inescapable.

"We miss her."

"So much, yes."

Jack and Eleonora went to bed. That night they did not make love.

Sitges emptied but they had nowhere else to go.

Jack had a call from Franck in Paris, advising him that the trail left behind by Giulia had now grown cold. Something about some papers left behind at one of the main railway stations, indicating she had left the country. His contacts in officialdom had effectively closed the case. Jack has asked whether it was the train station from which passengers travelled to Italy? No, it wasn't. No, Franck informed, him, you could only reach the south-west of France and Spain from there. He thanked him and bid him good-bye.

So, their instincts had been right, to come here. But she could be anywhere or might have already moved on. Jack and Eleonora took heart from the information, but their hearts were no longer in it; deep down, they did not believe they would find Giulia any more.

Skin against skin.

Sharing the same bed but often worlds apart. Grazing softness, the mechanical comfort of remembered embraces.

"Don't think of her, please …"

"I'm trying."

"Doesn't it feel different with me?"

"Yes … and no. It's difficult to explain. I'm sorry."

"I know. Me too, I also think of Henry, you know. It's not just you. You touch me nice, but he touch me differently. It doesn't mean better. Just different."

"We think too much, Eleonora."

"Yes, but is not possible to switch brain off like a machine or an instrument, is it?"

"Sadly no."

Memory persists.

From week to week, the colony shrank or grew in size as the ebb and flow of arrivals and departures continued. Either dots in the sand or a small shantytown of tents and a handful of huts clumsily assembled from wooden planks and discarded roofs of corrugated iron. The only constants were the huts where food and basics could be purchased from local fishermen and budding Arab entrepreneurs and the souvenir stall held by Haroun and Jamel, who were also the principal source of dope for the motley group of Europeans. Supplies came in at night, whether by sea or across the dunes. No one had ever witnessed their actual arrival.

Once the beach and endless vistas of waves and horizon had been a thing of beauty. Now it looked to most eyes more like a bleak field of dreams. If they had been living in a movie this is where there would have been music on the soundtrack by Erik Satie or the camera would have panned down the shore to the sound of melancholy of an American indie tune of woe.

Giulia's lost months began.

She still shared the same tent as Stieg and Marta. The couple were becoming closer, and in the dark she could track the steady progress of their tenderness and affection as their lovemaking grew less noisy and more furtive, just as their moans grew deeper and the silences between each thrust lengthened. Giulia listened and touched herself inside the cocoon of the sleeping bag, her own frantic movements mimicking the rhythm of her friends, somehow attempting by thumb and index finger to reach her climax as they came in unison. But Giulia would studiously keep her lips closed and not a sound would escape when the moment came, so as not attract attention to her own climax.

Although the nights were growing colder, there were still occasions when it felt too hot inside the exiguous tent or the waves of desire flying across from the embracing couple just made her dizzy with lust and longing and loneliness and she would discreetly slip out and walk a hundred metres or so down the beach to cool down, watching the sea, dipping her toes into the fresh nocturnal water, daydreaming, imagining, looking down at her body. Invariably she would not find herself alone on the sands and one or another would join her. Sometimes she would allow a man, or two, to shyly touch her and would not resist their advances. They would fuck her on the beach. Or she would follow them to their own tents. Some proved tender. Others were rough. But Giulia always remained silent. She had no wish to bond with them or know them better or even look at their faces. It was just some ritual in the dark that tempered her emptiness.

She didn't think of herself as some slut or a fallen woman. At the colony, sex felt natural. The casual intimacy came easy. Something that just happened. And required no emotional investment. Even though she was overcome with terrible waves of sadness after the act. Because, as pleasurable as it might have been, it was never enough.

She took refuge in the dope.

Spending days in a haze, lazing in the sand, catching up with her sleep inside the now empty tent vacated by the rutting couple, swimming, taking endless walks up and down the beach and into the vastness of the neighbouring dunes, gazing at the sea and imagining pirate stories full of blood and daring that reminded her of her own bookish youth when she had spent days buried inside the world of novels and exciting adventures.

Briefly she recalled the whispered words of the bad man in Paris one night, as he had painfully taken her anal virginity on a violent whim and as he dug ever deeper inside her, and the burning sensation spread like wildfire through her body, he kept on threatening and cajoling her. How he would train her to become a sheer beast of pleasure, a wonderful whore; how he would sell her to pirates or was it slave traders, who would take her to sea, cage her, strip her of every last veneer of civilisation and turn her into an animal fit to service every single sailor on the ship before she was auctioned on the coast of

Africa, displayed naked in some flea-ridden market, shaved, painted, examined into the deepest recess of her intimacy by potential buyers before disappearing into the desert for the rest of her life. At the time, the words, the prospect of such degradation had actually excited her in a perverse sort of way and the images had imprinted themselves indelibly on her mind. Again and again Giulia watched the sea.

But most of all she would waste the hours smoking the powerful local grass the Arab boys in the shack dispensed.

Soon the money she had stolen in Paris ran out.

She could always cadge food, fruit from others in the colony. She wasn't a big eater anyway. But she was now dependent on the grass. It kept the world at bay, offered her a form of serenity she could no longer do without. Following a couple of days in a mild, but increasing state of need which surprised her, she resolved to do something about it.

One evening she finally nervously walked up to the shack where the two Arab boys traded their wares. She had actually never really looked at them closely before, and realised now that she was facing them that they were in fact fully grown men, probably in their mid-twenties she thought. Tall and lean, dark eyes buried deep into their sun-lined features. One had a thin beard obscuring his pockmarked cheeks. She had slipped on her bikini bottom. Feeling it would be more appropriate for the occasion, even though the majority of the women in the colony ventured all over the place in the nude throughout the day.

Communication with the locals was unusually in a halting mixture of English and French, but lengthy dialogues had seldom proven necessary before.

As she approached, Jamel held up a straw hat with a long band of silk circling its diameter, trailing well beyond the hem, waving it at her with exaggerated theatricality, indicating with a smile that it might suit her. Giulia noticed for the first time the long pink scar that bisected his left cheek.

"No, no," she shook her head. "I'm not looking for a hat …"

There was a rictus of disappointment on his face at her reaction.

"You want something else?" he said Haroun kept silent, looking her up and down, his eyes visibly lingering over her uncovered breasts. "More food deliveries they come tomorrow. Is too late already today."

Giulia was now facing the two young men, noticing how one was her height but the other one only reached her cheeks. She hadn't noted their disparity in height previously. Their musky smell reached her nose.

"I want *herbe* … grass …" she said. Then hesitantly continued, "but no money right now. Soon. Is it possible to have a few day's credit?"

"You not pay, can't pay" Haroun sought confirmation.

"Money is coming, From home. From my parents. It's OK," Giulia lied.

"Maybe not money," Jamel suggested. "Something else you give us, no?"

She knew others had traded for watches or jewellery. But her watch was just an old battered Swatch, and the only jewellery she had was worthless. Her leather ankle chain and the cherry and leaf necklace Jack had bought for her just before she had decided to leave him, which he had given her on the occasion of their last time together. She didn't even wear any rings on her fingers.

“What?”

“What have you got?” the taller Arab asked.

“I don’t know,” Giulia answered. “I don’t want that much grass. Just a little.”

“Just a little?”

“Yes.”

“What will you do?” one of them asked.

A veil of weariness fell over Giulia. One part of her knew all too well what the men had in mind while the other half of her brain struggled to accept the fact she had reached such a low of emptiness that the prospect of agreeing to their demands could be dismissed as just another necessary chore.

They were observing her. She lowered her eyes. In lassitude or in shame.

Haroun and Jamel took this as a sign of acceptance.

“You come inside, to the back,” one of them said, pulling up the improvised hinged wooden counter top that normally separated sellers and buyers.

In a daze, Giulia walked into the shack and was guided to the back where their sparse merchandise was stored.

“You French or Algerian?” Jamel asked, his hand rudely grabbing one her buttocks, feeling for firmness,

“No. Italian.”

“Ah, I know you are from south. Dark hair and eyes.”

Haroun’s breath smelled of pungent spices as he breathed down her neck and weighed her breasts in the cup of his hands.

“Is small, but nice.”

“Thank you,” Giulia couldn’t help herself responding, as if the past year of wandering and bad mistakes could not totally erase the politeness bred by her upbringing.

“You do everything?”

“Yes,” she whispered, guiding her mind away from her body, attempting to detach herself from the situation.

“Show us your body,” Haroun ordered.

Giulia straightened her back and pushed her chest forward.

“No. Completely naked,” he pointed at her off-grey bikini bottom.

She obeyed. After all, everyone in the colony past and present had witnessed her nude, and so had the two Arab merchants, albeit from a distance inside their shack with an open view across the beach.

She stood there, exposed.

“You not like lots of other European girls. You not shave there?”

He was referring to her unkempt bush, the pubic hair she had never enjoyed trimming, let alone thinning or carving into all sorts of shapes on the borderlines of smoothness.

“No,” she replied. There was no point explaining why to them.

“You dirty girl?”

She wanted to protest, but quickly realised he was not referring to personal hygiene.

“I think you be very dirty girl with us, if you want good *herbe*. You work hard to earn it, Italian girl, no?”

Giulia kept her silence. Her breath shortened. Images of sea pirates, violators, torturers, despoilers racing through her imagination.

“Open legs and bend,” Haroun said, moving behind her while Jamel placed himself in front of Giulia and began loosening his belt.

A stray finger rudely forced its way past her sphincter, followed by a gob of spit pearling down her rump to lubricate her dry opening. Jamel’s cock stood to attention in front of her eyes, uncut, a long thin envelope of brown, protective skin dangling past his hidden glans.

Giulia closed her eyes.

In darkness there is no sin, just shadows.

The finger in her rear was joined by another as the Arab man stretched her in readiness for his assault.

"Giulia! Giulia! Where are you? Are you inside?"

It was Stieg, loudly calling out for her.

The finger roughly withdrew from her anus, a long nail scratching her deep as it did so.

"Hell! What's happening here?"

The dreadlocked Swedish backpacker had suddenly rushed into the shack's storage room and surprised them.

Jamel, almost out of shyness, quickly pulled his trousers up to his waist and tucked his semi-hard cock inside. Haroun drew back behind Giulia, and turned to the unbelieving Stieg.

"Is OK," he protested. "The girl she come here happily. We agree. Is deal. We give her *herbe*, she offer herself to us. Is not wrong."

"The fuck it's wrong," Stieg exclaimed in anger. "Giulia, you cannot do this. It's so wrong. You should have talked to Marta or me. You mustn't do this."

Giulia was still bent over in the degrading position she had been assigned when he had rushed in. Stieg placed his hand on her shoulders. "Come with me. Now."

Giulia rose to her feet and followed him out the souvenir and provisions shack. She realised she had left her bikini bottom on the ground. He took hold of her hand and pulled her away from the area of the huts.

"You come back anytime, Signorina. We always have *herbe*. Is the strongest and the best," Haroun shouted out behind her. "I know you come back," he sneered.

*　　*　　*

Both Stieg and Marta were unmercifully angry at her. How could she do what she had done? Or been prepared to do, as Giulia feebly pointed out. Nothing had yet happened.

"I don't know. I was in a daze," she tried to explain to them.

"You must never do it again," Marta pointed out. "Go to the Arab men. They will give you disease."

"You smoke too much, Giulia. You must stop, cut down. It's just not good for you so much," Stieg added.

Giulia nodded in agreement.

"I will. I promise."

Like adrenaline in steep overdrive, the realisation of what she had just done overwhelmed Giulia. It was madness, there was no other way to describe it. Her shoulders slumped. They were inside the tent where Giulia sat cross-legged on top of her crumpled sleeping bag. She had slipped on a T-shirt and panties.

"The others have set up a big new campfire down the beach," Marta said. "It seems it's Halloween. I'd lost all track of time being down here. The German girls have brought their guitars. Come with us. We'll sing, drink a little, dance, relax. It will do you good, Giulia," she suggested. "Take your mind off things."

"No," Giulia said. "I feel tired now. I'll sleep instead."

"Are you sure?"

"Yes," she crawled into the sleeping bag. Marta tucked her in with care.

But sleep wouldn't come. The earlier scene she had been involved in flashing like a movie behind her eyes. In slow motion. Speeded up. Every word said, every single gesture captured in the amber of memory. Giulia couldn't help herself crying. What had become of her? How could she have stooped so low?

Distant sounds of laughter reached her from the campfire down the beach where the winter stragglers of the colony were enjoying themselves but it felt like a world away.

One hour or so later, or maybe it had been longer, Stieg unhooked the tent's flap and looked in.

"You're crying?" he queried.

"Hmmm …" Giulia sniffed.

"I thought I'd just come and check how you were. Not feeling better, are you?"

"No."

"What is it?" Stieg asked.

"I feel abandoned, lonely."

"There's no need. We love you, you know, all of us. You're our little girl lost …"

Giulia tried to regain her composure. She wiped her tears away with the back of her hand, raised herself halfway out of the sleeping bag and sat up. The night was cold and she felt a chill fly across the thin material of her T-shirt.

"I didn't say thank you, Stieg. You arrived just in time."

"I'd seen you wander away towards the huts, and you were such a long time returning, I sort of wondered what was you were up to," Stieg explained.

"You saved me," Giulia said.

"You're our friend. I would have felt rather guilty had I not." He lowered himself to his knees and leaned over to take Giulia into his arms and held her tight.

Giulia drew a deep breath and held in his fraternal embrace quietly wallowed in his warmth. He smelled of the sea. It had been such a long time since a man had held her like this, in invisible chains of tenderness. He loosened his grasp on her. A voice at the back of her throat was screaming silently that she wanted to stay like this for ever. She moved her chin from his shoulder where she had buried herself during their clinch, moved her lips towards his and kissed him, her tongue desperately darting past the wall of his teeth and connecting with his wetness.

Stieg initially displayed some hesitation but soon surrendered himself to the moment. He firmly strengthened his hold on her, squashing Giulia's thin frame against his hard chest. His outstretched hands circled her back.

Giulia lowered her right hand from his shoulder and felt for his penis through the torn jeans he was wearing.

"I want you inside me now," she begged.

"This is wrong," he whispered.

"Who cares?" she said.

Marta returned to the tent a short while later to find Stieg and Giulia fucking on the ground between the two sleeping bags, sand flying wildly across their bodies as they convulsed. They were grunting like animals in heat. It was desperation, not lovemaking.

Stieg did not see her enter, too busy ploughing the young Italian woman who lay on her back opening herself wide to him.

Across his heaving shoulders Giulia caught a sight of Marta and the look of first surprise and then sheer disgust spreading across her features.

Giulia silently hoped Marta would recognise the note of regret in her eyes, explaining in the language of emotions that it wasn't Stieg really, it could have been anyone, any man right now. That it wasn't personal.

"Bitch," Marta mumbled and turned back and ran down the sand away from the tent.

Stieg came loudly. Giulia was unable to reach orgasm

despite the savage intensity of the fuck. They separated in darkness, neither willing to speak. Both slipped into their respective sleeping bags, as if nothing had happened.

When morning came, Marta had not returned to the tent.

SHE'S COMING HOME

MARTA HAD CAREFULLY FOLDED her clothes, taken off her bracelets, ankle chains and watch and removed her wallet, placed them all in a neat pile and, without a word to anyone, walked out as the sun rose and plunged into the still cold waves, as fearless of the elements as she had been all her life.

Marta never came back. Her body was not recovered, and Giulia's whole world fell to pieces.

The sea near the improvised colony had always been treacherous but there was no one around to look after matters or raise a red flag warning that it was sometimes unsafe to swim. No one knew if she had done this deliberately or if had been an accident. Both Stieg and Giulia kept their own council, and mourned her silently, while all the others who had not known Marta as well as they had ambled silently up and down the beach for the next couple of days, watching the horizon in the vain hope of her surfacing again, or at any rate her inert body floating on the waters.

She kept on sharing the tent with Stieg, but an abyss of silence and blame quickly grew between them. Giulia wanted to feel guilty, but could not summon the right emotion. She wondered whether she had lost the capacity to feel for others, as if the cold heart Jack had once accused her of harbouring had now become a fact of life.

She'd never wanted it to be that way. She'd dreamed of love, meeting the right one, having children. Where had this terrible dissatisfaction with normal life begun, she wondered?

Soon, the colony was almost deserted as others left, one at a time or in small groups, to migrate back to the world they had left behind. Winter was approaching. Barely a dozen tents survived, scattered across the immensity of the beach. Haroun and Jamel had boarded up their shack and disappeared one night.

"What do you plan to do?" Giulia had asked Stieg.

"I think I'll stay," he said. "Maybe she will come back."

He kept on refusing to believe that Marta had drowned. Insisted she had just gone travelling and would return when her anger had faded.

"I'll keep you company," Giulia said.

He greeted the news with indifference.

Today, she would smoke that final joint, one she had found in Marta's corner of the shared tent, half-buried in the sand beneath a pile of months-old women's magazines she had picked up on her travels. Some sick form of inheritance, she realised. There was no more grass to be had, by any means. She convinced herself she could survive without it. Reality wasn't that bad, was it?

Jack sat on the hotel room balcony facing the marina, counting the pregnant women walking by outside. Eleonora had gone into town to look at the shop windows, now that the siesta hour was over. He'd done that useless pilgrimage too often by now, and was long tired of the sight of leather belts at premium prices, cut-price swimming costumes and colourful and flimsy summer dresses and pharmacies advertising herbal

Viagra substitutes between the handful of tapas bars.

The score was pregnant women: seven vs. prams: five. All in the space of one hour.

A small boat came swanning in and slowly inserted itself into its assigned gap and moored.

The smell of grilled fish wafted up from the parade of restaurants below that stretched all the way to the harbour's gates.

For the first time in weeks, he had booted up his laptop and gone online earlier. Several Google Alerts for Giulia. Though not one of them actually concerned her, the search engines extracting her first name and her family name from separate locations on the web. An avalanche of e-mails, two thirds of them spam or newsletters he no longer took any interest in. Few people appeared worried by his disappearance from London. Only a few pointed comments from his literary agent. He had churned out three of his monthly book comment columns while still in Paris and the next deadline was still a few weeks away. He could always improvise another here without the need to refer to any of the actual books he was writing about. His online bank statement was still in the black. An editor in San Francisco was inviting him to contribute a new short story to an anthology on the theme of decadence. Twenty-four people wanted to become his friends on Facebook, none of whom he'd even met. He deleted messages wholesale.

The blank screen on his computer just glared at him.

He had once told Giulia, when they were still together, that he would never make her a character in one his stories or books. But he now realised he was now about to break that promise.

Writing about her would keep her alive. In his mind at least. No doubt she would hate him for doing this, he knew she would see this as a particularly perfidious form of betrayal, but then how much worse could things be? She probably hated him already. Years ago, he would have written pages and pages full of sound and fury in the hope one woman or another would return to him, understand the savage nakedness of his love, the purity of his affection. He was older than that now and no longer held such romantic notions. It would just be a story, not a bottle in the sea.

Maybe he could try and imagine, novelise what she had been up to since she had left him behind and taken her own road on a journey where he could not follow.

Yes, she would take a train to the south and there could be guns, drugs, bad men, all the normal clichés, maybe even pirates on the high seas. A life imagined. There are no new stories, Jack reflected, just the craft of knitting familiar elements together and coming up with a new angle and enough surprises to keep the reader intrigued. The minor art of fiction.

He opened a brand new folder.

He was thinking about his opening line when Eleonora arrived back, with a baguette and a bottle of mineral water under her arms. They already had Serrano ham in the room's fridge and had agreed to eat in tonight. She kissed him on the forehead.

"Any news?" she asked.

"No," Jack replied. "Just doodling."

"Doodling is what?" she looked at him and the empty laptop screen with round eyes.

"Just trying to write something."

"I never see you write," she said. "Is good if you start again."

"Watching someone write is no spectacle, Eleonora. Most of the time, I just sit there, scratching my scalp or other parts, picking my nose, drinking Pepsi or coffee. There are better things to see, even on Spanish TV …"

Jack closed the folder and switched off his laptop.

The writing could wait.

Stieg opened his eyes, rubbed them, watched Giulia rise from the sleeping bag that had once belonged to Marta. Bent over to avoid brushing her unkempt head of black curls against the canvas of the tent's roof, she slipped her jeans on, a pair of old socks and her scuffed trainers. He stretched his limbs, his vision of her still blurred by sleep as she stood there, her now-tanned skin and pert breasts contrasting with the off-blue of her washed-out jeans as she delved into her backpack where she finally found a well-creased T-shirt and a woollen cardigan he had never seen her wear before. He noticed her dropping various small items into her pockets, her purse, some papers – was it her passport? – and watched her slip out of the tent in silence. Stieg remained silent throughout.

Giulia aimed straight for the dunes, retracing the path that had brought them here months before. The upwards journey through the sand was arduous; she had grown used to wading barefoot through the sand for so long now, and her trainers now felt awkward and didn't provide her with any grip. Half an hour later, she had reached the road which she remembered travelled north. The sun had barely risen. She sat down, took a sip of water from the plastic bottle and waited for some sign of traffic. By the time a van stopped for her, she had almost run out of water. The driver was an Arab with a lined face, his sun-ravaged skin drawn tight across his features. He was only driving to the nearest village, where he said she might find drivers journeying to Tangiers.

The next day, seven vehicles later, Giulia finally

reached the city and caught a bus and then a ferry to Gibraltar where she rang her father back in Rome from a public telephone booth on reverse charges.

"I want to come home," she told him. "I need your help."

He asked her no questions, just listened to her explanations and what she needed now. First he would wire her some money at the General Post Office and would then arrange for a flight to be booked. There were no direct connections between Gibraltar and Rome, and she would have to catch a connection in Madrid where she would have a six-hour wait. Giulia smiled: what were a few more hours in the general scheme of things?

"Please," she asked him. "One thing … When I am home, I don't want you to ask any questions, OK?"

"You're my daughter," he said. "The important thing is that you return to your family. I will ask no questions, that's a solemn promise."

"Thank you."

The cash would likely not reach her until the next day, she knew. She sought out the beach where she would sleep tonight. A final night on the sand would not do her any further harm, she reckoned.

Eleonora was reading on the hotel room's balcony, while Jack took a shower. Their conversation these past days had reached a total impasse, as if they no longer had anything to say to each other. Words no longer seemed necessary. They both cared immensely for the other, but there was a wall that now separated them. They slept in the same bed but no longer touched, almost like a couple who had been married or together for decades. It had only taken them three months to reach this awkward stage of comfortable companionship.

He heard her cellphone ring.

Jack was washing his hair when she came into the bathroom.

"Anything?" he said, brushing the water away from his eyes.

"Yes."

He switched the water off and Eleonora handed him a towel. Her face was inscrutable.

"So?"

"It was Il Dottore ..."

He stepped out of the bathtub, still dripping profusely onto the porcelain tiles. He held his breath as long as he possibly could. Please, not bad news. Please. Please.

"She's returned home."

The weight on his shoulders and heart just swept away in an instant.

They looked at each other. Extraordinary relief. Pleasure. Questions galore.

"Good," Jack said. His vocabulary had been drained and he could thing of nothing better to say.

"Yes," Eleonora confirmed.

"So here comes an end to our lives as amateur detectives," he joked.

She managed a crooked smile.

They walked back to the bedroom, where he slipped on some clothes. She closed the window to the balcony to keep out the cold.

"I'll be leaving tomorrow," she said.

"I see."

"It's better that way. I'm not sure if I want to see Giulia again, in Rome. But my life is there. I'll have to find a job, do something with my life. It's been good being with you, but we both knew it would come to an end. You understand?"

"I do."

The quest for Giulia had finally brought them together. Its ending could only tear them apart. That was the way of things.

"I'll call reception to let them know we'll be leaving tomorrow then."

"What will you do?" Eleonora asked.

Jack had a wry smile. "Go back to my wife, I reckon." He had never mentioned her before. Yet another unseen presence in his affairs of the heart. "If she will have me back."

Eleonora moved over to the kitchen area to boil some water for coffee.

Jack called out after her.

"Maybe the next time we meet, we can make things work out better," he suggested. "All you have to do is call me, you know that. Anywhere in the world, I will take you. Just say where and when, OK?"

"Yes, I think we need time for reflection," Eleonora pointed out. "If we meet again, it must be a new chapter. We start again. Just us. No more Giulia and Henry looking, how you say, over our shoulders?"

Eleonora would return to Rome and he to London. She spoke to Giulia once on the phone, neither of them willing to reveal much of what had happened in the intervening months since Giulia had left for her studies in Paris.

She would find a job in Naples as the official photographer for the local sports arena where a variety of rock and jazz concerts were held. It wasn't much but it was a living. Jack began writing stories again, in great part influenced by the past months. She had a brief affair with a drummer but she knew he would never be faithful to her. Six months later, in the throes of abominable loneliness she rang Jack. She knew he was not perfect and that they could not seriously envisage a future life together, but right there and then all Eleonora wanted was a bit of tenderness.

He sounded exactly the same. Both positive and melancholy.

"Another chance?" she asked him.

"Absolutely."

"You won't believe it, but I have missed you."

"Me too … Swear."

"That's good," she said. The sounds of Naples at night were crowding outside the window of her first floor apartment.

"Where?" Jack asked her.

They made the necessary arrangements.

Giulia's flight landed at Fiumicino. Her father was unable to pick her up as he was on hospital duty, but her mother and brother had come to greet her instead. Tommaso was driving her old banged-up car, which she had been given on her nineteenth birthday. She was surprised it hadn't yet fallen apart.

Both were careful not to ask her too many questions as they waited for her luggage to emerge along the conveyor belt.

They both remarked on how tanned she was and that she had lost weight.

The drive back into the city was loaded with long silences.

Rome seemed so quiet and provincial after all this time away. So dead. But she knew it was not the city that had changed in her absence. She was a different person now.

Giulia briefly remembered Ernesto. He was nice, but a

bit boring. Years ago, during the course of her first year at University, together with two other friends they had organised a film club. He was the only boy she had brought home that her mother had approved of. Well-bred, polite, somewhat shy. But she knew he had a soft spot for her. Had been hurt and resentful when he had heard through common friends that she had become involved with a man twice her age. He'd begun to avoid her as a result. Maybe she would agree to see him again.

They reached the Circonvallazione. Tommaso's driving manners had not improved, she noted with a wry smile, as her brother cut across the next lane of traffic with a total disregard for other cars. Her mother was wittering away about aunts and uncles and the whole gallery of their relatives. Giulia felt it difficult to feign interest.

Yes, she would phone Ernesto.

Maybe boring was what life was meant to be about.

THE FLIGHT OF THE ANGEL

HAD ENRICO NOT BEEN so suspicious, Cornelia would at some stage have cited the pretext of a previous business engagement in Paris and left the villa that very evening. And swiftly disappeared back to America to deal with the perilous loose ends. It wasn't the people in France who represented a problem now, just her own faceless principals in America. And all for that moment of unnecessary kindness when she had briefly caught a sign of loss in Giulia's eyes.

"So are you just an unusual girl in search of kicks or something altogether different, Marti?" he'd asked. "That is my dilemma."

"That's for you to decide," she replied.

"And is your name really Marti?"

"Why do you doubt it?"

"Because you carry no papers, passport or anything that might provide a clue in your handbag. Somewhat unusual, no?"

"My mother always warned me about the danger of pickpockets in Europe."

"Is that why you don't even have a single credit card in your purse. So uncommon for an American."

"I happen to be something of an uncommon gal."

"So I'd noticed earlier. I've never come across a handbag so Spartan and anonymous in a woman. You certainly travel light: a handful of bank notes, a tube of lip salve, a few commonplace pills, a map of the city, Métro tickets, a vial of perfume, a spare set of underwear and paper clips. Or have I forgotten anything?"

"I like to travel light. Most ungentlemanly to go through a lady's bag, Enrico."

"At least it's French perfume."

"Duty-free has its advantages."

Santaclara gave her an amused but probing look.

"You will stay in the house tonight, Marti."

"Is that an order?" she asked.

"Shall we say I'd prefer it if you did."

All she had was the bathrobe now wrapped around her nudity. She had no clue where he might have stored the clothes she had arrived in. She had little alternative.

"As you wish."

"Just a precaution, you see. These have been strange days. Our friend's demise and then a few days ago one of the security men from the club was found dead in somewhat ugly circumstances, so you must understand my caution. He had been on duty the night of the hit. We're still wondering if there is a connection."

Cornelia didn't bat an eyelid under his intense gaze.

He emptied his glass.

She declined a refill.

"Actually, I am famished following our earlier exertions. Have you any food? Nothing elaborate, some snack maybe? I'd rather not have to go to sleep on an empty stomach. Or play further."

"Of course, my dear. Let's repair to the kitchen. Right now. Can't have you hungry, can we?"

Cornelia was beginning to piece together the lay of the land and getting her orientation around the sprawling house. This had now become more than a recce as she actively concentrated to raise herself to combat mode. Santaclara was no fool and wasn't going to dismiss her presence as lightly as she had initially hoped. There was no easy retreat. Normally, she would have accepted the prospect of a further rough fuck or two with a light heart and mind, but she now knew he wouldn't be satisfied with such a basic outcome before setting her loose. Why would he have revealed so much under her less than probing questioning if that was the case?

Now, she was no longer certain whether he had even told her the whole story. Maybe he and his remaining partners in the club were also actively involved in the trading of women and the elimination of the man she had been assigned to kill was just a way to increase their share of the proceeds.

Did he maybe consider her to be a potential piece of no doubt valuable merchandise?

She idly wondered what sort of price she might fetch. After all, she had displayed an abnormal willingness to be stretched to her limits and had offered no resistance and she knew that white meat, blonde at that, could fetch a high price, even more so as she wasn't Eastern European and therefore even more exotic and rare. The Middle East, Africa, South America. The possibilities were endless.

Not that she had any intention to allow herself to be funnelled further down the flesh pipeline. Her complicity had always been a means to an end, and she felt no inner need to submit or serve.

They had shared bread, cold cuts and a chilled bottle of white wine at the wooden kitchen table.

"You will have your own room, of course," he had informed her. "I'm sure you will find it comfortable. I think I have tired you enough for today. We will have more time on our hands tomorrow. I certainly wish to explore further with you, Marti. You have the beauty, and the right body for our games but you also clearly have a brain, a most favourable combination. You will have to tell me more about your past experiences. Explain a bit what makes you tick."

"Tomorrow," she willingly agreed. Her buttocks were still on fire. He had carefully marked her there stopping just before drawing blood in earnest.

"Good. Oh, and my German shareholder will be joining us. I rang him earlier while you were showering. Told him about you. He is intrigued. I hope you don't mind. He is driving down. Should be with us shortly before lunch I expect."

"Do I have an alternative?"

"No."

"Am I to be the main course?" she asked.

"How witty," Santaclara said. "Now, let me show you around the house. I'm very proud of it." Cornelia welcomed the guided tour. It would serve her well.

There was an indoor pool in the east wing of the villa, its surrounds festooned by a profusion of orchids spanning most of the colours of the rainbow, earthenware pots circling the perimeter walls of the pool. "You should swim," Enrico suggested.

"I've just eaten," Cornelia protested feebly.

"It was so light. Anyway, it's an old wives' tale that one shouldn't swim after a meal. Didn't you know that?"

"They forgot to teach me that at university."

He beamed.

"Educated. Even better."

"Do you have a lady's swimming suit you could spare, then?"

“No need, Marti. Throw that bathrobe of yours off and let me see that sleek, charming body of yours. Your pallor will blend so perfectly with the blue of the water. I reckon it’s too late now to be coy, no?”

Whatever kept him happy. Cornelia discarded the robe, dipped a couple of toes in to check the temperature. She’d always disliked bathing in the sea, it was always too cold for her, even in warmer climes. And she’d never been a very good swimmer, which had been a great disappointment to her parents. She lowered herself in and swam a couple of lengths while he watched her with a satisfied grin spreading across his features. He was holding a large towel out for her as she later emerged dripping from the water. He massaged the thick material against her skin to dry her.

“Wonderful. Now let’s escort you to your bedroom. You need a good night’s sleep.” He hadn’t returned the bathrobe and she understood he wanted her to walk the rest of the way stark naked. As she stepped up the stairs, she felt his eyes as he followed below her looking straight into her most intimate parts.

The upper floor was a labyrinth of corridors and bedrooms furnished with care and taste. The room she had been assigned was right at the end.

“Get your energy back,” he said, gently guiding her past the door with a firm hand on her bare and still damp shoulder. “You’ll need it.”

The door was locked behind her. The room had no windows.

Cornelia slumped on the bed and pulled the covers and sheets towards her.

Sleep came easily.

She heard the key turn in the lock. Wiped the night away

from her eyes and glanced at her watch. Past ten in the morning already. She had been so tired that all dreams had been kept at bay.

"Join me in the kitchen, whenever you feel ready to face the day," she heard Santaclara say, as he retraced his steps down the corridor and the stairs leading down to the ground floor.

When Cornelia opened the door, she found another bathrobe, still smelling cleanly of detergent and fragrant conditioner on the floor outside. At least she wasn't expected to parade nude again. She slipped it on and tightened the belt around her slim waist.

"Good morning," Enrico called out as she emerged into the brightly lit kitchen. He was sitting at the table sipping from a large bowl of coffee.

"Hi," Cornelia tentatively said.

"Bread, coffee, jam?" he offered, pointing at the spread scattered across the breakfast table.

Cornelia smiled at him, with as much innocence as she could summon.

"Actually, would you mind awfully if I took another dip in the pool. It would be a nice way to start the day, invigorate myself for later rigours. May I?"

"Absolutely," he said. "What a splendid idea. In fact, as I watched you swim and then later walk yesterday evening, Marti, it made me think of a dancer. Yes, that's what you reminded me of. Do you like dancing?"

"When I am given the opportunity, yes," she said.

Was he playing with her, or was it just a coincidence? Cornelia was unsure.

"I won't be that long. Just a few lengths and some exercise. Stretching and all that. You could even join me, why not?"

He looked at her, weighing up his options.

"An excellent idea," he finally responded. "Let me finish here. I'll be with you very soon. Go along,"

Cornelia made her way to the wing of the vast villa where the indoor pool was situated, rapidly scouting her surroundings as she made her way forward for anything that could suit her purpose. The final room to her right before the four-step descent into the pool area was a large, cavernous and lushly-appointed lounge with a massive home cinema screen covering its back wall and a row of deep, leather seats. To keep the light out, the windows were shielded by heavy mauve brocade drapes. Right now they were open and offered a partial view of the leafy walled garden. Cornelia swiftly advanced into the room and threaded out one of the knotted curtain cords holding the drapes in place. On her way out, she closed the door to the room. And briskly continued her short journey to the pool. It had only taken her a few seconds.

Shedding the robe, Cornelia slipped into the water, still holding the thick cord bunched up in her hand. Standing, submerged up to her chest, she looked around her and spotted the small circular outlets through which the pool's pumping system recirculated the water. She stuffed the cord inside the furthest cavity, waded back to the other side of the pool and waited for Santaclara's arrival.

She didn't have long to wait.

She peered up at him, her wet hair momentarily unfurling its blonde curls all the way down her back.

"It's so long," he said. "You're like a true siren."

She had carefully avoided getting her hair wet the previous evening.

"You're wearing trunks," she protested. "It's not fair. Makes things quite unequal. I get the distinct feeling you like to hold the upper hand, Enrico."

Enrico laughed.

He took an elegant dive into the pool, splashing her wildly as he cut through the water. He quickly resurfaced, straightened out and whizzed past her, swimming with grace as he completed his first length. Cornelia just stood in place, her hands and feet fluttering idly, content to feel the lukewarm soup of the water wash over her body. Santaclara appeared determined to put in some genuine exercise. Which suited Cornelia just fine. With her back to the pool's rim she inched back and pulled the cord out of its cranny and waited for him to make another vigorous turn and pass her.

Her outstretched arm holding the soaking thick curtain cord in a loop, she caught him in full flow as the improvised weapon circled his neck. It wasn't enough to hurt him badly, but it took Santaclara by surprise and the impact and sharp pressure of the material against his Adam's apple forced him to open his mouth wide and swallow too much water. His body jack-knifed as he floundered badly. Cornelia pounced and pulled on the cord with both her hands and all her strength while digging her right foot into his back to increase her leverage while the agitated man began to struggle like a drowning puppet, half choking, half gasping for air.

Cornelia knew he was in good physical shape and would eventually regain some instinctive form of composure and would likely be strong enough to resist being garrotted in this manner. Still pulling hard on the cord, she released her right hand and keeping her foot buried in the small of his back, she moved the freed hand to his wet scalp and viciously forced the man's whole head under the water. She couldn't strangle him, but drowning would suffice. Like a fish both caught in a whirlpool and speared by a hook, indistinctly becoming aware that the dual attack was getting the better of him, Santaclara began to convulse. Cornelia increased the downwards force on his head, resisting his attempts to surface for air. He squirmed unexpectedly and she briefly lost control of the upper part of his wriggling body but she sharply adjusted her stance and fiercely dug her knee into his back, without losing any of the advantage the position gave her.

The whole scene took place in complete silence, bar the splashing and the ripples coursing outwards through the water where Santaclara's head was submerged.

Cornelia drew her breath, hoping her lesser bodily strength would hold out against the man's diminishing energy before the balance between them might turn against her.

Gradually his frantic movements slowed, the remaining air inside his lungs thinning, undermining his strength to fight her and Cornelia knew she was winning the struggle to maintain him under the pool's surface.

Time ground to a halt.

There was a final jolt and Santaclara's body went limp under her hand and against the vicious downwards pressure applied by her knee. This was it. Cornelia waited an extra couple of minutes to ensure this was no unlikely ruse and eventually let go. The man's body, face downwards in the water, just floated there. He was dead.

Throughout the struggle, Cornelia had managed to stay totally calm, emotionless. A detachment born of experience although this was the first time she had actually killed someone with her bare hands. It was only now that she pulled herself out of the pool that the adrenaline began to flow throughout her body. She sat down in one the plastic deck chairs scattered around the swimming pool's perimeter and the wall of orchids. The sensation was intoxicating. It was better than sex.

The German associate arrived two hours later. He was a short, swarthy balding man with an annoying imperious manner.

Cornelia had lingered in an energy-restoring bath, washing all the chlorine off her skin and shampooing her hair until she felt normal again. She had located where Santaclara had stuffed her clothes and dressed and spent an hour or so exploring the villa at leisure. Her plan formed.

"So you're the American woman?" the German said, looking her up and down with a superior manner after she had opened the front door for him. She had buzzed his car through the electronic gates of the property. A metal grey BMW 318i Estate, she noted.

"Well, I don't see any other gals around," she smirked, letting him in. He wore a grey pinstriped suit and black shoes polished to within an inch of mirror shade perfection.

"Where's Santaclara?" he asked.

"Went out to the shops," Cornelia replied. "Normal stuff, bread, milk, we'd run out, he said."

The German looked surprised. There was an innate meanness about him. Like an aura of menace. This was a man who knew how to inflict pain and revel in its effects. Cornelia experienced a sense of relief that she would not now be used further by him and Santaclara. This bastard would have certainly displayed a cruel imagination.

"Enrico said I should entertain you, of course."

"Good."

"You've been driving a long time, I understand. We can go to the kitchen. Drink something," she suggested.

"Perfect," he curtly said. He dropped his brown leather attaché case to the floor and followed her.

"Water, juice or something stronger?" Cornelia offered.

She was keeping her fingers crossed he wouldn't go for beer. There were only cans, which she had been unable to spike. She had earlier found a large cache of sleeping pills in one of the bathroom cabinets, enough to despatch a whole battalion into the arms of Morpheus. She'd wondered whether they had been for Santaclara's sole use or were kept in such abundant reserve for possible female visitors. If that was the case, there was some poetic irony in the situation. She had emptied every single tube and bottle and carefully ground the white pills down to a fine powder which she had evenly distributed across a strategic number of bottles and carefully ensured they had fully dissolved throughout the respective liquids.

The German guy looked around the kitchen shelves, still eyeing Cornelia with some suspicion.

"Will he be long?" he asked.

"I don't think so."

Cornelia sat down at the table, not wanting to rush him in any way. She had hoped to locate a suitable gun somewhere in the house, but even after breaking into a handful of closed drawers, she had been unable to get her hands on one. Forensics however would have been a bastard and she was hoping to depart the scene later, with no obvious evidence of her passage hanging around. A bullet lodged deep inside a skull would warrant too thorough an investigation. Drowned men didn't.

"Well, we are in France, after all. Is there some white wine in the fridge?"

There was.

He was out cold within a half hour. Much too long as far as Cornelia was concerned. Throughout, as they sat together uncomfortably in the kitchen, taking sips of wine and waiting, she could virtually read the German's mind as he mentally planned her use and degradation later, and a manipulative smile spread across his thin lips at the thought of the abuse and how he would enjoy it.

While she had been waiting for Santaclara's German acolyte, Cornelia had been thorough in her explorations and established the fact that the villa's garage housed all the right ingredients for her purpose.

She had never torched a house before, but had watched enough TV crime series or read enough books to understand the basics. She also felt confident that French fire investigators did not have the same technical resources at their disposal as their American counterparts, fictional or otherwise. And, even if she slipped up, it was most unlikely that the source of the fire could be tracked down back to her. There would be no prints. Not that hers were on anyone's records. Just a dead body drowned in the pool, and another burned to a crisp in the kitchen area whose stomach contents would by then have turned to ashes.

Once the flames had caught hold and began spreading rapidly, licks of fire streaming across drapes, swimming like a horde of lemmings over ceilings, consuming furniture and wall hangings in their hungry stride, Cornelia retreated to the front door and slammed it behind her. She had picked the German's pockets earlier and retrieved his car keys and drove to the centre of town, where she abandoned the vehicle in an underground car par under St Germain des Prés.

She made her way to her hotel, paid the bill in cash,

retrieved her meagre belongings and took the Métro to the Gare Du Nord where she took the first Eurostar train to London. She knew that neither the British or French border officials at the station or at London's Kings Cross scanned passports in view of the sheer amount of passengers passing through. It was better to avoid her particulars being archived a few weeks in a row departing Paris. The muddier the waters the better.

She spent a week in London, acting like a normal tourist, visiting museums and theatre shows on Shaftesbury Avenue, enjoying Indian meals, walking in the plentiful parks, openly using her credit cards for the first time.

For her flight back to New York she had a choice of seats to either Newark or Kennedy. She chose Kennedy.

TAKE ME TO CARNEVALE

JACK AND ELEONORA HAD arranged to meet the man in a small café on the left-hand side of Campo Santa Maria Formosa, right opposite the church and the hospital. It was February. It was Venice. A thin morning mist still shrouded the city, floating in from the lagoon, like a shimmering curtain of silk, half obscuring the old stones, the canals and the normal sounds of the floating city.

They'd been communicating by e-mails since parting months before in Sitges.

They both knew there were still things left unsaid between them.

Thought they would give it one more chance. To see if they could banish the ghost of Giulia and past relationships.

Jack hadn't even brought his laptop with him on this Venice trip, but the apartment they were staying in, which he had agreed to house-sit for friends travelling in India, had a computer in almost every room and a wi-fi connection and it had been, for both of them, almost too much of a temptation. Like allowing their fate to be decided by the vagaries of electronic availability.

Eleonora had been sitting on one of the sofas, half reading and half daydreaming, while he listened to music on his iPod. Right then the soundtrack by Nick Cave for *The Assassination of Jesse James*, he would remember later.

"I don't know," Eleonora had said, and he had recognised exactly the precise words she had uttered, just from reading her lips behind the threnody in his ears. It was something she often mumbled when things were not quite right.

He'd switched off the music and turned towards her.

"What is it?"

The green of her eyes emerged from a sea of sadness.

"You know …" she replied.

He knew. Oh yes, he knew. They were just going nowhere, and no earnest conversation could put them back on track. Even in Venice.

They had reached the city a week or so earlier, arriving at Marco Polo airport. To save money, they had not gone to the extravagance of taking a water taxi but, instead, the bus which took them across the Ponte Della Liberta to Piazzale Roma where they had caught a *vaporetto* down the Grand Canal to the Rialto Bridge stop and, following the map they had been e-mailed by his friends, had somehow made their way on foot to the apartment, dodging the customary labyrinth of small bridges and lesser canals.

By now they had visited a multitude of churches, several handfuls of Titian and Canaletto paintings, eaten too much exquisite food to jade the best of palates and suffered an indigestion of baroque and classical architecture and the silences between them were growing longer.

From their bedroom window, they could see St Mark's Place and the Doge's Palace and the Campanile across a bend in the Canal. But the weather was cold and humid and the old building's heating was stuttering at its best and they'd had to wear sweatshirts most of the time both inside and outside.

Maybe he should have chosen the Caribbean where they could have lazed naked on a beach and the warmth might have seeped into their mood. But Eleonora had never been to Venice and he had promised her he would take her anywhere she wanted, and she was aware that Roberto and Barbara had once offered him the apartment here should he ever wish to visit. Jack had been to Venice several times before, and to be frank had never been too much of a fan. In summer, the canals smelt and he disliked being just an anonymous part of the tourist crowds. In truth, he was not a great traveller.

Eleonora, on the other hand, was twenty years younger and always sported an enthusiasm for new places and experiences that he no longer could pretend he had. And he secretly knew he'd never possessed the joy or curiosity even when he had been younger himself.

Although neither wanted to broach the subject they both knew to a different degree that their relationship was doomed. The age difference, the opposing temperaments, the cultural differences, the weight of his own past, her own ambitions in life. But loneliness still bound them. His, full of despair that she would in all likelihood turn out to be the last significant love of his life; hers, full of wonder that Jack had somehow become the first genuine love in her life – yes, she had now realised, Henry had just been a youthful infatuation – but with her mind, her imagination nagging her daily about the roads not taken and all the future roads that were still to be reached.

In an effort to negate the due date on their affair, they had agreed to come to Venice. In her mind, she had wanted to confront beauty. In his, it was just a melancholy vision of past literary memories of Thomas

Mann, Byron, Dickens or Nic Roeg which resonated in the greyness of his soul, the delusion that a trip to a new place could repair the stitches that were coming apart in his life. The magic of Venice as suture.

"Carnival begins tomorrow," he had pointed out to her.

"Really?" she had exclaimed, her eyes widening in anticipation.

"Yes."

"Will you buy me a mask?" Eleonora had asked.

"Of course."

"And I will get one for you," she suggested. "Something darkly romantic, that would just suit you."

"Why not?"

"And we acquire them separately, and they remain secret until the first evening we go out and wear them. A surprise!"

"A lovely idea," Jack had readily agreed, the fleeting thought of Eleonora quite naked except for a delicate white Carnival mask shielding her face, and her green eyes peering through the disguise already warming his heart and suggestible loins.

His finger lingered on her knee, and he shuddered. The electricity between them still worked.

"Can we go online and read all about the Carnival?" she asked.

"Of course," he said. They made their way to the guest bedroom where the nearest connected computer stood on a rickety trestle table their host used to mix his paints on.

Above it, by coincidence, hung slightly crooked on the wall by the window, was a gaudy painting of a woman in chains wearing only a black mask which obscured her eyes. Roberto's latest BDSM variation.

They surfed freely for the next couple of hours,

learning all about Carnevale and its origins, the tales of Casanova, the types of masks and their significance. One link led to another and yet another until an aimless stroke of the keyboard took them to the website where out of sheer prurient curiosity they arranged for the meeting in the bar on Campo Santa Maria Formosa the next day.

At first, Jack had been somewhat hesitant, but Eleonora's enthusiasm had swayed him.

"It will be an experience," she said.

"I suppose so," he answered.

"Don't act so old and blasé," she added

Jack smiled wryly. She always knew how best to silence him.

"Yes, it's all because of Attila the Hun."

They were sipping espressos at the back of the small café. The man was in his fifties and had white hair and was explaining how the earliest inhabitants of Venice had been exiled all the way to the lagoon by the invasion of their native lands by foreign hordes.

"Fascinating," Eleonora commented.

"And the bridge that connects us to the Italian mainland was only built by Mussolini under a century ago. Before that we were isolated and you could only reach the city by water."

Jack ordered another round from the hovering waitress. Mostly San Pellegrino mineral water; neither he nor Eleonora could cope with too much coffee at this time of day.

"It's a party," the man who called himself Jacopo said. "But we try and organise matters so that we adhere to all the old traditions of the Venice Carnevale, not the diluted versions that have sadly evolved over the years since Carnevale's heyday."

"We understand," Jack said. Eleonora looked him in the eyes, and nodded.

"It is strictly by invitation, of course," he continued. "Normally, we try and restrict attendance to pure Venetians, but as you know, there are fewer of us now. The younger generations are all leaving the city. So sad."

He looked at Eleonora. Her dark hair shone glossily; she had washed it just before they had left the apartment to walk here. When wet her hair then extended to the small of her back like a long curtain of silk. Jack observed her, too. She looked luminous. Already excited by the prospect of the party they were being informally interviewed for. As if a fire was rising inside her, bringing light to her features, heat to her hidden senses. Jack recognised that gleam in her eyes. It was invariably present when she had been fucked. He kept on watching, transfixed as Jacopo's words swept soundlessly over him. The man with the white hair also kept on observing Eleonora, as if weighing her in his steady gaze.

Jack returned to reality, reluctantly abandoning his vision of Eleonora's fascinated attention to the man's words.

"Naturally, you remain masters of your destiny. A polite 'no' will always prove an acceptable response to any overture, although it is hoped that all guests will participate freely and openly in the proceedings."

Again, Eleonora nodded, her chin bobbing up and down.

Jack sighed discreetly.

It was true that they had often discussed the remote prospect of others joining in their games, their lovemaking. But they had never reached the stage where they had actively done anything about it.

Something inside him – something rotten or diseased?

– had always imagined what it would be like to see Eleonora mounted by another, harboured the curiosity to witness how another man would touch her, make her moan. Because he found her so beautiful, part of him felt she should be shared with the whole world, so that all and sundry could truly understand why his love for her was so strong and overpowering. But it was a long road from mere thoughts to the realities of the flesh.

She had even asked "Would you be jealous if it actually happened?" and he had been obliged to dig deep into his thoughts and had finally answered quite truthfully "I'm not sure. Maybe if I could watch. I wouldn't want you to fuck another man behind my back, that's for sure."

"Wonderful," Jacopo said as he rose from the café table. "You are a lovely couple. I think you will enjoy our parties a lot."

They had jointly agreed to attend the opening of Carnevale the next day. He had slipped over a piece of paper on which he had scribbled the address.

"Every party takes place in a different locale," the man with the white hair had said. "They can only be reached by the canals, so you will have to make arrangements accordingly."

They all shook hands and he departed.

Left alone, Jack and Eleonora looked at each other. He tried to smile, but couldn't raise the right rictus. He knew already that they would go. Eleonora had always been a woman of her word and once a decision had been taken, only hell and high water could ever change her mind.

"Well," she said.

"Hmmm …"

Eleonora was dressing.

"Don't wear panties," Jack suggested.

"Really?"

"Yes. I think it would fit in with the spirit of the occasion."

Eleonora chuckled softly.

"If you say so. Anyway, the dress is quite heavy, so I shouldn't feel the cold …" She gave him a twirl. He applauded theatrically.

"Flattery will get you everywhere …" she said.

They had been shopping in Mestre. In Venice, the prices were much too unaffordable. She had found him a sleek black silk suit made in Thailand which Jack wore with a black shirt and a scarlet bow tie.

"My prince of darkness!" Eleonora laughed. As if he now reminded her of a vampire.

In contrast, the dress they had acquired for tonight's event for her was white and made from thick linen, falling to her ankles with ornate elegance from her bare shoulders downwards, thin, almost invisible straps holding the dress up above her small, delicate breasts, unveiling just a discreet if appetising hint of gentle cleavage. Underneath she wore just dark hold-up stockings reaching to mid-thigh, their shapely black veil as sharp as her luxuriant pubic hair. A perfect conjugation of nights, when she cheekily raised the dress to her midriff, exposing herself to him.

God, she was stunning! Her lipstick was fiery red and she had surrounded her eyes with a grey circle of kohl.

They had found masks at Mondonovo, on Rio Terra Canal, near the Campo Santa Margherita, where masks could still be found that were replicas of the old historical, traditional models, and were different from the traditional fare on offer to gullible tourists in search of local colour.

For Jack, in his black outfit, they had chosen a *larva*, also called a *volto*. It was white, made of fine wax and should have typically been worn with a tricorn and cloak, which he had of course absolutely no intention of doing. After all, this was the twenty-first century! The shape of the mask would allow him to breathe and drink easily, and so there was no need to take it off, thus preserving anonymity.

Eleonora, on the other hand, had been coaxed by the old wrinkled lady at the store to select a *moretta* instead of the more traditional *bauta*. It was an oval mask of black velvet that was usually worn by women visiting convents. Invented in France it had rapidly become popular in ancient Venice as it drew out the beauty of feminine features. The mask was finished off with a veil, and was normally secured in place by a small bit in the wearer's mouth. As this was not appropriate to participate in a modern party, Eleonora's model had been modified so it was held by a clip at its apex that was attached to her mountain of curls.

"*Bella*," the old woman had said when Eleonora had tried the mask on.

"*Bellissima*," Jack said in turn, with a painful stab of fear coursing through his stomach, as Eleonora stood, fully attired in dress and mask, and the jungle of her curls peering impudently above the formal mask.

"*Grazie mille*," she laughed.

There was so much more he wanted to say to her. Like "Do you really want to go?" or "What will you do if another man proposes to you?" or "Do you still want me?" but the gondola they had booked had just arrived. They walked down to the waterside entrance of the building. The night air was cold and the sky full of scattered stars whose reflection glistened over the waters of the small canal like a million phosphorescent fish.

Jack read the address out to the gondolier in his French-accented Italian.

"It's party time," Eleonora said.

The half-abandoned palazzo dominated the Grand Canal halfway between the Ponte del Rialto and the Ponte dell'accademia, with the Campo San Polo visible from the ornate balconies on the land side of the building.

The tall man who wore the white mask with the elongated beak, similar to the head attire medics had worn in the years of the Plague, when pepper had been lodged into the furthest reaches of the bird of prey-like beak to shield its wearers from the illness, had been hovering near them most of the evening. They had briefly been introduced by Jacopo, earlier on in the festivities. Occasionally he would approach them with new glasses of champagne and would whisper in Eleonora's ears, or casually allow his leather-gloved hands to brush against her bare shoulders. His English was nigh perfect, albeit with West Coast American inflections. Jack couldn't remember his name. Real or otherwise. They had been introduced as Byron and Ariadne. No one here used their real name.

As neither Eleonora or Jack were particularly sociable or voluble, they had been isolated in the margins of the party and its flowing conversations. They had both drunk too much by now. Which meant he was retreating, as he often did, into longer and longer silences, whereas her demeanour was becoming looser, more joyful by the minute. How many times now had she wondered at the sheer elegance of the evening and its incomparable setting, the candles illuminating the cavernous, marble-floored rooms, the gold dishes laden with fruit, the never-ending flow of booze. She was intoxicated by both the alcohol and the sense of occasion. Was this the adventure she always claimed she was seeking whenever he would raise any questions about the future?

A hand took hold of his. Jack turned round. A woman in a red velvet dress and a white powdered wig pulled him a metre or two towards her. He looked up at her. She had endless legs enhanced by thin six inch heels. Behind her mask, he could see her eyes were the colour of coal.

"You are English, no?"

"Indeed," he answered.

Her scent was sweet, cloying almost.

"So you like our Carnevale?"

"Absolutely," he responded, ever polite.

Her purple-lipsticked lips moved into the shape of a kiss.

"Is it your first time in Venice?" she asked.

"Not quite," he answered. "But the first time I've been here at Carnival time, though."

"Ah …"

She moved nearer to him.

He realised they were now alone in the large room; the woman with purple lips, Eleonora, the tall guy and him. Somehow all the nearby partygoers had drifted out silently into the other neighbouring rooms, leaving faint echoes of conversations and the tinkling of crystal glasses eerily suspended in the tobacco smoke-infested air.

He took a step back.

"Oh … shy?"

"No," he muttered.

"So?" She extended her left arm and her fingers swept across his dry lips.

"Your woman isn't anywhere as shy as you are, I see,"

she remarked.

Jack's heart dropped all the way down to his stomach as he glanced around. Eleonora was now being embraced by the tall stranger, who held her tight against the far wall of the room, his hand burrowing under her dress, his face muzzled into hers. Her eyes was closed.

"Come," the woman with the white powdered wig said, taking him by the hand and leading him to a low couch at the opposite end of the room.

He followed, as if in a trance. Time slowed down to a crawl.

Her cunt tasted of exotic spices. Pungent, strong, savage. His tongue lapped her generous juices with quiet and studied abandon.

She spread her legs wider apart and pressed his head down firmer against her. Jack momentarily gasped for breath.

"Lick me harder," she ordered him.

Once she had tired of his worshipping the thick folds of her labia and the invisible radiating heat pulsing through her opening all the way from her innards, she pulled him on to the worn-out couch and firmly pulled his trousers down and began sucking him off.

Somehow, even though she was talented and imaginative, he failed to get totally hard, and she gave up within a few minutes.

"No worry," she said. "It happens."

Red-faced, he looked her in the eyes, attempting to guess how old she might be behind that mask. Her skin was spotless and taut and her long, defined legs were those of an athlete at the peak of her form. He gulped and instantly recalled the taste of her and its striking flavours. She had been on her knees and rose to her feet. He just stood there, his black silk trousers bunched around his ankles.

"Undress," she said. It was more of an order than a suggestion.

He meekly obeyed.

He wanted to turn around and see where Eleonora was. And the tall man. Their own noises had been muted, distant, but nevertheless insidiously present all the while he had been involved with the purple-lipsticked woman. She sensed this.

"Do so as you are. Don't turn round," she said, unclenching the black leather belt that circled her thin waist. "Look down to the floor as you undress."

He noticed the smudged purple stains of lipstick on the mushroom tip of his cock, like dried wine against the ridged flesh of his masculinity. He pulled the trousers down over his laced shoes. Then kicked the shoes off and quickly slipped off his socks. Surely there was no more ridiculous sight than a naked man wearing just black socks? He then pulled himself up and began unbuttoning his shirt. As he did so, he saw the woman reach for her matching red handbag, which had been lying on the couch and pull a devious contraption out, all leather straps and ivory trunk, from it.

His stomach froze.

There was a faint cry from the other end of the room.

He was now naked.

The woman pulled her ruched dress upwards and belted the strap-on to her waist. The artificial cock jutted ahead of her like the prow of a boat. Hard, inflexible.

"Maybe this will give you a hard on?" she suggested. "Word has it that English men are much appreciative or should I say receptive?"

He knew he could say no, and just leave the room with

no further expressions of protest. But the words wouldn't pass his lips. And he also knew he could not leave Eleonora here alone anyway.

She indicated the couch and how he should bend over its sides and she positioned herself behind him.

Now, through the corner of his eyes, he could finally see Eleonora and the other man. She had also been stripped naked, and wore only the hold up black stockings. The pallor of her body was unbearable to watch. As was the shocking contrast between her skin and the dark-as-night material of the remaining stockings.

The other man's cock was thick and dark pink and was ploughing her roughly and systematically, pulling out of her almost all the way with every stroke and then digging back into her up to the hilt with every return thrust. Machine-like, metronomic, like a deadly instrument of war.

He felt the pain explode through his own body as the woman's artificial member breached him with one swift movement. He swallowed hard, almost bit his tongue

As he did so, he realised why Eleonora was so silent. A red handkerchief had been stuffed into her mouth, as her face rhythmically banged against the wall with every repeated movement in and out of her. He couldn't help noticing the handkerchief was the exact same shade of red as the lipstick she had decided to adorn herself with to attend the party.

Also, her hands were tied behind her back with brown fur-lined metal cuffs.

She must obviously have agreed to the restraints.

There was another huge stab of unbearable pain as the strap on began stretching him and he felt himself being filled like he had never been filled before. For a brief moment, he feared he was going to defecate, as the pit of his stomach went totally numb then perilously loose, but the pressure against his inner walls soon reasserted itself and the pain slowly began to recede. Not that being fucked in this manner gave him any pleasure. He felt as if he was becoming detached from his own body as it was being so cleverly defiled by this woman whose name he didn't know.

And his eyes kept on hypnotically watching the abominable movements of the other man's massive member inside Eleonora, the way the tight skin around her opening creased inwards and then outwards again as she was being implacably drilled, and the eyelet of her anus winked open and shut with every movement below it. There was sweat dripping from her forehead. Her calves tightened, her arse cheeks shook, her hair was undone, her curls spilling in every conceivable direction as if moved by an invisible wind rising from the nearby lagoon and flying over the Giudecca to shroud the city on its way to the marshes and Trieste.

From the tremors now compulsively coursing through her body, Jack knew Eleonora had come. The stranger had succeeded in raising her senses, playing her like Jack had rarely been capable of doing.

But the man did not cease.

He would visibly continue fucking her until she begged for him to stop.

Would she ever?

Back at the apartment, they at first could not bear to look each other in the eyes. They went to bed in total silence, still coated by the dry sweat of their exertions, of their shame.

They slept late into the morning.

After breakfast, they took a *vaporetto* to the Lido and later to the Isola di San Servolo. A trip they had agreed to undertake a few days before they had stumbled across the website which had lured them to the party.

Over dinner in the San Polo district, they began communicating again.

"Talk about an experience!'

"I suppose you could call it that …"

"Regrets?"

"No."

"Sure?"

"Absolutely not."

"Were you jealous?"

"A little, I suppose."

"You?"

"No. It's … how can I put it … life …"

"Certainly one way of putting it …"

They tried to go for coffee at Caffé Florian, but it was closed on Tuesdays in winter. They made their way back to the apartment. There was no power. They tiptoed their way through darkness towards the bedroom.

"It doesn't change anything, does it?"

"I don't know," she replied, spooning against him.

It was at that precise moment Jack knew he was about to lose her. First Giulia, now Eleonora. His radar had enough practice.

That it was too late to plea, beg, affirm his love, however impure it now was.

He didn't sleep that night. He stayed awake in the darkness, listening to the vague sounds of the Canal delle Due Torri lapping against the building's rotting stone facade and the imperceptible melody of her breath, as her chest moved peacefully up and down against him under the duvet.

He smelled her, listened to her as if trying to fix these memories in his brain once and for all. All that he would one day be left with.

Jack finally succumbed to sleep around seven in the morning.

When he awoke, she had left the apartment.

The morning went by. He tried to read, but couldn't concentrate on the lines, whether a week-old newspaper or an anonymous serial killer thriller.

Eleonora returned at the beginning of the afternoon. She was wearing that black skirt he remembered buying her in Barcelona and which held so many memories. The one with the giant sunflower patch sewn into its flank. And a T-shirt he had once loaned her in the early days of the affair when their lovemaking had proven a tad rough and messy and he had left compromising semen stains across the blouse she had been wearing that day. The T-shirt that advertised *McCabe and Mrs. Miller* across the Aubrey Beardsley-like face of a woman.

He was sipping a glass of grapefruit juice at the kitchen table.

He welcomed her.

"Had a good walk?"

"No."

"Oh …"

A shadow passed across the room shielding her eyes from his examination.

"I saw him again," Eleonora said.

The pain inside returned.

"Have you fucked him again?"

"No."

"I see."

"There is another party tonight. A different palazzo this time, near the Campo San Silvestro. He's invited me.

Wants to introduce me to some of his friends …"

"Do you want to go?"

"Yes."

"Without me?"

"Yes."

"Why? I still like you, you know."

"I know. But liking is not enough. I need a life, you see. Alone. I don't want to be owned … Anyway, you still think of Giulia, don't you? Don't deny it: every time you touch me, when you close your eyes, you think I might be her …"

"I've never tried to own you, you know that. You're too much of a gypsy to be kept in a cage." He hadn't answered her question, as if he already knew she was right.

Eleonora smiled.

"You can come, if you wish, I reckon. As long as you promise not to interfere and allow whatever happens to happen …"

"I don't think so," Jack said. "Don't much care to repeat yesterday's foursome. Just didn't feel right to me somehow."

"I understand."

She walked to the bedroom they had been using; she was holding a large Mondadori canvas tote bag.

"What have you got there? Been shopping?" he asked.

She looked away.

"No …," she hesitated, then came clean. "Well, it's the outfit he wishes me to wear tonight."

"Can I …"

Eleonora interrupted him.

"I'd rather you didn't see it, Jack."

That evening, he left the apartment to wander the narrow streets and have several coffees in a row to allow her to dress in privacy.

By the time he returned, she had already left for Carnevale or had maybe been picked up.

She did not return that night or the following day.

His days and nights were haunted by obscene visions of her with other men, and the abominable images of alien cocks of all shapes, sizes and shades invading her. Her mouth, her cunt, her arse, her hands. Orgasmic flush invading the delicate pallor of her skin. The indelible marks of hands, ropes, whips and paddles across the familiar geography of her body. And the sound of her voice just saying 'Yes', 'Yes' and 'Yes' again, like Bloom's Molly. And the grateful acceptance of her smile, of her eyes. And then the terrible visions would repeat again and again, as if captive in some infernal porno film loop, and Eleonora's face would become Giulia's until Jack could no longer recognise who was who, and they were both determined to be unfaithful to him for ever, leave him until he burned in hell.

Finally, she reappeared halfway through Carnevale.

She looked radiant. More beautiful than ever.

"You haven't shaved," she remarked. "The stubble on your cheeks is so grey."

"Couldn't bother," he said. "So, you're back."

"Not really," Eleonora said. "I've just returned to pick up my stuff, my clothes and all that."

"I'm sorry," Jack said.

"It's the way things are," Eleonora remarked. "After Carnevale ends, Master has promised me that the adventure will continue. He wants to take me to Mardi-Gras in New Orleans and also the Carnival in Rio one day …"

"How exciting," he said bitterly in response.

"Don't be like that, please, Jack," she protested. "You

should be happy for me. Respect what I am doing, surely."

"I find that difficult, Eleonora. I would have given you everything. Surely you realise that."

"I know, but it would never have been enough. You know that. I'm young. I have a life to live. My life."

Her skin shone in the pale light coming through the window, the curls in her hair like the gift of Medusa.

Jack closed his eyes. Promising himself he would not open them until she had left with her belongings.

Jack never saw Eleonora again. He stayed in Venice until the end of Carnevale. At dinner one evening, he met another woman, a legal interpreter from Arizona. They had a few drinks together and he was pleased to see that he could still chat a woman up, be reasonably witty and seductive. But when he took her back to the apartment and undressed her after some willing fumbling and a cascade of mutual kisses, he wasn't capable of fucking her. Just couldn't get hard enough, despite her assiduous ministrations. Lack of inspiration or wrong person, he wasn't sure.

The next day as he sat at an overpriced café by the Rialto bridge, he caught a glimpse of a small water cab racing down the Grand Canal. A woman was standing at its prow. For a brief moment, he thought he recognised Eleonora. Same skirt and T-shirt, but the cab was moving too fast for him to be positive it was actually her. At any rate, she was alone on the small boat, standing erect behind the driver, facing the breeze. And for a brief moment, the wind shimmered, the image in his eyes blurred and he thought it maybe was Giulia, not Eleonora any longer. And then his vision blurred and she looked like yet another woman. Unknown, though.

*   *   *

Shortly after, his friends returned from India and he promptly made his way back to London.

He left the two masks they had worn on that fateful evening behind. Not quite the sort of apparel you could wear for the Notting Hill Carnival.

Jack would never go back to Venice.

THE SIMPLE ART OF RETRIBUTION

IVAN NEVER RETURNED PHONE calls. You had to ring three times at ten minute intervals and leave an identical message and a number where he could call you back. Never on a landline.

If he was otherwise detained and did not return the call within the hour, you had to repeat the process at the same time on the following day. Those were the rules.

Cornelia reached New York mid-afternoon and was home by four. It was the best time of day to fly in, when the traffic into the city was still sparse enough. First she showered and then, still dripping water, immediately rang Ivan on a spare cell phone she had acquired at the airport, for which she had picked up a spare SIM card from a small souvenir and touristy bric a brac store on Broadway South of Houston.

There was no answer, as she expected. She slipped on her dark blue silk kimono, stretched her long limbs, and adjusting a cushion at one end, lay down on the frayed leather sofa on which she liked to do most of her reading and thinking. She tried Ivan twice again, repeating the succinct message. And began her wait. Outside, the sun was setting over the park. She tried to concentrate on a new book she'd been waiting to read by some English crime writer she'd heard good things about. The opening pages grabbed her attention, but soon her tiredness got the better of her and she dozed off.

She awoke in the dead middle of night. Her kimono's thin, tenuous belt had come undone and the flimsy material had parted and the skin across her stomach and thighs was littered with goose bumps. Cornelia shivered and realised with disappointment that it would be at least a further day until matters could move on. Too much time to kill. She moved to the bedroom and slipped between the sheets, shedding the kimono in her stride. She always slept in the nude, no matter the weather.

It took another three days for Ivan to call back. Maybe he had been out of town.

"Cornelia?"

"Yes."

"I didn't realise you were back."

"I am. Reporting back like a good little soldier."

"So, everything cleared up? I haven't heard back from my principals. Surprising. I'd assumed they would have told me the matter is at an end. In which case, I'm owed," Ivan said.

"Lucky you."

"Any problems?"

"Quite a few as a matter of fact."

"Oh."

"I think we should speak about it in the flesh. Meet."

"That's quite irregular."

"I know. But it's important, I assure you."

"Something the client should know?"

"Not until you and I have spoken," Cornelia said.

"This is most unusual, my dear Cornelia," he continued.

"But necessary," she added. "I insist on meeting."

Ivan reluctantly agreed. She would have to come to him.

It took Cornelia just over an hour from Grand Central Station on the New Haven local train to reach Westport, Connecticut. By then, the sky was already darkening, sombre clouds floating menacingly over the surrounding woods. Ivan had sent a driver to the station to pick her up in a grey four-wheel drive Jeep.

The metal gates to the property slowly peeled open from the centre as the chauffeur operated a remote electronic switch on the car's dashboard, drove in, and the gates behind them closed in their wake. The man at the wheel, a short black guy in a green woollen cardigan and heavy brown cord trousers had not spoken a word during the short fifteen-minute journey across the bridge and then through the forest roads and a labyrinth of left-hand turnings which Cornelia memorised carefully. Nor had he even glanced at her in his rear view mirror. She was wearing black from head to toe, a thin cashmere sweater which felt soft against her skin, tailored Armani slacks and flat ballerina slippers.

The car pulled up along the side of a large, architect-designed single-storey country house. The driver parked on the gravel path, at a right angle to a closed garage door.

Just as the chauffeur was about to pull the car keys from the ignition, Cornelia swiftly pulled out the small Beretta she had brought along in her slim handbag and pressed it in a single movement against the back of the man's head. She'd screwed on a silencer before leaving Manhattan. The detonation barely echoed within the car's interior, a hushed, repressed sound that no one inside the main building could possibly have heard.

The man slumped against the wheel just as the engine died.

Cornelia checked his pulse.

He was dead. A single bullet was generally sufficient.

She experienced a clear sense of relief. She had not used the weapon for ages. Always avoided having to utilise her own gun. Normally, each new job was supplied with its own, which was either disposed of following the hit or returned, depending on the arrangements concluded beforehand.

She hoisted herself off the back seat, gave the dark house a rapid glance. There was no movement at any of the visible windows on this particular side of the building. She opened the door and stepped out.

There was a soft breeze billowing between the building and the nearby stream that lay at bottom of the house's small lawn.

She could feel the uneven gravel under her feet through the thin leather sole of her flat ballet shoes. On this particular surface, it felt almost like walking barefoot.

She reached the front door. It wasn't locked. Cornelia walked in.

The corridor beyond was lined with bookshelves. Cornelia couldn't help herself giving the spines a rapid glance. But she couldn't afford to be distracted. Maybe afterwards she would have some time to give the books a closer look, although at first glance they were mostly art books, not the sort of titles she collected.

The entrance passage led to a large open-planned space with a high latticed wooden ceiling, bordered on one side by wide bay windows which overlooked the garden and the stream, and on the other by a massive stone fireplace. A couple of deep and lush leather sofas were scattered at a right angle around a low glass table. Someone was sitting in one of them, with the back of his head to her, smoking, a newspaper – the *Wall Street Journal* – spread in front of him, held up between his two hands.

Cornelia coughed.

The man turned round. Looked at her. Set the newspaper down next to him on the sofa.

"Cornelia, I presume?"

"Indeed," she said.

He kept on gazing at her.

"Mmmm … Even prettier than I was unreliably told."

"Ivan?"

"Yes. And you are my sweet angel of death? So we finally meet …"

Cornelia smiled. In the flesh there was nothing particularly impressive about the man. The master of ceremonies she had been put in touch with nearly five years ago, the man who had assigned the jobs to her, paid her fast, no questions asked, made the arrangements, set the targets.

He was in his mid-fifties, a tad overweight, thin grey hair just that little bit too long for social conformity, wore horn-rimmed glasses and, she noticed, had terribly thin lips. He was dressed in nondescript dull pastel colours.

"You're on your own?" she asked.

"Of course," he replied. "I assumed that what you wanted to discuss was of a private nature. It's only me. No stray ears."

"Good."

"And, as you know, I've asked the driver to remain outside, in the car."

"Perfect," Cornelia said.

"Anyways, I am being a bad host; can I offer you a drink?"

"A coffee would be nice," she said.

He rose from the couch and walked over to the kitchen section, separated from the main space by a thin wooden partition.

"The Paris job?"

"Yes," Ivan queried.

"What was it about?" Cornelia asked him.

"You know I can't reveal who my customers are, Cornelia. That would be quite unbecoming and disloyal and you should know better. I think we've had this conversation before, no? Why are you asking?"

"Because …"

"You did clean up, on your second trip? The witness – was it a young woman with dark curling hair, I was told? – has been eliminated, has she?"

"No, she hasn't, Ivan. First of all, she was a totally innocent bystander who just happened to have come across a bad man and, in all likelihood, knew nothing about his other activities. Furthermore, I just couldn't find her. She's just faded away into thin air, presumably returned to her own, quite ordinary life."

"But she saw you, didn't she? There's a link. The trail could lead back here."

"Yes, she saw me kill him. But I know she will do nothing about it."

"That's just not the way it works, Cornelia. You're making me angry. So what the hell have you been doing all this time?"

"Uncovering a whole hornet's nest."

"You should leave it undisturbed, you know that."

"It's too late."

"And what does that mean exactly?"

"It means that we are both in agreement that the whole affair must come to an end. We both want it dead and buried."

"So?"

"So, Ivan, you will identify the client for me, and I will take over from there," Cornelia suggested.

"That is quite ridiculous. I can't. How many times must I remind you of that? Our sort of business has its rules of conduct and they cannot be modified just because an innocent bystander was in the wrong place at the wrong time. Anyway, even if you were to make contact with the primary client, what would you do then: plead on your knees and with your eyes wide open for the girl to be spared?"

"No," Cornelia said enigmatically.

Ivan shrugged his shoulders in exasperation. "Oh Cornelia, what's happened to you? You were one of the best. I don't understand what's come over you." He took a final sip of coffee from his cup, weighing his thoughts. Cornelia remained silent.

"Tell me, Cornelia dear, in the hypothetical case where you were to discover the client's name and location, what were you proposing to do, to say to make him change his mind?" Ivan asked again.

Face impassive, Cornelia said "Kill him."

"You must be joking," Ivan said.

"That would certainly put an end to the whole matter. Clean up the mess once and for all," she added.

Ivan frowned. This was getting beyond a joke. "You're not serious, are you?" he asked her.

"Deadly serious, if you will excuse the inappropriate vocabulary."

Ivan looked at her. There was the hint of a smile on her lips and her eyes appeared ice-cold. And it dawned on him how efficient and utterly ruthless she had been in the past on the many occasions she had been assigned a hit. His frown grew deeper.

The woman was dangerous. And, right now, unbalanced.

He slowly began to rise from his seat.

Cornelia gave him a darting glance.

"I think I need another coffee," Ivan explained.

"I don't think you do, Ivan." He looked down and saw the gun she was holding in her right hand, pointing straight at his stomach. It had appeared out of nowhere. He frantically looked at the large bay window.

"Your driver won't be coming to help," Cornelia said. "No cavalry to the rescue."

"Bitch," Ivan muttered under his breath.

"No need for profanity, Ivan. It's just business, isn't it?" Cornelia pointed out, getting to her feet, the Beretta still aimed steadily at Ivan's midriff.

He was about to swear again, but thought the better of it.

"What now?" he asked.

"You tell me who ordered the Paris hit and where I can find him or her."

"And if I don't?"

"You know the cliché: we can do it the easy way or the painful way. It's up to you. Your call."

Cornelia now stood facing him. He could even smell her perfume and the heat her body was generating. She towered above him, his black-clad angel of death, her blonde hair spreading like a halo against the recessed lighting in the room's ceiling. Even with the rivulets of fear now rushing through his system, Ivan could not avoid finding her beautiful. And strangely serene.

"You wouldn't …" he protested.

But deep inside, he knew she would.

"Get up," she ordered him.

He meekly obeyed. There were no alternatives, he realised, his thoughts scrambling in every possible direction.

She was a full head taller than him. The line of the gun did not deviate a single inch.

"Undress," she enjoined him.

He expressed puzzlement, but Cornelia's gaze stood firm and he began to strip.

Once he was down to his smalls, she insisted he continue until he was fully naked. He became painfully aware of how out of shape his body was, the love handles he had always meant to exercise away, the round overhang of his stomach, the pasty texture of his thick thighs. Cornelia insisted he get rid of his socks too.

"There is nothing more ridiculous than a naked man wearing socks," she remarked. "That's what was always wrong with so much sixties porn," she even chuckled.

His cock had shrivelled – cold or fear? – and partly retreated into his ball sack.

Cornelia looked him up and down, quite unjudgmental in her gaze.

She raised the gun and Ivan's throat tightened. But all she was doing was pointing it in the direction of the bathroom.

Cornelia marched him there, the muzzle of the Beretta forced into the small of his naked back, metal hard, his bare feet brushing the stone floor as he wearily lifted himself up the two small steps that separated the living space from the corridor.

"You don't know what you're doing," Ivan protested.

"I do. Absolutely."

It took Cornelia just over one hour to break Ivan's resistance down. She had hoped it might take less time and not prove as messy.

The Beretta wasn't enough of a threat. Its use was too final, and her handler knew that.

His hands tied high above his head to the shower rail, Ivan stood inside the bathtub in a distorted parody of crucifixion. Cornelia had kicked his legs apart and his genitals hung limply between his legs. She had switched the shower on and the increasingly hot water poured down across his stretched shoulders. Ivan grimaced and squirmed. Cornelia ignored him and explored his medicine cabinet. There was a small container of old razor blades, some rusting across the edges. She took hold of a couple and taped them with surgical tape to the end of a toothbrush. Improvised but a worthy instrument of persuasion, Cornelia knew. She turned back towards the bath tub and the immobilised man and sat herself on the edge and faced Ivan. Switched the water off. His pasty body was all now blotchy in all shades of pink. When Ivan saw what she was now holding in her hand, he shuddered briefly.

"All I want is a name and an address, Ivan."

Ivan remained mute.

"Just a name and an address. No need for explanations or anything else. It's irrelevant. I already know what these people are all about. It doesn't please me, naturally, but all I am concerned about is eliminating any evidence of this unfortunate job you gave me. I want to draw a line under it. Get back to my life. It's nothing personal. If I don't do it, you know it well, Ivan, I will have to keep on peering behind my back for ever, not knowing if anyone is a threat or not. I want to live in peace. It's simple."

Ivan closed his eyes, refusing to communicate. Braced for the worst.

The first cuts were to his cheeks, deep but short and

Cornelia then drenched the wounds with a generous splash of his own cologne. She knew it would sting badly. That was the intention.

Ivan swore. She looked him straight in the eyes.

"No," he whispered. "I just can't."

"I'm sorry you feel that way."

The next cut was savage and sudden and scythed into the already taut stretch of skin in his left arm pit and would have severed his arm from the shoulder had sinews and bone not proven an obstacle to the blade. Ivan screamed and blood began pouring down his flanks to the bathtub floor where it pooled quickly around his bare feet.

Cornelia worked slowly but systematically down the man's body, selecting targets at random, trying to imagine where the pain would be at its most acute but not fatal. When she sliced into one his nipples, his bladder inadvertently loosened.

A dozen cuts later, Ivan finally relented as the razor blades began a series of small and delicate incisions into his balls and thighs. The tears streaming down his cheeks now rivalled the myriad small rivers of blood pearling down the upper half of his body. His breath was short, his voice croaking.

He gave her a single name. It meant nothing to Cornelia, but she hadn't expected it to achieve any recognition.

She waved the gerrymandered toothbrush in front of his eyes and with her other hand took hold of his cock and squeezed it hard. She felt it pulse in her grip, almost as if he was going to have an erection.

"And?"

He supplied her with an address outside Los Angeles and a California telephone number.

Cornelia lowered her arm. Set the improvised weapon down over the nearby sink and walked across to the main living quarters where she had previously left her handbag.

Returning to the bathroom, she became aware of the strong combined smell of blood, urine and fear that now permeated the enclosed space. It reminded her of previous scenes of carnage she had been involved in. She was also aware that what she was doing now would automatically signify an end to that part of her life. But Cornelia had never been sentimental. She would adapt. There were other ways to make a living. It's not as if she had ever experienced any form of vicarious thrill executing contracts on total strangers. It had just been a means to an end. Initially, just an extra job to raise enough money for a rare book she had coveted.

Ivan's head had partly fallen across the top of his chest as he was suspended like a sorry, dangling puppet from the metal shower rail. He didn't look up when Cornelia entered the bathroom again. He was broken and had lost all capacity for added curiosity.

"I'm sorry," Cornelia said and raised the gun to his forehead and killed him. The familiar fragrance of cordite rose, soon blending with the other smells in the exiguous quarters.

On her way out, Cornelia carefully wiped every surface she remembered touching while in Ivan's house. Pushing the dead chauffeur's body across onto the front passenger seat, she drove the car to New Haven station and abandoned it in a side street two blocks away from the station car park. The station was deserted and she spotted no surveillance cameras. She already had a return ticket and there were only two other people at the other end of the platform waiting for the day's final train.

She reached Grand Central just past midnight and took a cab directly to the gentlemen's club near Wall Street where she volunteered for a shift. She had half an hour to kill before the time to go onstage came around and, much as she hated the facilities at the club, took a long shower. She had to wash the smell of death off her skin, and out of her mind.

As she waited for her dance music to begin, Cornelia looked out from the wings of the small stage into the audience, and breathed a sigh of relief, noting that her hedge fund guy was not in tonight. She didn't think she was ready for more questions or sympathy tonight. Just the usual Friday night crowd in search of tits and ass. Well, if they wanted to see pussy, that's what she was here for, she reckoned. Not that she ever referred to her sex as pussy. It was just cunt, no more, no less. No need for euphemisms or poetry.

G IS FOR GYPSY

JACK HAD RETURNED FROM Venice and slowly attempted to put his life together again. Wrote more stories and idle journalism, but his heart was not in it any longer. However, he had no other alternatives. A writer just writes. He doesn't investigate missing person cases, after all. That just made a mockery of everything, didn't it?

He got an assignment to another festival abroad. Not by coincidence, the place he and Giulia had first come together. Of course. Those fickle ways of fate …

Jack had always been a man who travelled a lot.

Which meant he used hotel rooms on almost all occasions.

If asked what his strongest memories were of foreign cities, he'd always remember the hotel, the room. Not the monuments or the museums or the architectural and cultural wonders of the place. But then he wasn't much of a tourist.

Every time he walked into a new room, shortly after arrival in a new town, Jack would sigh. He knew this particular home away from home for the next few days would prove both exhilarating in its potential for sex or eroticism, or just damn lonely if, yet again, he was to inhabit it alone for the duration.

Sex and loneliness. Two feelings that invariably went hand in hand these days.

"Here are the keys," the uniformed young woman at reception said, handing Jack back his passport and a small folded paper wallet with keys and breakfast time information. "We've given you room 411."

It would be room 411. Out of all the hotel rooms in the world, what were the odds on being given room 411 again?

"Just my luck," Jack thought, as his heart dropped or stomach sunk or whatever could best describe his body's reaction to the news. A feeling of sudden vertigo, of drowning in a sea with no water.

"Is the hotel full?"

Maybe he could ask to be moved into another room?

"Yes sir," the receptionist looked up. "It always is at festival time."

"OK."

The elevator.

The long, endless corridor, which had always reminded him of *Barton Fink*, the movie, albeit in more opulent ways. Or The Overlook in Kubrick's film of *The Shining*.

The door.

The key in the lock.

The light.

The room.

The bed …

Jack dropped his luggage to the carpeted floor. Opened the window slightly to let some air in and lowered the heat level on the thermostat.

He sat himself on the corner of the bed. Closed his eyes. Opened them again. It made no difference. He could still see the long silhouette of her pale body spread across the double bed, her legs apart, her slight breasts barely hillocks amongst the blinding, white landscape of her torso as she lay on her back and earth's gravity pummelled them down to almost non-existence, the soft brown pinkness of her nipples like two minuscule beacons in the sea of flesh. The billion ebony dark curls in her hair washing over the sheets. The way the sun on a summer day past had caressed her dormant skin as its rays whispered their way through the open windows and caressed her nakedness.

It was as if she were still here.

Or maybe it was the ghost of her, following him along from country to country, from hotel room to hotel room, like a Flying Dutchman's curse as he sought to escape her memory. But he knew inside he never would. You don't forget the unforgettable.

His brain cells, out of control, now began to focus on all the sharper details of her anatomy, the angles, the curves, the indelible memories of her softness, the smell of her breath, the colour of her teeth, the longing and the thousand questions ever present in her eyes and it was like yet another stab wound piercing both his heart and his gut in one swift decisive movement.

Tears welled up inside him. He loosened his belt and pulled his trousers down to his waist and his fingers took hold of his half-hard cock and began caressing its velvety mushroom tip, arousing himself, allowing all those lost images of her to inspire him, to stimulate him. Had she not one day revealed that waiting for him to arrive from the airport in another hotel room in another southern city she had not been able to suppress her urgent need for him and had eagerly masturbated herself to a thunderous climax even though she knew they would be reunited just a couple of hours later following his own flight's arrival?

But today Jack could not achieve sufficient hardness,

and soon gave up.

It was as if the hotel room itself was alive and was whispering to him on the sly that he would never know her again in the physical sense of the term and there was no point jerking himself away to her memory, to her spirit, but then, the room suggested in his ear that there were other options, weren't there?

Pulling his black trousers back up to his waist and tightening the belt, he moved over to the travelling bag in which he kept his laptop, pulled the computer out of its protective sheath.

He opened the lid and booted up.

Scoured the familiar chat rooms in search of sex.

There were some possibilities but after a few lines of dialogue with various other seekers of nsa activities, he realised there would be too much work, explanations and lies involved to convince any one to actually meet quickly enough, let alone do the deed. Unless he moved on to the gay or bi rooms, which on this occasion he was not yet in the mood for. Or desperate enough.

Jack checked his mail. Mostly spam and the customary offers of cheap Viagra, Levitra or no money back penis- and breast-enhancing products.

He undressed.

Looked at himself in the bathroom mirror. Wished he looked better, slimmer, younger, less morose.

Back in the room, he balanced the laptop on his knees and began writing Giulia a letter. Maybe now she was back in Rome she would finally respond.

Dear G.

I miss you. Terribly.

I know I have no doubt written this many times before, but you have left a hole inside of me. A deep, hollow cavern full to the brim with love and longing and despair.

You no longer even answer my messages and ignore me as if I were dead, but I don't mind. Writing to you in this way – which you probably find either despicable or pitiful – keeps you alive in strange ways. I can't let go of you, I just can't. Sorry.

I miss you. I hope you are happy, even if it is others who are now pleasing you, touching you, making your heart flutter somewhere, far away from here and me, which I foolishly, mistakenly still believe is where you should really be.

I'm in X. It's festival time again. You won't believe this, but I am in the very same hotel room. Room 411. Remember? I didn't ask for it. Maybe the hotel staff had a record of me being in the room before or it was sheer coincidence or again the bookings computer proving mischievous.

Being here evokes such strange feelings, Giulia.

Little since you has ever been the same. I am now nothing without you, but in the same time you have made me a better man. A man who knows what love is, can potentially be. No woman had ever given herself to me so freely, without reservations, so wildly, and made me realise the terrible strength of love unleashed as you did.

From that first, sometimes hesitant evening in room 411. Unveiling the beauty of your body, inch by inch, touching the paradise of your small breasts with my rough, undeserving touch, silent in awe at the perfect delicacy of the combined shades of pink of your nipples (which I had somehow expected to be much darker), slipping my fingers inside you, experiencing the divine heat of your cunt, spreading your wetness across my hand and learning the musky, hypnotic smell of you, fingertips travelling slowly through the mass of your pubic curls then moving into more dangerous territory towards your rear hole. And the worried "No, not there, please" of your voice. "Why?" "Just not there, please."

That first night we did not even fuck.

Once stripped, we caressed each other, hardy explorers of new-found lands, we cuddled, we merged, we embraced rather frantically, skin against skin, lips against lips, sweat against sweat. You rode me repeatedly, like a young stallion. Dry-humping me like no one had ever done before. Rubbing your cunt and protruding bone against my hard cock, until I was even hurting but would never ask you to stop. I thought you would even tear my cock's outer skin off in the savage assault of your passion, while all the time I tried not to come, as if ejaculating on you would have been a crime, a sad admission of my innate vulgarity.

We writhed that way all night, between torrents of words, endless stories of our respective pasts and inevitable questions about what might lie in our future. From the very first mail, months before, we knew this could only be an impossible love. But then it was also more than just animal attraction. We were so wrong for each other: ages, geography, past, activities, personalities. But, on the other hand, we were also so supremely right, weren't we? Remember how when apart we were almost telepathically in touch, always knowing when the other was about to call or do something particular. E-mails criss-crossed the web with mighty abandon; SMS messages littered the airwaves.

But mostly we were creatures who lived in hotel rooms, as we could not be seen publicly by others, irrespective of the foreign cities we travelled to.

I told you stories about the women who came before, the other hotel rooms I had lived in, seen. How, when once staying at the Algonquin in New York one night I had been kept up until the small hours of morning by acute sounds of pleasure from a woman in the room on the other side of the thin wall, who kept on achieving incredulous orgasms one after another for hours on end. Never had I heard a woman so vocal in the throes of sex, moans, loud sighs, cries, shouts, rumblings, she went through the whole gamut of possible sounds, time after time. The bed in the opposing Algonquin room would bang repeatedly with every new thrust of her lover inside her against our common wall, and the anonymous woman would shriek, purr, scream; it was primeval, basic, awesome. And arousing: I must have come myself at least three times during the night, manually, provoked by the hurricane-like waves of pure sex streaming through from the other room. It was unavoidable. All I had to do was close my eyes, imagine the reverse image of the room I was staying in, and myself fucking her in every conceivable position of the Kama Sutra, with every new variation evincing a new kind of explosion from deep inside her throat. To say she was both loud and enjoying herself was something of an understatement. I even imagined that no man was capable of extracting such sounds of pleasure from a woman alone and that it must have been a sheer procession of men entering the room and taking turns with her as she lay there with her legs splayed open and her apertures moist and slick and ripe for plundering at every turn.

Towards four in the morning, I finally managed to get some sleep.

The next day, I had to leave the hotel shortly after breakfast to go to a business meeting downtown and just as I exited my Algonquin room, the door to the next room opened and a woman walked out. I had imagined the creature being so royally fucked in countless, alluring incarnations: sleek, blonde, redhead, brunette, tall, dusky, pale, opulent and skinny, beautiful and mysterious, but none of the visions I had evoked throughout the night corresponded with the reality!

She was a tiny little Chinese woman in her mid-fifties, with a wrinkled face and a shapeless body over which she had draped a faded brown fur coat which had known better days. She looked up at me and her face betrayed no feelings of recognition or any embarrassment at having likely been overheard in the demented throes of her sexual exertions by a neighbour.

We both walked towards the elevator in silence and went our own ways for ever.

I wonder, Giulia, whether others ever heard us and tried to imagine what we looked like, or with less obvious difficulty, what we were up to?

Not that we would have cared. Would we?

After we had technically become lovers at last, your own appetite and curiosity for the pleasures of the flesh no longer knew any bounds, surprising even me, as you wanted this whole new world and wanted it now. Within a day we were taking baths together with no shame. By the end of the first hotel room episode, that taboo word 'love' was already leaking freely from our hearts.

We quickly became experts at living in a world of our own, a world within the existing world of rules and conventions, rules which we openly flouted, oblivious to the eyes of others.

Like the half-assed leers of the men at the front desk of the hotel in Barcelona as they saw us pick up our key and walk arm in arm towards the elevator, noticing the disparity in our ages and looks and guessing all too well the boundless fornication we were about to embark upon.

In that room, in the shadow of Gaudi's Parc Güell, where we fucked mercilessly, leaving blood all over the sheets, as your period caught us in ambush, but never slowed our frantic ardour.

The breakfast room at the Washington Square Hotel in New York, where the Filipino waiter imprudently (or was it unprofessionally) remarked how much my daughter looked happy. The only time I saw you blush.

A bathroom in a hotel in Sitges where my sense of transgression knew no bounds and I burst on you sitting peeing and harvested your hot stream in the cup of my hands, a sensation of heat that has marked me for ever and which I have craved after ever since, not just on my hands but all over my body in my desperation to capture the sheer essence of you.

Was it Paris, New York, Calcata, Washington D.C. or somewhere else where I hastily withdrew my cock from inside you and came too early, my white seed pearls like beautiful stains across the thick jungle surrounding your cunt lips? A mishap that provided us with an unholy scare as you feared a most inopportune pregnancy and all future fucks had to be lessened with a condom from then on.

"Oh, how you fill me," you would say.

"Oh, how I want you," I would say.

Oh, how my heart would break into a thousand shards every time I took you from behind and the incomparable sight of my dark cock stretching your pink lips and burying itself deep inside you while the eyelet of your arse would almost wink at me, as if inviting further depredations. And the obscene thought that one day other men would see you thus, would contemplate the tragic pornography of your indecency, was enough to make me cry.

But I did not have the right to ask you to be mine and mine alone. I was scared to do so. Not because it would have been wrong; it would have been. But because I was in fear of your answer. Knowing your awful pride and will for independence. Later I realised that there were actually days and nights when you would have wanted me to do so and offer a more permanent form of commitment. Becoming genuine girlfriend and boyfriend, whatever that meant or entailed. Move to the city where you lived so we could see more of each other or you might be able to call me at any time of day to meet up, however innocently, for a coffee and a chat.

Why is it that love grows at different speeds between people who care for each other, need each other badly? Not fair, is it?

Many hotel rooms later, you finally left me. You wanted to live your life. You wanted other adventures. From the very first night, you had told me you were a gypsy and that you would not allow any man to ever catch you, imprison you. Let alone me.

An urban gypsy flitting through the lives of men, destroying hearts and souls with cheery insouciance, a falling star amongst us mortals. Oh, how you burned me.

Where are you now, embarked on what beautiful adventures with witty and sexy strangers, witnessing horizons I know nothing of? The last time we spoke, you would no longer even tell me of your plans because you guessed right: whatever news you provided me with would be betrayed by me one day, used in a story somewhere as some exotic fictional character which only you and I would recognise. You did not want to be a character in a book, Giulia. Forgive me. But then all I wanted you to be was a lasting character in my life. Fiction is only second best, you know, a consolation for the unworthy.

I still want you badly.

The warmth of your mouth around my pulsing cock.

Your fingers weighing my swollen balls, learning how a man is constructed at his most intimate.

The generosity of your eyes.

The foolishness of your wonderful youth.

The ghostly pallor of your body in a hotel room where we have just made love. The flowers in your hair when you accompany me to an official function and are proud to say "This is my man".

So, here I sit in room 411 of the Palace Hotel. I am naked. I am pitiful. I am lonely. Hotel rooms remind me of sex, of you.

Oh, just to hear the sound of your voice.

You belong here.

I send you this forlorn kiss.

Jack

Jack pressed "Send" and the e-mail made its way to wherever she would pick it up, if she ever did. He expected no answer, of course. That would be asking for too much. Things were clear cut by now and he would never see her again. Maybe occasionally hear about her through third parties (although not Eleonora he guessed), but then even that was unlikely. Different countries, languages, ambitions.

He exhaled.

Washed his face with cold water and slipped on the white terry cloth bathrobe and returned to the computer.

The emptiness weighed on him. Once again, he clicked his way into a chat room.

A sharp sense of unworthiness settled on his mind.

As if Jack finally realised that he had done Giulia wrong.

Guilt was a dangerous thing.

It called for punishment.

Oh yes.

There was a discreet knock on the door. Jack walked across, still wearing the white bathrobe. Outside the hotel room windows, night was falling and the sound of distant sirens – police? – ambulance? – firemen? – echoed through the town as it pursued its descent into darkness. He opened the door.

The stranger looked even larger than the photo he had posted online and forwarded to him during the course of their conversation and ensuing brief negotiation.

A swarthy guy, gym-sharpened and feral.

"You 'slave of G'?" the man asked brusquely.

"Yes," Jack lowered his eyes submissively. It was the unimaginative handle he had earlier used online.

"Good," the man said, taking a decisive two steps into the room. He looked Jack up and down, maybe checking that the few details he had been willing to reveal during their halting chat room conversation and then over the telephone were correct. He appeared satisfied and slammed the door shut behind him.

A point of no return had been crossed.

"So, this what you want? You're sure? No going back now?" the visitor asked.

"Yes," Jack meekly answered. Fear was now turning to resignation.

"Yes, sir,boy," the man ordered sharply.

"Yes, sir," Jack said in a low voice.

"That's better."

The taller man approached Jack and forced him to take

a few steps back into the room, until he was standing by the bed. The visitor lowered his hands and took the bathrobe belt and undid it, then quickly pulled the garment off Jack.

Jack stood naked.

Again, the visitor looked him up and down. And smirked.

Jack had already obeyed the initial instructions he had been provided with once the assignment had been arranged. He was fully bare, having shaven all the hair around his cock and balls while the stranger was en route to the hotel. Jack shivered briefly.

"Nice cunt, looks clean enough," the man remarked, examining him.

"Thank you, sir," Jack answered obediently. The act of shaving down there made him feel even more naked, available, ripe for all sorts of humiliation.

"On your knees, slave,"

Jack duly obeyed.

The man untied his trousers and exposed himself, presenting a thick, half-hard already cock to the kneeling, naked host.

"Open your face hole wide," the visitor said.

Jack took the semi-tumescent cock inside his mouth, where it hardened like rock within a few seconds, thrusting hard against the back of his throat, as he tried not to choke. The man took a violent hold of his hair and conducted his movements with brutal, steady regularity.

The man's penis had an acrid taste and its texture was surprisingly spongy, which Jack had not expected. As he mechanically continued sucking the stranger's member, the room surrounding him seemed to murmur to him "See, now you know what it felt for her, and all those other women, to take your cock into their mouths … now you know what it must feel like to be a woman, to be on the receiving end …"

There was another gentle knock on the door.

The visitor pulled his cock out of his drying mouth.

"Who is it?" he asked.

Catching his breath, Jack said "Another guy I spoke to in the chat room. I wasn't sure whether either of you would actually show up. You know how it is with chat room meets. I reckoned if I made two appointments, there was a better chance one of you at least would show up. We don't have to open the door, if you don't want to."

The other man smiled, cock still at full mast.

"Why not? The more the merrier. Let him in."

He rose from the floor and went over to the door and opened.

The new visitor was a wiry Oriental guy. His gaze greedily focused on Jack's exposed, bare cock. The earlier stranger walked over and explained the situation, offering the Asian man the opportunity to withdraw, should he wish to do so.

The new visitor seemed to enjoy the possibilities afforded by the new situation and elected to stay.

"A greedy slave, indeed," one of the men remarked.

They both undressed.

The Oriental man lay on the edge of the bed offering his uncut but already unsheathed erect cock and the larger of his two visitors took hold of their new found slave by the scruff of his neck and forced Jack down to his knees again.

"Suck him, worship his dick," he ordered.

The new cock was thinner, veiny and tasted differently. Jack diligently set to work, already mentally comparing the experiences.

As he did so, the first visitor to the room sharply took hold of his soft cock and balls and pulling both backwards and slightly upright by his genitals, forced Jack into the position he required. He spat across his raised, exposed rump and with two fingers lathered the abundant saliva into his anal opening, testing his elasticity and resistance.

"Nice and tight," he remarked. "That's how I enjoy my slaves." He suddenly slapped Jack's arse cheeks and then violently thrust himself inside him, breaching the moist ring of flesh in one single movement.

Jack couldn't help himself from screaming. It burned like hell as the foreign penis buried itself deep inside his innards. But he still managed to keep on sucking the cock now fucking his mouth.

"Good boy, good boy," the Asian man said.

Later, the two men changed places and used him thoroughly in all his available holes.

Jack's mouth was dry and the muscles in his cheeks hurt, come dripped from his well-stretched opening and inside it felt like the fires of hell still and as the men dressed in silence and he lay on the bed, exhausted, willingly degraded as he had wished, he briefly imagined the strangers keeping him in slavery together, abducting him from this luxury hotel room, putting a black, studded leather collar around his neck and transporting him still naked under a coat to another seedy hotel room which would smell of piss and shit and stale tobacco, where he would be offered to all-comers, fucked, whipped, beaten, peed on and hosed like an animal until death would prove a welcome release.

But they just walked out, closing the door to room 411 behind them in continued silence.

Maybe it was a form of penance, Jack imagined.

Or more likely just more self-pity.

"Oh Giulia," he wrote inside his head, "this is what I now am without you, a lost soul, a creature of sex of loneliness. A man who travels a lot and gets up to abominable things within the sacred secrecy of hotel rooms. Without you."

Just another letter he would never send.

And decided to go to Rome.

ROGUE FEMALE

CORNELIA WAS SITTING ON a high stall in an open all-hours bar called Phillies with her back to the nocturnal street. Across from her to the left, a man and a woman silently stared straight ahead at the white-capped, blonde barista busy cleaning dishes. The fedora-wearing man negligently nursed a cigarette while the woman, red-haired, in her late thirties she guessed, peered down at her well-manicured nails. There was no juke box or ambient muzak, no noise except for the occasional gurgle of the twin coffee percolators on the nearby counter; it was a perfect three in the morning form of silence, made for nighthawks and lonely hearts. The woman was thin, even gaunt, the silky fabric of her red dress draped across her shoulders, opening up across a V of indifferent, pale flesh. She sported cerise lipstick, just like one imagined vamps did in black-and-white forties noir movies. The couple hadn't spoken to each other since Cornelia had walked into the joint. But their body movement clearly betrayed the fact they were a couple. Only deep familiarity expressed itself, communicated with such a display of common silence.

Outside, it had been ages since even a car had driven by. They were enveloped in a sea of dead time, listening to the mute voice of the downtown Los Angeles night. Figueroa Boulevard was just a few city blocks away, even more of a desert at this forsaken time. There was no game tonight at the new Staples Center Stadium by the nearby convention buildings, so no stragglers ambling by or zigzagging their way past the flaming radiance of this old-fashioned street corner bar in search of a car parked forgetfully around the block some hours earlier.

Cornelia was sipping her second glass of mineral water. The ice had long melted and a lone wilted slice of lemon floated over the bottom of the thick square-shaped glass. She kept on watching the couple, idly imagining their back story, mentally embroidering a whole scenario to justify their presence here, explaining the way they had once met and the unknowable reasons that seemingly kept them together when they visibly had so little to say to each other any longer. Surely, they had somewhere to go back to? Cornelia hadn't. In a few more hours she would call a cab and get him to drive her back to LAX for the first morning flight of the day to La Guardia and her apartment on Washington Square Place full of books and CDs, where she would while the days away until the next telephone call, improbably in view of recent circumstances, summoned her for a job. No rush, she didn't need the cash. But practice made perfect, they said and she had never said no in the past when offered a hit. She had a reputation. She would always find new customers, somehow.

She quietly wondered whether the other insomniacs keeping her company in Phillies also speculated about her own presence there? She didn't think so. She was anonymous. No one remembered her face. She was wearing a dark, dull bobbed wig and librarian glasses and her two-piece standard issue female junior executive suit was a boring anthracite blue, her hair shielded by a shawl and her shape somewhat indistinguishable behind the suit's dull material. She wore flat shoes, to distract attention from her height. She guessed she looked like any other anonymous office worker. Good; it was a suitable appearance. Forgettable, indifferent. Safe. She should know by now. By hook or by crook she had learned the rules of the game, the occult conventions, the precautions, the limiting of risks since she had undertaken her first job. When had it been? Nearly five years back already. Once you'd swum with the sharks, it all became second nature, even if this particular job was not being done for monetary reasons. Just a final necessary evil to get these people off her back and close the chapter. It was a pity about Ivan. But there would surely be other handlers. She was too useful a commodity. She now knew what to do and what not to do. And Cornelia had never much been encumbered by rules and regulations, or least of all morality.

So, now she was just a woman in a bar whose true face others would never see or remember, watching the world go by. Your average, anonymous contract killer. Working on her own account for a rare occasion.

Killing off what is left of the night.

The woman at the bar in the red dress briefly glanced her way, but she visibly didn't note Cornelia's presence, her gaze passing straight through her and likely alighting on some passer-by walking outside, turning the corner on a slow journey towards Chinatown just a mile or so away to the east. The other woman's eyes were rimmed with too much kohl; didn't suit her, made her look older than she was, Cornelia reckoned. She looked away, her indifference returning. The woman's partner lit another cigarette while the attendant refilled his cup of coffee.

Cornelia attempted to recall the eyes of the other woman earlier this evening. The younger one. What colour were they? She just couldn't. Much of what had taken place did so in semi-darkness, an oppressive penumbra in which she had played the leading, murderous role. There had been a haunting quality in those eyes when she had pleaded for her life. She had just been in the wrong place at the wrong time. Yet another one. Damn!

"My name is Sarah," she had said, looking towards Cornelia with a sadness full of resignation, as if she already knew she could not be swayed. There were rules in this unholy game which must not be ignored. And even though Sarah was not a player, she had instinctively been aware of the fact.

Cornelia had not responded immediately.

"I will do anything you wish me to," the young girl had continued. "Or rather you can do anything to me you want. Anything."

Maybe it was the cold heart she saw in Cornelia's eyes that made her plead with such desperation. She had once been told by someone she trusted that they were sometimesgrey, steely and unfeeling. When she cleansed herself every morning with cold water and no soap and examined her features in the mirror, she saw no such thing. Eyes are just eyes. They convey nothing. Colours changed somehow.

The body of the man she had tracked down to this hotel room was sprawled just a few feet away on the carpeted floor, stone cold dead. One bullet had sufficed. It seldom took more; don't believe what you see in the movies. Killing a man with a gun was simplicity itself if you knew where to aim and had a steady hand and, of course, the advantage of surprise. Ivan had supplied her with his address on the West Coast when she had forced him to spill the beans and Cornelia had quietly observed him for several days to identify the patterns he followed, trailing him from his office as a realtor in Beverly Hills (no doubt a cover, but that wasn't her concern) to the Figueroa, a rococo hotel downtown with a fascinating over-the-top decor that blended equal doses of terracotta Mexican colours with Indian artefacts and monstrously sized potted plants throughout its dark lobby area. The guy had parked his Chevvy in a lot at the back of the hotel, which had given her time enough to move ahead and innocently share the elevator with him up to his floor. He hadn't even given her much of a look. She'd jumped him just as he was opening the door to his room. As the lock clicked Cornelia had put the gun to his head and sharply shoved against his shoulders and forced him into the room.

It had taken her barely a second or so to take it all in. The young woman sitting on the bed adjusting her stockings, looking up at her and the man barging through the door. The way the girl's mouth formed a puckered O of surprise. The man was just about to say something in protest when Cornelia had pressed the trigger, and the muffled sound of the weapon's silencer had interrupted the *nature morte* of the scene unfolding in overdrive. He slumped to his knees, and then almost in slow motion to the hotel room floor, his limbs spreading incongruously across the floor, his face three-quarters burying itself into the lush softness of the carpet.

The young girl's mouth returned to its normal thin-lipped shape and she froze on the spot, no doubt a million emotions, questions and fear spreading through her body.

The hit was clean. There wasn't even that much blood, yet.

Cornelia looked at her again.

Their eyes locked.

A torrent of communication surging through the darkened, pastel room in the utter stillness of the late afternoon. All things unsaid but sadly clear in both their minds.

Witnesses have no rights.

This was when she told Cornelia her name. In a forlorn bid to humanise herself. To make Cornelia reshape her resolve.

But there was no way she could commit the same mistake again. Giulia, Paris. Was this a circle of hell through which she was wading, every event cursed to repeat itself in infinitesimal variations?

Cornelia didn't respond, just stood there, her legs now straddling the inert body of her appointed victim.

"I can't offer you money. I haven't any," the girl continued. "But I promise I won't say anything. Please. To anyone …"

She certainly didn't look like a whore he had picked up somewhere. Not a cheap one at any rate. Maybe a girlfriend, or another man's wife he was enjoying on the side? Or another woman he intended to groom? That's what hotel rooms were for, weren't they? Perfect havens of anonymity where anything could happen. Sarah's white blouse and pleated linen skirt had a conservative cut, only spoiled by the fact that the skirt had been hoisted up to mid thigh as she had been straightening the line of her stockings as Cornelia and the man had forcibly entered the room. The upper, uncovered half of her thigh was creamy, white, almost virginal, above the darker, flesh coloured fabric of the hold up stocking. No garter belt, Cornelia couldn't help noticing.

"Will you let me go?" she asked quietly, as if she no longer even believed it could happen.

"I don't think so," Cornelia replied. "I just can't. Not

this time."

"Why?"

"Because."

Sarah lowered her eyes.

Cornelia felt unbearably sad. There was no enjoyment to be found in killing innocents. She was not a sadist. Didn't they call it 'collateral damage'?

"Now?" the young woman enquired, seemingly resigned to her fate, her voice low.

Cornelia walked up to the bed where Sarah was sitting.

Looked down at her.

"A waste, I know," as if apologising.

"Yes," Sarah agreed, her voice a thin sliver escaping from her mouth, touching the very root of Cornelia's heart, or was it her stomach? Sometimes, emotions affected her in curious physical ways.

All of a sudden, she wanted to ask the girl so many questions. Who she was, why she was here, the nature of her relationship with the dead man? She desperately wanted to know her. But she also knew it was impossible. She didn't have the time. Yet another unnecessary risk.

Her name was Sarah. That was all she could allow herself to find out.

"Get up," she ordered.

Sarah rose from the edge of the hotel bed, and stood, her gloved hands by her side. She was shorter than Cornelia had initially estimated.

The young woman looked towards her, waiting for further instructions, a veil of sadness drifting across her pale face.

"Had he paid you in advance?" Cornelia asked her.

Sarah blushed. Cornelia wasn't sure if this was caused

by embarrassment or anger. Or even pride.

It made her look quite beautiful, though. Her cheeks an attenuated shade of pink that served to emphasise the sharp delineation of her cheekbones.

"With him," Sarah answered, "it had nothing to do with money. Absolutely nothing."

"Love?" Cornelia continued.

"No. Nor lust either," she said. "You wouldn't understand."

No, Cornelia would never understand truly why certain women invariably agreed to surrender themselves to the wrong men.

When Cornelia ceased responding, Sarah brazenly straightened out her whole body, almost growing by an inch or so as her back snapped into position.

"You just wouldn't understand," Sarah defiantly continued. "Not in a month of Sundays."

No, Cornelia couldn't.

"Undress," she asked her.

Sarah obeyed unconditionally, and Cornelia knew it was no longer because of fear. Just submission. Like many women when they shed their clothing, she began by the bottom. She unzipped the invisible fastening on the right side of her skirt and the light fabric of the garment slid to the floor where she elegantly stepped out of it. She wasn't wearing any undergarments, revealing that her plump mound was shaven totally smooth, which Cornelia somehow hadn't expected, although she did the same to her own genital area, but then it was something the punters in the clubs preferred. Standing there motionless now, Sarah allowed Cornelia a minute of oppressive silence to collect her thoughts and drink in the vision of her obscene nudity, upright in her stockinged legs and nothing else.

Her sexual slit was a straight line gash from which no inner or outer labia protruded, like a raw wound, a scar that hypnotised Cornelia. Like an image in a mirror. She felt another twinge in her stomach. She couldn't help but stare at Sarah's cunt.

Then she quickly shed the rest of her clothes, the opaque white silk blouse and a small, and somewhat unnecessary brassiere, which then unveiled slight dark-nippled breasts even the smallest of men could cup in one hand, delicate hills in the porcelain landscape of her body.

Cornelia kept on peering at her.

Forgotten desires of school crushes on other girls flooded back. It had been ages since she had been with a woman.

Having taken in Sarah's prominent sexual characteristics, Cornelia quickly noted that the whole geography of the young woman's body was dotted with small bruises. These blemishes travelled across a whole spectrum of colours from dark, almost blue to brown and pale yellow as the skin had begun repairing itself.

These bruises had been created over a period of time; there was no way they could have happened on the same occasion.

"Turn round."

Sarah did so, with elfin grace.

The bruises also generously populated her back, prominently spread across her thighs, with even redder lines, like the forgotten remnants of whip lashes or continued caning, criss-crossing her slightly androgynous buttocks.

In the small of her back, there was the tattoo of a Chinese ideogram, which Cornelia was unable to recognise. She should have asked her, but she didn't.

She still had a million questions for Sarah, but none could travel the tortuous journey from her brain cells to her lips.

"Touch me," Sarah pleaded.

It was her turn to give orders. Topping from below?

Hesitantly, Cornelia moved an arm forward, brushed her fingers against one of the younger girl's shoulders. Her skin felt damp. But electric. She slowly moved upwards, sliding her fingers through the short ash blonde hair. Like a journey through silk.

She noted one of the more prominent bruises on Sarah's body, a soiled few square inches of skin between her navel and her cunt where the skin had almost broken and still waltzed between dark tones of black and a borderline crater of yellow. She tenderly touched her there. The softness was divine. She perversely pressed harder.

"Does it hurt?" Cornelia asked.

"No," she replied.

Her fingers lingered over the flatness of Sarah's lower stomach, bathing in the nearby heat emanating in concentric circles from her sexual opening outwards. The pink gash was short and as straight as a ruler, highlighted by her depilation. Cornelia had witnessed a variety of shaven cunts in the clubs where she had worked, but it was the first time she had been allowed to look at one so close, so long. Is that what I look like, she wondered?

"Not him," Sarah said. "Others."

"More than one?"

"Yes."

"I see," that was all Cornelia could prosaically say in the circumstance.

"I don't mind," Sarah said.

"Really?"

"You can, too, if you so wish." Sarah was inviting her to hurt her, defile her, mistaking the confused signals Cornelia was putting out.

"I'm not that sort of girl, you know."

"How do you know?" she responded, with the bare hint of a smile on her lips, as she glanced over at the dead body by the door.

"I just know," Cornelia answered.

"Anything you wish to do," Sarah suggested. "I'm available, I'm here, I'm yours for the taking, any way you wish. I won't scream."

As she said that, all Cornelia's imagination could conjure was the image of the young girl willingly being punched and whipped by other men, while she carefully kept silent and tears rolled down her cheeks.

How could she enjoy it, she wondered?

"You know I can't," Cornelia finally said. Then added "But you are indeed very beautiful. Really."

The nude girl sighed.

"Do it now, then."

But Cornelia knew she couldn't shoot her. Not like this. Not after seeing the wonder and questions of her nude body, feeling the tremor of life and softness coursing through her skin, the unknown history buried inside her soft southern voice.

If she shot her, it would be showing her total disrespect, assimilating her to that piece of shit now dripping dark blood over there by the door across the hotel room flooring. And whose bowels had undignifyingly now opened.

She deserved better.

Cornelia nodded to her, indicating the window that opened onto South Figueroa Boulevard. Sarah's eyes questioned her silently. Cornelia blinked once and she understood.

The flight of her naked body through the air was not unlike the dance of a butterfly in the summer breeze, weightless and beautiful, as she swam towards the ground in seemingly slow motion, fluttering her invisible wings, the bruises like a kaleidoscope of colours inked across her white skin, floating, smiling.

Cornelia looked away before she hit the ground.

She was now waiting for the long Californian night to end so she could catch the first flight back, wasting the remaining hours of darkness in an almost empty bar called Phillies. The couple across from here were still communicating in total silence.

Not long to go.

She had a bit of a cramp, a muscle giving her grief in her right shoulder, maybe caused by the recoil of the gun earlier. She must be getting older, no longer properly absorbing the reverse shock wave in her gun arm. She shifted imperceptibly in the high stall and across her shoulder she saw a man outside in the street sketching on a pad. For him, she guessed, we must be bathed in an eerie pool of light and an image worth remembering, just anonymous shapes in a composition of light and darkness. Not unlike an Edward Hopper painting. He was quite tall and balding, an imposing man with a Patrician allure.

As Cornelia turned around a bit more to look into his eyes, the sketch artist drew a final flourish on his pad and, satisfied, closed it and began to walk away, almost immediately melting into the night's surroundings.

Cornelia adjusted her position on the bar stool, took another sip from her now lukewarm glass of water.

When morning came, she left the all-night bar and

walked up the Boulevard in search of a cab, like a night ghost fading into day.

REMEMBER ME WITH KINDNESS

JACK'S BUDGET FLIGHT LANDED at Fiumicino. It was a hot, humid summer day.

Even though he held a CEE passport, the uniformed border officer at immigration control looked up and actually asked him whether he was visiting Rome for business or pleasure. As inquisitive as an American airport official.

"Sentimental reasons," he answered, and was then allowed through with no further comment.

Maybe the border guard had been bored or something, as he had never been asked any such question on the occasion of his previous, numerous visits.

He had only hand luggage so went straight through into the main terminal's arrivals hall and made a beeline for the car-hire desks. He had no need for anything fast or fancy in the way of transport, but he still had to convince the rental clerk that he actually did prefer a car with manual gearshift rather than an automatic. Habits die hard. After filling in the necessary forms and signing in all the dotted places, Jack was handed the keys to a dark blue Fiat and given the directions to the parking lot where it was kept.

He walked out into the midday sun and looked around. On his last time here, Giulia had been waiting, with her usual both wanton and joyfully innocent smile, wearing a white skirt and carrying a huge canvas bag embroidered with sunflowers, an accessory she'd bought six months earlier in Barcelona and which made her look like a schoolgirl rather than a full-grown woman. Three years ago already.

He settled into the driver's seat, keeping the door open for a few minutes to allow the heat to escape from the car's interior before the air-conditioning kicked in, while his feet got the measure of the pedals, getting himself accustomed again to driving a car on the opposite side of the road, and having the steering wheel on the left-hand side of the car. It always took a little acclimatisation, however many times he had to rent cars abroad.

And finally, he drove off towards the city. Considering it was the main road connecting Rome to one of its major airports, there was something old-fashioned and narrow about this road which made him think of all the legions of Caesar and past emperors and despots who'd in all likelihood marched down these avenues upon returning or departing for battle many centuries before. No modern highway this, more of a cobblestone alley in places, with twin ramparts of trees on either side and occasional low stone walls pouring with ivy, possibly erected long before even the Mussolini era.

It was as if the twenty-first century hadn't yet broken through here despite the gleaming modern cars racing up and down the road, all splendidly oblivious to any hint of a speed limit. Jack was in no real hurry and, irritated by his leisurely pace, some of the other drivers would hoot at him repeatedly.

He'd found a room on the Internet in a small residential hotel close to Piazza Vittorio Emmanuelle II. It was a quiet side street and easy to park, even though he wasn't sure if the parking space he had chosen was illegal or not. At any rate, he couldn't be bothered about parking tickets and was confident the Fiat wouldn't be towed away since it wasn't blocking anyone, and many other local vehicles were lined up on the same side of the street. The hotel was situated on the fourth floor of a massive apartment building and suited him fine: a clean, spacious if somewhat Spartan place, just a reception desk manned by a young student busy revising her exams, she informed him, and a small breakfast salon at the other end of the corridor. Jack didn't require anything more. There were bars all across the city, and anyway he wasn't much of a drinker. Never had been. More taste than principle, even if he found that some people gossiped behind his back back in London, and he was often suspected of being an ex-alcoholic. Print the legend, he thought; it's miles more glamorous than the truth.

He changed into a clean shirt and walked toward Via Cavour and Stazione Termini. Here, the parcel he had ordered was present, as promised by Timbers, who had set it all up back in London when Jack had phoned him with his unusual request, left in the luggage locker he had been posted a key for the week before. The transaction had not proven cheap, but then again, money was now the least of his worries. The gun had been left at the bottom of a plastic Rinascente bag in which the seller had buried it, with no sense of irony, under a crumpled mess of seemingly used women's silk lingerie. This was not the ideal place to check the weapon out, but it appeared in good shape, and should contain six bullets. He would not require more. He treated himself to an espresso at one of the station's countless cafeteria counters and watched with melancholy how the two spoons of sugar drifted slowly towards the bottom of the small cup. Just the way espresso coffee should behave, he recalled her teaching him when they were still together. He sketched a wry smile for any curious onlookers. The coffee and sugar boost gave him a new sense of purpose, renewed his determination to see this all through.

He walked away from the bar and the busy train station and took the direction of the Campo dei Fiori, past the inescapable ancient monuments surrounded by wide-eyed tourists. Shortly after crossing the Piazza Vidoni, the Roman streets became quieter again, as if foreigners no longer ventured this far, beyond their self-circumscribed tourist enclave and he made his way down Corso Vittorio Emmanuelle II until he reached the Feltrinelli bookshop. He walked upstairs and ordered his second espresso of the day and a panini and sat at the edge of the shop's balcony watching the customers mill below as they picked up random books and browsed at their leisure. She had once written to him, a long time ago before they had even slept together and were still enjoying a mildly flirtful stream of e-mail communications, that this was her favourite spot in all of Rome to waste time, meditate, observe others, casually do her homework. On his fateful initial visit here, this was also the first place she'd taken him and they had spent an hour here, nervously silent most of the time, knowing that a few hours later they would be in bed together for the first time. He remembered every single moment – the perfume she had worn, the heat radiating from her white skin as their knees brushed against each other and she contrived to make her cappuccino last forever as if scared to move on to the next, concrete and physical stage in their affair.

He didn't expect to find her here today. She was now

studying in a different area of the city, he'd found out,but still he had to come and visit the place again. Just in case. To commune with the past. To reopen old wounds. To feel the hurt inside. It was foolish, he knew, but if he had to march down this Calvary road of his own making, the Feltrinelli bookshop could not be avoided. The latest novel by Walter Veltroni and the Italian edition of the final Harry Potter book were piled high by the cash registers and staff kept on replenishing the displays on a steady basis. He'd sent her the English-language edition of the Rowling when it had appeared but by then they were no longer on speaking terms and she had not even thanked him or acknowledged the gift, one of many over the months they had known each other. The first book she had sent him as a gift was a collection of stories by Italo Calvino. Strange how he remembered every single, irrelevant detail.

Finally, his stomach reminded him he hadn't had a real meal since a dim sum in London's Chinatown the day before, so he left the bookshop and headed across the Corso Vittorio Emmanuelle II towards the Campo dei Fiori and the Pollarolla Restaurante where he had a pleasant memory of *fragole di bosco* with a fine dusting of sugar. Of course, he had also taken her there, once upon a time. Because of a stomach condition, she was not allowed to eat any spicy food, which Jack had always considered something of a tragedy. But the meal today, *insalata verde* and *risotto ai funghi,* could not feed the pain inside and later, as he walked back to his hotel, he made a detour by Stazione Termini and under cover of darkness surrounded by rushing commuters and loitering teenagers he slipped his left hand deep into the plastic bag he had now been carrying for half of the day and felt the hard grip of the gun down there. It felt real. By

Stazione Termini Jack sat down and wept.

He woke up early.

Escaping the inevitable dreams of her, of them. The sheer epiphany of her body, the ever so subtle and patently unique colour of her nipples, the broadness of her smile, the terrible harshness of her words on the phone the last time he had called her, the luscious sound of her sigh every time he had penetrated her. The places they'd been, the things they'd said.

He always woke up early these days, maybe as an automatic reaction to the sleeping memories of her and the abominable pain they invariably inflicted on his soul.

He adjusted his eyes, wiped the night away and moved his right leg.

Yes, he was back in Rome.

Alone.

He passed on breakfast, picked up a map of the city from an older woman now manning the hotel's reception desk and, avoiding the lift and its ornate metal grille, walked down the stairs to the street and found his rental car. He hadn't been ticketed, after all. Small mercies.

Jack pulled the gun from the depths of the Rinascente plastic bag and moved it to the glove compartment. Not an ideal place to keep it, but there were few possible hiding places in the hotel room. He would just have to drive carefully and not attract undue police attention. The busy Roman traffic would help.

Before driving off, he phoned Alessandra, Giorgio and Marina and made appointments to see them separately throughout the day. They were all surprised to find out he was in Rome, but sounded happy enough to meet him.

With the festival organisers he gossiped freely about books and movies and cultural politics. As they always did when they met at events. It was amazing how buoyant they remained every single year in the face of mounting difficulties in obtaining funding, grants and sponsorship. Of course, they asked him why he was in Rome. "Just passing through", he would answer, with a fake smile and this seemed to satisfy them. They embraced and made a vow to see each other again at the next festival and went their separate ways.

Alessandra knew a small *trattoria* in the Trastevere, concealed in a labyrinth of cobbled streets and small churches only a local could navigate with impunity and find a way out of again. Jack meekly followed her. Night was falling. Inside, he felt ever so empty. Following the break up with Giulia, he had almost once fallen into bed with Alessandra as both had been on the rebound from heart-shattering affairs. But it hadn't happened. They knew each other professionally, and she had also been aware of his relationship with Giulia, as they both freelanced for the same magazine. Maybe it was because neither Jack or Ale were sufficiently head over heels over the other, or maybe lacked the energy for purely recreational sex. Sometimes you want the tenderness and the feelings, and the physicality wasn't enough to conquer the inner thirst. At any rate, after a failed attempt at meeting up in Paris for a tryst, they'd both drifted apart, either to other adventures or, in Jack's case, his desert of loneliness. He expected nothing of tonight either. It was just a way of saying farewell to a friend. No less, no more.

The cuisine was Sicilian and for the first time ever he tried pasta with sardines, followed by great bowls of steamed shellfish, with a succulent sauce they both soaked up with freshly-baked local bread. The small piazza outside the restaurant was shrouded in darkness as he looked out of the windows of the restaurant, somehow expecting Giulia to walk by at any moment, like a revenant straight out of the past.

"Still thinking about her?" Alessandra asked. He had sometimes used her as a confidant .

"Yes," he answered. "It's a sickness. I know. Don't tell me."

"There's a character in Marquez's *Love in the Time of Cholera* who tries to cure himself of a case of unrequited love by later bedding 622 women," she remarked, as if proposing a cure.

"It would feel too much like revenge," Jack pointed out. "Anyway, it wasn't unrequited. I have pages and pages of e-mails, text messages and letters to prove it. And I know every square inch of her body at rest and play, every obscene crease and every single silky surface, intimately," he said.

"You always had a wonderful way with words …" Alessandra sighed.

"But now, words are insufficient," he answered. "Powerless. She no longer answers my messages, won't ever listen to me, answer the telephone. She probably thinks I've gone mad. And she's probably right."

"Did you come to Rome to try and see her?" Alessandra asked.

"No," Jack said. "Oh, I don't know any more. Maybe I just came for myself …"

He offered to drive her back to her apartment on the other side of the river.

The car moved along the Tiber on the Lungotevere heading north. Even at this time of night, the traffic was thick. Alessandra insisted on smoking a cigarette. He opened his window and looked out. Across the river was an old-fashioned building, white and functional under the light of a three-quarter moon: the San Filippo Neri Hospital. A knot twisted inside his stomach – wasn't this where she had been born or where her father, the surgeon, worked? Or both?

Alessandra invited him up for a final coffee, but he declined.

"I have to get up early in the morning," he said. It would have been pointless.

Back on his hotel bed, Jack prayed for sleep. When it finally came, hours later – the sounds of the Roman night punctuated by sirens and the odd boisterous laugh of passers-by in the street outside – it carried an ocean of despair and memories he just couldn't banish. It was a warm night and he kept on wiping away the sweat between his legs and under his chin, as he thrashed around feverishly between the crisp white sheets.

Even sleep was no longer a refuge.

Giulia lived in the hills behind the Stadio Olimpico.

He painfully managed to find his way there, manoeuvring the car with difficulty with an unfolded map on his knees and dodging cars that sped past him. She had pointed out the area to him when they had driven nearby on the way to secret places where they could fuck, but he had a hell of a time today finding his way past the Stadio Olimpico. Once in the hills, it was no better and he arrived at the top by mistake, enjoying a view of both central Rome and all the neighbouring hills he remembered from his history and Latin lessons all those years past. Oh, there was the Vatican. And there was the road that led out of town to the lake and Calcata, past the neglected area whose name he couldn't recall where, she had told him, prostitutes and low-life came out at night, then further down the road the RAI buildings. She had confessed to an unholy fascination with the whores there when she had been a troubled teenager and how she had always imagined what they were doing or how she would act if she were one.

Jack studied the map carefully and found her street. He drove off downwards in its direction.

Via Luigi Credaro was a cul-de-sac and a small supermarket occupied the ground floor of the apartment building where she had returned to live with her parents. He managed to park a hundred metres away on the opposite side of the road.

Though he had never been here, he seemed to remember Giulia saying that the family's apartment occupied the top two floors of the building. Did her bedroom overlook the street, or was it on another side of the building facing the hills or another part of the city?

So, this was where she had mostly grown up, apart from those years in the country when she had commuted to school in the city by train. It felt strange being here. He kept his eye on the door to the building; the supermarket was now open and customers trickled in and out.

Jack opened the glove compartment and took out the gun and placed it between his thighs on the car seat. He'd never fired a gun in his life, let alone owned one. But he had read enough books and articles and knew the basics – the safety, the calibre, the damage it could invariably cause.

I'm crazy, totally crazy, he thought. He'd been in love before, of course, but never had he been so obsessed by a woman, a girl, or missed her so much. Without her, he had sadly realised, he was nothing.

However much he knew that things could never have worked out between them after the initial yearlong honeymoon of covert meetings and fiery fucks in forbidden places and foreign cities, Jack still couldn't give up on her totally, admit defeat, let her, and him, get on with their respective lives. She was younger. She still had a life – *adventures*, as she'd so often put it – ahead of her. Even after whatever she might have done since Paris and that other older man. He didn't. Not without her.

It was a few weeks before when he had been researching for some still unfinished story that he had stumbled across a pornographic website replete with photos actually submitted by non-professionals; openly voyeuristic images of nudity, both simple and extreme, and of couples enjoying sexual intercourse. He had distractedly spent a quarter of an hour surfing through the images and noting the monotonous repetition of positions and angles, when he had come across a series of eight shots in which the woman's face was always out of the frame but her opulent white arse stood front and centre, her wet, pink gash circled by unruly black curls, fully exposed along with the puckered, darker areola of her back door. The young woman was on her knees, her rear right in the camera's face. From image to image the arse came nearer and nearer to the fore and in the final three photographs a resplendently thick and hard penis took aim at the woman's cunt and was then seen entering it, finally ending deeply embedded in it up to the ball sack.

He had of course seen a thousand photographs of this kind before, but this time the shape, the colour, the details of the woman's arse recalled Giulia's in indelible resemblance. Jack had been violently sick, rushing to the bathroom and spewing out all the contents of his stomach over the carpet long before reaching the safety of the ceramic bowl. It had been like a knife to his heart. Naturally, Jack knew there could be no way she had not moved on to other men after him and the sad episode with the dead man in Paris in the years following their break-up, and since when do women in their twenties have to act as nuns? But somehow the images on his laptop had brought it all home, the sheer reality of another man fucking her, owning her, playing with her and, worse, getting her to allow him to even broadcast photographs of their terrible intimacy across the web.

A few hours later, he had hesitantly peered at the photographs again and realised it wasn't her, couldn't actually be her. A few meshes of the woman's hair were in the frame of one of the images and the shade was assuredly not hers; also, there was also a distinctive mole absent in a familiar area of her lunar landscape, he discovered, to his relief. But the scar was still there. Inside Jack. Who was she with now? Who did she love now, she who had once loved him?

The door to the building opened and a woman walked out, plump, dark-haired, almost a vision of what Giulia might look like twenty years later. Her mother? Would Giulia also age badly and put on so much weight around her waist and backside?

The heat of the day hammered against the parked car, but Jack couldn't switch the air-conditioning on or the battery would rapidly go flat.

Was she now alone in her room in the large two-floor apartment?

Or maybe she was now in a small hotel room by Lake Bracciano, being ploughed by another man? It had been, after all, she who had once discovered that hideaway.

Enough. Enough.

I am sick. I am sick.

Sick enough to climb the stairs to the apartment, ring the bell, confront her when she opened the door and brandish the gun? *If you can't be mine, you can't be anyone else's* ...? The pitiful stuff of tabloid journalism. Come on!

He could sit here all day and not see her, he realised. And even if she did emerge, what would he then do? Follow her? Stalk her? He'd lose her in traffic most likely.

In her anger, when he would refuse to let her go and beg for a last meeting, a final embrace, a penultimate conversation, she would always fire back that he had no respect for her and could not accept what she felt. She had these crazy ideas about respect, but he understood what she meant.

In a letter, one of so many, too many, he had written that loving her was also knowing when to let her go, but it was a precept he had proven incapable of adhering to.

What the fuck was he doing in Rome? What the hell was he doing with a gun?

There was just no way he could kill her. Let alone a sensible reason ...

Damn.

Jack drove off, found the highway that led out of town, past the desolate and empty market place where the whores were said to congregate at night like in a Fellini movie, sped past the RAI buildings and into the countryside.

The sky was blue.

Maybe he could find peace after all.

There was a junction with a road that led to Lake Bracciano and Trevignano. He sighed and drove past it, his mind assaulted by more memories of nearby hotel rooms where they had made love and had once been unbearably happy. Watching her emerge from the shower, her wet, unfurled hair hanging all the way down her back. Jack putting that cheap necklace around her throat. His final gift.

The next turnoff was for the medieval town of Calcata. He was just over forty kilometres from the city, in the Parco Treja Tuscia region. Here, behind the high, fortified ramparts in a small stone house, where the February cold had chilled their bones to the marrow and forced them to spend almost two whole days in bed – talking non stop between the tender fucking, learning about each other, getting accustomed to the taste of each other, growing bolder with mind and body and plunging headfirst into transgression – he had moved inside her for the first time and fallen in love with her. For ever.

Calcata looked the same. In all likelihood it had not changed in a few hundred years. Once abandoned, the small town had been repopulated several decades ago by hippies and was now turning into a historical arts centre, with medieval summer houses for rich Romans, artists or visiting lovers, art galleries and a handful of tiny country restaurants. The whole town, whose population still didn't number more than nine hundred people normally, was built on a hilltop of volcanic rock.

He parked the rented blue Fiat outside the ramparts and walked up the stone street into the town, past the arches and fortifications.

The small cottage where they had frozen and spent a whole thirty-six hours all that time ago was still there. He wondered what sort of couple was now inside in that unforgettable bedroom you could only access through a shaky wooden ladder (aaahhhh, the vision of her climbing those stairs, stark naked, his eyes looking straight at the voluptuous and bouncing flesh of her arse as he ascended behind her, his cock hard and ready, his mind aglow with tenderness and desire …).

Jack walked past the steep stone steps leading to his forgotten paradise and ventured past narrow alleys, closed craft shops and freshly washed clothes hanging loose from windows until he reached the narrow promontory that dominated the valley below.

The view was quite beautiful, rugged, untamed. In the distance, forests dominated the far landscape, but below the damaged stone walls protecting this side of Calcata was a lunar expanse of rocks as far as the eye could see.

Jack sighed.

Best remember the good times.

When she smiled at him and her eyes expressed a million things unsaid.

He pulled that silly gun from the plastic bag and hurled it into the gaping void. It fell in a large arc and it felt like almost a minute before he saw it actually hit the ground some five hundred metres below. It didn't go off. He had left the safety catch on. No need to draw attention to himself even though there didn't appear to be a soul for a mile around.

He closed his eyes.

"*My sweetie,*" she would call him.

He took a deep breath.

"*My wild gypsy,*" he would often say to her.

Jack pulled his left leg over the wall, raised himself energetically so that he now stood on the edge of the precipice.

Looked down one final time.

Those fierce and distant rocks should do the job, he reckoned.

And jumped.

Sex in the City Range
Edited by Maxim Jakubowski

Sex in the City - London
Paperback - 9781907016226
eBook – 9781907726392

Sex in the City – Dublin
Paperback - 9781907016233
eBook - 9781907726378

Sex in the City - New York
Paperback - 9781907016240
eBook - 9781907726385

Sex in the City – Paris
Paperback - 9781907016257
eBook - 9781907726361